Praise for the work of

Mabel and Everything After

In *Mabel and Everything After* we are gifted with a heartwarming story of Emma and Mabel's circuitous journey to each other. Safren has a distinctive voice with her writing style. She displays a depth and maturity with this being her second novel. Her storytelling reflexes have been honed to perfection. This is by far my favourite novel of 2022.

-Della B., *NetGalley*

Mabel and Everything After was everything I wanted it to be and more. A lovely coming-of-age new adult, college... romance, that was very lovely to witness. Loved spending time with Mabel and Emma.

-Simone R., *NetGalley*

All the feels! This is a book for those who believe in love at first sight. But it's not only about it, it's what happens after, when it's not the right time to be together, but it's a soulmate love. I rooted so much for Emma and Mabel in those four years. Their summer love was beautiful to read, but their growing up was what I needed to read as well.

-Caroline B., *NetGalley*

I loved this book. Emma and Mabel are everything. This book was everything. Thank you so much Hannah Safren for writing your love story for the world to see.

-Jessica R., *NetGalley*

Mabel and Everything After by Hannah Safren is a new adult coming-of-age romance that highlights how important timing is with love... This is a heartwarming romance but has some bittersweet moments as well. They both have a lot of growing up to do and must go through some painful truths before they're able to find their happily ever after. This really touched my heart, and I was on pins and needles wanting them to finally get together. I highly recommend this and can't wait to see what Safren does next.

-Leah M., *NetGalley*

SHE MET HER BY THE SEA

Hannah Safren

Other Bella Books by Hannah Safren

Mabel and Everything After

About the Author

Hannah Safren's adoration for the enchanting Carolina coast shines through in her latest Bella Books novel, *She Met Her by the Sea*. Having relocated to Wilmington with her wife and their two small children in the winter of 2021, Safren finds inspiration in the orange sunsets, the bright pink azaleas, and the ever-present humming of seagulls.

Safren balances her creative endeavors with a career in architectural sales for a roofing manufacturer out of Florida.

She enjoys golf and bourbon and Saturdays in July on Topsail Island, but more so than anything, she enjoys watching her kids relish in the simple pleasures of childhood: Popsicles poolside, splashing in rain puddles, screaming bloody murder when she asks them to put their shoes on, or comb their hair, or go to bed.

SHE MET HER BY THE SEA

Hannah Safren

BELLA
BOOKS
2024

Bella Books, Inc.
P.O. Box 10543
Tallahassee, FL 32302

First Edition - 2024

Editor: Heather Flournoy
Cover Designer: Heather Honeywell

ISBN: 978-1-64247-543-2

PUBLISHER'S NOTE

Acknowledgments

I prayed for dear friends battling really scary cancers. I mourned with friends that have lost siblings, and parents, and pregnancies, and jobs, and checked in on those that have moved on from their spouse. I celebrated the birth of my own two babies (joys of my life!), and I cheered on others as they welcomed their own little humans into this wild world.

I know all these things, or things like them, become more common as we grow older. Life goes along like this. High highs and low lows. But these very real, amazing, beautiful people are my reason, my reminder, my inspiration to handle each day with care. To move with purpose. And yes, though it seems trifle in comparison, to complete this very manuscript here. Special love to Brittany Deal, Shelby Forsyth, and Nikki Kuhn for your time, the greatest gift one can give. I am endlessly appreciative!

To Bella Books, I am beyond grateful for another opportunity to showcase my dearest passion with you.

And finally, Heather Flournoy, the world's greatest motivational coach and editor. I am so, so appreciative of your guidance. You are the best!

Dedication

To my wife. Everything in me loves you.

CHAPTER ONE

Emily

April

Emily Brynn inhales a final gulp of smog and siren. "Today is the day, Dad."

She had started planning her New York City escape just nine hours earlier, standing in this same spot on this small balcony of her two-bedroom Tribeca condo. Sure, she was two glasses of red wine into the midnight hour when the revelation hit, but she knew it then, and she is sure of it now.

She is leaving New York.

She is leaving The Brynn Company.

She is moving to Wrightsville Beach, North Carolina.

It's not entirely out of the blue. Leaving the rush of the city has been on her mind since her fruitless fling with Zaya Bloomsburg when she questioned, for the first time, if there was a single woman in all of New York City that could savor a holiday without turning it into some social media spectacle.

That was four years ago.

A loud knock sends her scrambling for a to-go coffee mug before opening the door. "Good morning, Mike."

"Hello, Ms. Brynn." She watches him scan the room. "I see why you need the luggage cart today. Where are you off to?"

"I'm going to spend some time in North Carolina. Have you been?"

Mike lifts bag number one as he speaks in his thick city accent, methodical and often disregarding the pronunciation of the letter *R*. "Back when I was about your age, I was a private driver. One of my regular guys had business in Raleigh. I'd drive him down there a few times a year. Don't know much about the state beyond that." Mike goes for bag number two. "What part of the state you headed to, Ms. Brynn?"

"Wrightsville Beach." Emily flings a large plum tote over her shoulder before handing the third and final bag to Mike for proper placement on his cart. She's known Mike since she bought her condo eleven years ago, and she knows if she places the bag on the cart herself he will readjust it, even if only slightly, to his liking.

"Right along the coast. I've got no doubt it'll be beautiful, Ms. Brynn."

She smiles tenderly at her old friend.

"Is there anything I can do to help you here while you're gone?"

"No thank you, Mike. I appreciate the help this morning."

"My pleasure. Julian should have your car out front by now. I'll follow you down."

Emily does not attempt to push the luggage cart. Mike won't allow it. She locks the front door and pats it with a "Farewell for now, home."

"I've got the lift," she says. "Least I can do." When the elevator doors open, she helps Mike guide the bulky cart in.

"How's Maria doing?" Emily asks.

Maria, Mike's wife of thirty-seven years, had a knee replacement last Monday. Emily has been checking in daily. Last Wednesday, she sent him home with a dozen yellow lilies and a woven basket full of fresh fruits to give to her.

"She's making progress. You know that physical therapy sure does wonders." He answers similarly every time.

"I'm glad she's continuing to make good progress."

"Thank you for always asking about her, Ms. Brynn. We're still working on all that fruit. She appreciated it so much, as did I."

"Good, I'm happy to hear you're enjoying it."

The elevator beeps twenty-seven floors down before opening to a white marble lobby. Emily greets Paula, the receptionist, and heads out of the grand revolving front door toward her shiny blue Mercedes SUV.

She's had it for over a year and has driven less than 2500 miles, opting more often for a chauffeur, or occasionally public transportation, but that's only when she's itching to feel more like the average thirty-seven-year-old city dweller.

Emily was never hunting for a vehicle, but when Mrs. Rebecca Langley, a good friend of her father's, opened a Mercedes dealership, she and her brother, James, were eager to support the new endeavor.

James was instantly hooked on what Mrs. Langley referred to as their "off-road icon." It mirrored a Bronco but with the class of a Mercedes: rugged, yet sophisticated. When he said, "That's the one," Emily had responded, "Make it two."

James was adamant about his black leather interior and matte black exterior, the grandest souped-up sound system, elaborate LED mood-tailoring interior lighting, and custom rims. Emily didn't share the same enthusiasm, so she leaned on Mrs. Langley.

"I think you'll be pleased with this light-tan interior, and this may be out of your comfort zone, but how do you feel about this Sea Blue Metallic?"

"I'll take it."

The Sea Blue Metallic feels serendipitous this morning as Emily Brynn heads off to the coast.

"You'll finally be putting some real miles on this baby, huh, Ms. Brynn?" Julian grins as he hands her the keys. Julian parks a lot of nice cars, but he's verbalized that Emily's is one of his favorites. "Feels like skydiving," he once told her.

"I'm looking forward to it," she shares.

Mike and Julian help her load the trunk with her three large bags. Mike pats the back when he has shut and secured it and double-checked his work. Much like her own father would do if he were here. "Good to go, Ms. Brynn," he shouts.

She hands them each a generous tip. "Thank you both for the help this morning. Stay well."

Emily takes FDR along the East River to the Upper East Side of Manhattan. She drives the entire way with the windows down, reintroducing herself to the noises of the city, something she's long grown numb to. She finds a parking spot right in front of her brother's 1876 brownstone, takes a deep breath, and heads up the stairs.

"Emmy!" Her two nephews, Clark and Briggs, and her niece, Blake, greet her loudly, slamming into her legs before she's fully in the front door.

"Come here, munchkins!" Emily hugs them all at once and then each individually. In the kitchen she expectedly finds her mother, Charlotte, and her brother's wife, Lilly, putting together a gourmet English breakfast spread—grilled tomatoes and roasted mushrooms, thick-cut bacon, baked beans, sourdough toast, and fried eggs with a runny yolk.

Emily gives them both a kiss on the cheek and a squeeze. "Is James in his office?"

She already knows the answer, but she lets Lilly respond. "He's in there."

Emily heads back toward the front of the house to her brother's office. She knocks lightly, turns the intricately designed brass knob, and peeks her head through the large wooden door. When she sees he isn't on the phone, she finds her way in. She sits comfortably on one of the two oversized leather chairs beneath a massive Arsenal FC pennant that hangs down from the high ceiling.

"I'm leaving the company, James."

Without looking up from his laptop, he responds, "You can't leave, you own it."

They own it together. That was always the plan. Not Emily's plan, but an implied plan since the moment she was born. James and Emily were destined to take over the family business, and that was that.

Their grandfather William Brynn started The Brynn Company in 1947. It originated as a commercial real estate company, specializing in the purchasing and sale of mobile home lots, a newer phenomenon at the time. By the mid-fifties, William had garnered over a dozen office buildings, small retail malls, and apartment complexes, and by the sixties he had cultivated a brilliant following. He knew where to invest, when to invest, and what to invest in. The real gold mine, though, was in the land itself. In the eighties, when the expansion of cell phones started to skyrocket, the city needed land to build cell towers—William Brynn's land. He sold off a few plots early on, but as the market kept evolving, he chose to forgo the steep initial buyouts for a lifetime of rent. A hefty, hefty rent. When Emily and James's father, Barry, took over in 1991, he expanded The Brynn Company brand, branching into accounting, property management, and, in his later years, historical preservation advocacy.

Barry would still own The Brynn Company if he hadn't died of an aggressive and cruel brain tumor one year and one day ago.

"It's all yours," Emily says.

James looks up with confusion in his eyes. "You're serious?"

"I am serious."

He shoves his computer aside and leans back in his chair, folding his arms against his chest. Emily sighs at how much he looks like their father. His thick head of ashy hair. Soft, welcoming brown eyes. Big hands, perfectly manicured. Broad shoulders always fitted neatly under an ironed shirt. Even on this Sunday morning.

"What's going on, Em?"

She takes a note from her pocket and tosses it onto his desk. "This is what Dad wrote me."

Their father had written James and Emily each a letter before he passed away. It was only four months from his diagnosis to death. A whirlwind of a season, but he managed to scratch out some final thoughts for each of them.

"You want me to read it?" James asks as he holds it up.

James had shared his note with Emily months ago. His was mostly about fatherhood, but there was a paragraph in there that said, "Much of our work comes down to knowing the difference between right and wrong. You are better than I ever was. Pick right. Every time." James reread it on repeat to Emily back in autumn when they were contemplating a billion-dollar deal that would have required them to relocate a flourishing eighteenth-century historic church.

With Barry's words as their motivation, The Brynn Company not only decided to decline the deal, but they spent the next four months helping the congregation legislate for protections so that they would never have to encounter a similar situation again.

James carefully unfolds Emily's note, knowing just how precious the writing on this flimsy paper is. She follows along from memory.

My Dearest Emily,

There's not a human I've met that works harder than you. Not even your brother. But don't tell him that. Might hurt his ego.

James smiles softly and Emily knows what he's just read. She's read it dozens of times since her father passed. Spent small parts of every single day over the last year thinking about these words.

Your work ethic, your natural knack for negotiation, and your brilliant personality are what make you the greatest employee I've ever had, and they will be what make you a great boss at The Brynn Company.

If that's something you want. And I wonder if perhaps that it's not your dream.

I wanted to share a little something.

I keep thinking of a vacation (your mother would kill me for using the word vacation instead of holiday) we took down to the eastern shore of North Carolina. Wrightsville Beach. You were four. We rented a house on stilts along the intracoastal. Watched every sunrise that week (you've always been an early riser!). We all fished. Or rather, you cast and reeled back in and the rest of us fished. You ate blue crab for the first time and way too much strawberry ice cream. To your dismay, it was sunny all week long, but on the very last afternoon it rained, poured, and you were so excited because you'd been wanting to run in the rain in your yellow rain boots and you finally got to! Stomped in all the puddles. Spread your arms and ran figure eights like an airplane.

In my final weeks here on Earth, that is what I think about when I think about the happiest moments of my life. The happiest you. You in those yellow rain boots running in the rain.

James sniffles, and Emily wonders if it's to stave off the tears starting to well up in his eyes.

I'll take the blame for your long work hours. For the pressure I've placed on you and your brother, which you've handled with extraordinary fortitude. It's hard for me to even believe I am writing this to you, but life, all of a sudden, seems a whole lot clearer when the end is so near.

I am telling you now, as your father (and your former boss!), to take more holidays. Limit those 65-hour work weeks. No more Sunday mornings in the office (remind your brother of this too, please).

Hell, take a whole year off. Why not?

Sure, work is winning and winning is satisfying, (that runs in the Brynn blood), but when was the last time you enjoyed a slow morning with tea? Went on a date? (Your mum made me write this.) When was the last time you played hooky on a Tuesday? Bought yourself a pair of yellow boots? Spent an afternoon jumping around in the rain?

You are great, my Emily Louise Brynn. Time is ticking.

I love you,

Dad

James refolds the letter carefully. "Well, I guess the ol' bloke confirmed my suspicion that you were the favorite."

"I can't believe you still had suspicions. It was so obvious." Emily winks.

James huffs out a chuckle. "So why now? One year since his death has ya in your feels, yeah?"

James's accent is much thicker than Emily's. They were born in London and spent their early years running around the streets of Mayfair in the city of Westminster. Emily hadn't yet begun middle school when their father packed them up and shipped them over the Atlantic to his hometown of New York City. James, however, was already well into his teenage years, so his lingo and love of Arsenal Football was too far down the aisle to be influenced.

"Probably. Yes. I've been thinking about it, though. I was out on my balcony last night and I couldn't see a single star in the sky. Not one. I'm thirty-seven. I have no kids. I have no life partner. Work is my life. And you know this business has never been my dream. There's got to be more to all this, yeah?"

James listens intently to Emily as she sinks into her chair, decompressing from the heavy burden she's just released.

"I actually don't know why it has taken me so long to pull the trigger," Emily continues, with a smile unraveling across her porcelain cheeks. "We're sitting quite well, James. We could buy the Knicks, terrible as they are. We don't actually need to work. It's just a bit of an addiction, yeah?"

James gags, and Emily knows it's because of her exaggerated *buy the Knicks* comment.

"Oh, stop it. You don't think I could negotiate us a fair deal?"

He nods in contemplation before laughing. "If anyone could, it'd be you."

Emily grins at the compliment.

"Well," James begins his rebuttal. "I'd argue that our company is not just work. We've been a part of building and protecting the greatest parts of New York City since the forties. We provide excellent jobs to over a hundred and seventy-five employees. We've started an incredible foundation, given millions to this city. And to top it off, you're amazing at what you do."

Emily has heard James give this exact same elevator pitch a hundred times. Even he can't stop himself from chuckling at how predictable his poor attempt at altering Emily's decision is. She laughs with him. "You're right. I do love this company. I'm proud of it. All we've done. But I'm still leaving, James. I need to."

James stares for a moment, clearly reflecting on the last year of work with Emily. She's never loved it the way he has, but she's always been very successful with it. "I get it." His thick eyebrows furrow. "You had me fooled, though. I thought burning the candle at both ends was your thing, no?"

"It was for a while, sure. Who doesn't like partying on the High Line with beautiful women and top-shelf cocktails?" They both chuckle, and Emily recalls one specific event, before James's kids were even born, when the two of them were the last standing, left to enjoy the sunrise on their walk home. "But when I think about my life," she continues. "I don't feel fulfilled. I want a family, like you have. I want something simpler. Smaller town, smaller projects, smaller impacts."

"Well, to touch on the love component, you could have had it with Parker, no?"

"She cheated on me, James. With a man."

He wants to burst into laughter. It's obvious in his beet-red cheeks and his clenched lips. "Oh, that was just a phase." He waves off his comment with a flick of his hand. "She's totally into ya, Em."

"No, James. She's not."

"Well, what about that movie star's daughter? Adam Kraves, is it?"

Emily's eyes widen. "Romi?"

"Yeah, weren't you shaggin' her?"

"How the hell did you know about that?"

He winks. "Word gets around, Em."

It does. The circle of wealth is small and quite loud. Everyone is sleeping together. Everyone is at the same parties, the same courtside suites, buying up properties on the same islands in remote areas of the Caribbean.

"Okay, so Kraves isn't the one. What does Maya think of all this?" He leans back in his chair, evidently giving up for now. "I frankly don't know how you'll live a day without her."

Maya has been Emily's best friend since she handed her a sharpened No. 2 pencil during a sixth-grade language arts class at St. Mary's Private Catholic School. Emily was the new girl with the weird British accent and Maya was the confident, kind, and beautiful best friend she needed.

"I haven't told her. I'm going to call her on my drive."

"Your drive? When are you leaving?"

"Today."

"Today!" James nearly knocks over his cup of tea. "You can't be serious."

Emily nods toward the window and he glances that direction to see her car parked out front, bags built up behind the back windows.

"You are serious." There is a sudden look of worry on his face. Likely deriving from the amount of work he's about to acquire.

"I am serious, but listen…" She reaches across his desk and grabs his hand. "I won't leave you in the lurch." She squeezes his hand to assure him further. "You know that. I will work remote as long as you need me to. There is nothing of importance that I can't do from North Carolina."

His tense glare relaxes a bit. Everything Emily does is calculated. It's certain. She is absolutely, one hundred percent not going back on her decision to leave and she will absolutely, one hundred percent not leave him to clean up any messes.

"You're going to Wrightsville Beach, aren't you?"

"Yes."

"How long?"

"I'm not sure. A year maybe?"

"One year. And then you better come on back up here, ya hear?"

Emily offers a tender smile. James reciprocates.

"I can handle everything," he assures. "Mark is up to speed on your files, right?" Under Emily's leadership, The Brynn Company has implemented more rigorous checks and balances to seamlessly handle vacations and any dire situations that may arise. Like one of the owners jumping ship.

"He's completely up-to-date," Emily assures. "There shouldn't be any hiccups. And he's excellent. I have complete faith in him."

"He's no Emily Brynn."

"I trained him. He's excellent."

James stands from his chair and stretches his arms up toward the ceiling. "Fine. Let's go tell Mum. She'll probably be excited. She's been telling me for years that you need to stop obsessing over work and find yourself a partner."

"Oh, I know."

CHAPTER TWO

Sara

"I know this happens, but I guess I just never thought it would happen to me." Sara presses her hand to her temple to massage away the frustration.

Jared finishes off his wine before responding. "No one does. The positive here is that he's not fighting you on the assets or the girls. It's hard. Of course it's hard working through years of marriage. You will get through it, and you will be happier for it. I'm sure."

Sara looks at him, thankful for his comforting sanity.

"Is this seat taken?"

Sara whips her head around Jared, thankful some stranger has interrupted her depressing vent session.

"Oh no, no, sweetheart." Jared pats the stool with flair. "Great timing, honey. Come sit with us. Are you waiting on someone else?"

"Just me."

"Love this for you." Jared pulls out the rounded rattan barstool for the woman with dark-brown hair and glamorous cheekbones.

"Vacation?" Sara has already run through her head why a woman this pretty would be solo at a bar on a Monday afternoon. She doesn't look familiar, or sad, or drunk, or lonely. Could be work, but she appears too happy for it. Vacation feels like the only option.

"No, I've actually just moved here." Speaking the words makes the woman beam with joy. A smile so wide, Sara finds herself mimicking it.

"Straight from England?" Jared asks jokingly.

The woman laughs. "Originally, yes. But the accent is a bit confusing. I've spent most of my life in New York. Manhattan. That's where I've just moved from." She waves her hand near her face. "My mother is responsible for this wonderful gift of an accent, though she'd tell you I sound like an American."

Sara chuckles, enthralled with this woman's bubbly personality. She wonders how her own deep Southern accent sounds to this glamorous creature.

"Well, you need to celebrate," Jared insists.

"Yes, yes," Sara concurs. "Hey, Jess." Sara grabs the bartender's attention. "Can you get our new friend a drink?"

"Cabernet, please," the woman says.

"I'm Jared, by the way."

"Hi, Jared, I'm Emily." She shakes his hand and then reaches across him. "And your name?"

Sara firmly shakes Emily's hand, noting how soft it feels against hers, the mauve color of her perfectly trimmed nails. "Sara."

"Listen, Emily," Jared says. "I'm so happy you sat down tonight because you seem like a great time and I'm meeting my husband for dinner, so will you keep my boss company?" Jared hops up from his seat, grabs his keys from the bar counter, and leans in toward Emily to whisper, loud enough for Sara to hear, "She's having a day."

Emily whispers back, again, loud enough for Sara to hear, "If she'll have me, I could use the company myself."

"Perfect."

"Bye, Jared," Sara says with a dramatic eye roll.

"Bye, love." He gives Sara a kiss on her cheek and heads off.

"So do you want to talk about your bad day, Sara?" Emily says with a squinty, humorful glare.

Sara huffs out a chuckle. "No. No. Not at all."

"Okay then." Emily lifts her wine and holds it up for a toast. "To my very first night in North Carolina."

"First night!" Sara's eyebrows shoot up as she clinks her glass with Emily's. "Now, this is something worth talking about. Spill everything."

Rather than removing Jared's empty chair between them, Sara leans into the conversation. Her elbow sits heavy on the bar as Emily shares that she had an itch to make a move. "I was working in real estate. Long days...that sound lazy, yeah?"

"No," Sara says matter-of-factly and sort of confused by the brashness of Emily's question.

Emily waves her hand toward Sara. "I'm sure you have plenty of exhausting days in your profession too. I don't mean to sound..." She trails off.

Sara nudges her along. "Sometimes, sure, but go on, go on. I'll assume you're not lazy."

A playful grin settles across Emily's face. Sara takes in her striking features, mesmerized by her eyes, almost golden.

"Well, thank you." Emily sips her wine with a touch of pompous exaggeration before continuing, "I was just done with it all, so I packed up a few too many bags of clothes and a bunch of very cute shoes that are completely unreasonable for a beach town." Sara lets out a giggle. Emily does the same. "I quit my job, and here I am."

Emily's eyes dart around before reconnecting with Sara. "I'm completely insane, aren't I?"

Sara nods in agreement. "Well, yes, it sure does sound a little crazy, but we're all a little crazy."

Emily shrugs in what appears to be agreement before holding up a single finger and pulling her cell phone from her small leather bag. "One moment," she whispers as she answers her phone. "Paul, how are you?"

Sara watches Emily intently, too soused to pretend to distract herself with the pecking shorebirds around the bar.

"No," Emily says firmly. "I made myself very clear to Ibrim at the preconstruction meeting. There will be no amendments. We are moving forward."

Sara scans Emily's entire face repeatedly. Her full lips, her wide hazel eyes, her model-sharp jawline. The single small freckle beneath her right eye. The power in her voice. Dominance that Sara finds oddly attractive.

"I expect there will be no more delays, correct, Paul." Emily says. A short pause lingers before she clicks off her call. "Sorry about that."

"I thought you quit?"

"Just wrapping up some things."

"Hmm." Sara lifts her glass. "I love your voice."

Emily stares for a moment, a slight upward bend on her lips. "Thank you."

"You sound proper. And smart. And important." Sara is still staring. Her elbow is still propped up against the bar counter, but now her head is against her hand. Emily smiles, and Sara notes that it favors the right side of her face. She is certain she has never examined a woman so intensely, but she is also certain that Emily is the most beautiful woman she has ever seen.

And also, she's tipsy.

"The accent is that good, yeah?" Emily's grin is wider. She doesn't appear nervous or uncomfortable. Quite the contrary. There's a natural ease to her that has made everything about the night feel so simple.

"Why here?" Sara continues in her forthcoming manner. It's not her norm, but this is what cabernet and an impending divorce will do to a woman's inhibitions. "I mean, it's paradise on Earth here, but I've lived here my whole life. It's home. For you, from New York, why did you move here to Wrightsville Beach? Why not Charleston, or Palm Beach, or, I don't know, San Diego?"

Emily breathes deeply, seemingly concocting a suitable story. "My dad passed a year ago."

Sara's lips purse together in a bit of pain at the news. It isn't what she was expecting to hear.

"We were on holiday here many years ago. He wrote me a letter before he passed, and in it, he talked about how I danced around puddles in yellow rain boots on our final rainy afternoon here. So I came back. To start something new. Settle down a bit."

Sara's eyes fill with tears. "Well, that is just perfect." She reaches across the empty stool, puts her hand on Emily's and squeezes it. "I hope you love it here."

"Me too."

Sara leans back in her seat. "Do you want another glass?"

"Yes."

The two sip down a second glass. And then a third, which is actually Sara's fourth since she was already one deep when Emily arrived. Two too many, but she is having so much fun rambling on about her favorite restaurants and bars. The Pilates studio she goes to and the preferred beach access of her two daughters. All the things Emily says she can't wait to explore.

"How old are your girls?" Emily asks.

Sara spruces right up at the very mention of them. Sometimes, lately, it feels they're the only reason she's stayed sane. "Six and eight."

"Are they home with your husband?"

"Ex-husband." Sara feels the fatigue from her family situation instantly drain her. "It's not technically official yet, but we're separated." It had been so nice going nearly two hours without thinking about the divorce.

"Oh gosh, I am so sorry. Did I just bring up the very thing you didn't want to talk about?"

"Yep." Sara smiles softly and nods her head, letting Emily know that it's all right. "We had a meeting today with our lawyer. It's all good, really. Just been tough. Coming home to a quiet house when the girls are with him. I miss tucking them in at night. Having them jump in bed with me every morning. I sound miserable, huh?" She forces a smile but knows the weightiness of her eyes can't be ignored.

Emily doesn't flinch. "You sound like you love your daughters very much."

"I do. We'll all get through it. We're a family."

Emily nods. "It is different," she says. "But we're both grieving in a way. Sometimes things are just shit, aren't they?"

Sara chuckles. A curse word in an English accent just sounds so much nicer.

"I don't know if this helps at all, but I measure my days in happiness. I'm happy more moments in the days than I am sad and I feel like that's a win, so hopefully the same goes for you. And if not yet, soon."

Sara smiles softly. "Soon."

Emily nods and takes a sip of wine. "Do you live around here?"

"I do. For now. I moved into my parents' condo." She points down the street. "It's just a couple of blocks that way. They live in Durham most of the year and this place is always empty. Just made sense to come here when Steve and I made the decision to part ways. It's only about fifteen minutes from our home in Wilmington. Well, his home in Wilmington now."

Sara notices Emily trying to bite back her uneasiness. It makes her chuckle.

"Listen, it could be worse. My parents' place is beautiful. Has plenty of space for the girls when they're with me, and waking up to the ocean really has been therapeutic. It's a nice fit for now."

The last four months of Sara's separation from Steve sifts through her. It's been four months since she moved out of her home. The home that she designed, loved, and brought her two baby girls home to. It's been four months since she found out about Steve's infidelity. Four months since the life she knew was no longer. She sighs, shoving her thoughts from the moment. "I'm real glad you sat down here tonight, Emily."

"Me too."

Sara breaks eye contact to look at her watch. "It's getting late. I should go."

"Yes. I'm going to head out soon as well." Emily's stomach rumbles loudly.

"Gosh, you never ate!"

"Was it that loud?"

Sara chuckles as she hops down from her stool. "Look at us, gossiping on like teenagers. Do you have any allergies?"

"None."

"Well trust me on this one, then." Sara waves over the bartender. The bar is much busier now that the dinner hour is upon them, and all the surrounding noise suddenly erupts. "Can you put in the dolphin Cuban sandwich for Emily and bring the check, please?"

Jess nods and hurries over to the computer. A moment later she's back with the check.

"Sara, good to see you as always." Jess redirects her attention to Emily. "It'll just be a few minutes, hun."

Emily hands her credit card to Sara. "Let me grab this."

"Not a chance. Consider it your welcome gift."

"Thank you."

Sara signs and neatly places the pen on the counter. "And hey, since we're neighbors now, let me give you my number in case you need anything while you settle in. Maybe we can do this again?"

"I'd love that."

The two exchange phone numbers and last names.

"It's Sara Dylan."

"Emily Brynn."

"Well, Emily Brynn," Sara says as she lifts her purse to her shoulder. "I hope to see you soon."

CHAPTER THREE

Emily

"Hi, Mum."

"Hi, dear, settling in?"

"I'm unpacking now. The place is gorgeous."

Given the spur-of-the-moment booking, Emily was pleased when she entered late Sunday evening. It was better than the pictures. Beautifully designed. Simple. Coastal. Bright. She went room to room, taking note of each detail. Copper mermaid tail handles on the white cabinets. A butcher-block island, pearl herringbone tile backsplash. Worn, color-coded books about fishing, and mermaids, and local ghost tales, and pirates filling the built-ins around the TV in the living room.

"It feels very…" She looks up at the A-frame shiplap ceiling with the large driftwood beams stretched horizontally across it. "Thoughtfully designed."

"Send me pictures!" Her mother is clearly elated for her.

"I will, I've got to send you a picture of this giant sailboat. It's bolted above the stairwell. Absolutely incredible."

"And how's the outside? It's on the water, right?"

"I'm walking out right now. It sits on the Intracoastal. There's a long wooden dock with an amazing view at the end of it."

A stone path out back leads Emily past a row of red, orange, and green fishing poles, two blue kayaks, an outdoor shower, and eventually to a long wooden dock. She walked this yesterday upon her arrival, and today she finds it even more romantic. There's tall seagrass on either side of her, draping over the marshland, mucking up her observations, but as she approaches the end, it tapers off, and a marvelous intracoastal waterway comes into view.

"I'm happy, darling. I'm excited for you."

"Thanks, Mum," Emily says as she plops into a navy blue Adirondack chair.

"Now, I don't want to annoy you with this, but I know you, and you'll be bored by this afternoon, so what's your plan, dear?"

"Then don't annoy me about it me, Mum."

"I just don't want you hopping in the car and finding yourself back in the office by this time next week."

Emily looks at her wristwatch. It's ten o'clock. Tuesday morning. She would have been in the office two and a half hours ago had she not left it all behind.

"I will not get back in the car, Mum." Emily rolls her eyes. "I'm staying here. You know that."

"You know you could not work for a while—ever again, in fact, if you like—and just enjoy the beach a bit. Scroll one of those dating apps?"

"Mum, please don't say that."

The privilege pounds in Emily's chest. The built-in benefits of being exceptionally wealthy have always bothered her. She was nearly eighteen when it first clicked.

She wanted to go to Columbia University, just as her father had, and she was accepted before the application was even submitted. After undergrad, she headed across the pond to get a Master of Science in Financial Economics from Oxford University, the alma mater of her mother. Again, applying was for logistical reasons only. She had a place there from the moment she was born.

It was the first time she realized the power of her family's name. And she's never forgotten it.

So much so, that she tried desperately to outwork it daily at The Brynn Company. From the age of twenty-three, when she first began working for her father, until yesterday when she quit, she was the first in the office and the last to leave. If there was a dinner, or a fundraiser, or a town hall full of angry residents, she was there. She was first. She was always prepared. Always ready to prove her worth.

Until now.

Here, on the coast of North Carolina, no one knows her name. Or her company. Or her billion-dollar family. No one cares about her bank account or where she went to high school or college or graduate school. The numerous houses she owns across the globe. Here, she is just Emily.

And here, she would not be caught dead sitting around basking in her riches.

She will work.

"Don't be angry with me for trying to get you to relax a bit. How'd Maya take the news?"

"Just fine."

Emily had called her best friend on the drive down. Maya's initial response was just like James's: "You can't quit. You own it."

Then she'd said, "You don't have to quit to go on vacation."

Then she asked if Emily just needed to "get laid."

But all that gibberish led her ultimately to say, "I'm proud of you, Em."

Emily adds, "She's happy for me."

"How's she going to survive without seeing you until August?"

The two did barre class together on Tuesdays, Thursdays, and Saturdays. Most Sundays they enjoyed mimosas while Maya's husband, Donovan, took their son, Ben, golfing.

"Oh, she won't. She said she'll be making a weekend trip down at some point prior to."

Her mother laughs. "Did you get some good seafood last night?"

"I actually did. Had this incredible Cuban sandwich with mahi on it. Odd mix, right?"

Recalling her dinner makes her think of Sara. Her rosy cheeks, shaped by long layers of golden hair. Her bright, ocean-blue eyes. Muted red lipstick.

She'd lain in bed last night thinking of her. If she had to draw up a storied Southern belle, it'd be Sara. She'd imagined that she's probably a lover of sun tea and wallpaper. Enjoys tuning in to a round of gossip. Wouldn't be caught dead in a pair of sweatpants. Not at school drop-off, not at the airport, not even in her own home. Knows how to bake a peach cobbler. Pours a strong glass of whiskey. Loves her babies more than life itself.

Emily had chuckled, forcing herself to stop stereotyping the woman she barely knew before finally falling asleep.

"It sounds delicious. All right, darling. I'm really proud of you. And I just want to add once more that I am proud of myself. Not to brag or anything, but I told your father that you wanted to do something different. You were just too darn good at your job for him to believe it."

Her mother loves that she was right, relishes it. Emily can hear the victory in her sprightly tone. If Barry were still alive, she'd be rubbing it in his face, but if he were still alive, Emily may never have left.

Life is strange like that.

"It's true, Mum. You were right." Emily feeds her mother's ego as she rises from her seat and heads back into her new waterfront home.

CHAPTER FOUR

Emily

"Hey! Emily!" Through her heavy breathing, Emily hears the smack of flip-flops against the pavement. "Emily!"

Emily stops midstride as she pieces together the familiar Southern drawl. She spins around to find Sara. Five days ago, when they shared too many glasses of wine, Sara was dressed professionally, her blond hair in loose spiral curls, her outfit ironed and well-tailored. Today, her hair is tied up into a ponytail. She's wearing brown leather sandals, fitted athletic shorts, and a razorback tank, a rolled-up plush yoga mat wedged under her arm.

"Hi!" Emily is winded and sweaty and, suddenly, a bit self-conscious in the presence of her new friend, who also happens to be beautiful and recently separated. And also into men, Emily reminds herself as she pops out her earbuds. "How are you, Sara?"

There's something different about her. Emily found her attractive the other night, but on this Saturday morning under this April sun, Sara radiates an easiness about her that feels magnetic.

"I'm sorry for interrupting your run." Sara squeezes Emily's arm. "I got excited when I saw you."

The charming remark swims through Emily, causing goose bumps to explode up and down her arms. Excited is exactly what Emily is feeling, but she's trying hard to ignore it since their definition of excitement is likely stemming from two different places.

"I'm happy to see you, too. I was just finishing up. That's my home there." She points to the wood shake house a block down the street.

"The Mayos' house?"

"Excuse me?"

"That white one there?" Sara points.

"Yes. Is that the owner? The Mayos?"

"Yep, Jared and I designed that house. Start to finish."

"You're a designer?"

Sara starts walking and Emily matches her stride. "Sara Dylan Design since 2016."

Emily gently leans in and nudges her. "You are quite the talent, Ms. Sara Dylan. It's a gorgeous home. I was just raving to my mum about it the other day."

"Thank you," she says. "Hey, I know you just ran, but I'm headed to a yoga class on the beach. Any interest in joining me?"

"Sure! I'd love to." Emily had been planning to do a thirty-minute barre session from her Peloton app, but an in-person yoga class on the beach sounds exactly like what she needs to be doing on this beautiful weekend in her new coastal oasis. "Do I have time to run in and change quickly? I'm a sweaty mess."

Sara peers down at her watch. "We've got fifteen minutes, go for it."

"You want to come up and check out your work?"

"Of course. I was gonna invite myself if you didn't offer."

Emily hurries up the stairs first despite knowing there is no time to straighten up. Upon opening the door, she takes note of the navy throw on the couch and the pages of the thick nineties' romance novel from the owner's bookshelf fanned out on the ottoman. She's pleased with the state of things.

"I'll be right back," she tells her.

In her room she finds her navy Lululemon spandex and a light-pink crop top. She splashes her face with lukewarm water and hurriedly applies mascara. "Earrings. That'll help."

While she puts on round gold earrings, she finds herself pushing down the tiny little crush on Sara that is encroaching on her sense of reality.

"My gosh," she says, chuckling. A deep exhale and she's back out in the living room.

"Nautical, simple, and airy were their requirements. It's been six years since Jared and I completed this job, and I must say I am still very pleased with both the hard and soft fixtures."

Sara rubs her hand along the butcher-block island.

"You should be. Is the sailboat your doing as well?"

"It is. Gosh it's still one of my favorite pieces. It's a replica of Mrs. Mayo's grandfather's sailboat. Those are his initials at the top of the mast." Emily had noticed them the other day, the LM intricately painted black. "And that sail there was created from the actual sail off his boat. I found an artist in New Bern that built this for them. A complete surprise to Mrs. Mayo. She had been telling me that they had nowhere to store the old boat but she couldn't find it in her to get rid of it, so I had this idea and worked with her husband to get it done."

"I would have enjoyed seeing her reaction."

"Tears! It was a good one."

The two hustle back down the steps and head off to find their spots on the beach. Emily takes note of each granule of cool sand beneath her feet. She's been to Hanalei Bay in Hawaii. Baia do Sancho in Brazil, the black sand beaches of Tahiti. Her family owns a small boutique hotel on Great Guana Cay. She's got a home in Salcombe and another in Brighton, but there's something she finds magical about this moment on the Carolina coast.

The two roll out their plush yoga mats side by side and sit cross-legged on top of them. Emily sees Sara, in her peripheral vision, instantly reach her long arms high above her head to stretch, but Emily is too distracted by all the beauty of this new place to prepare for the yoga instruction.

The seagulls are galloping around the early sky above her. Foamy waves roll up and stretch out across the sand, stirring up seashells and seaweed and small round pebbles. It's still quiet out. Too early in the season for tourism, but there's a handful of multicolored umbrellas claiming spots for unoccupied chairs along the shoreline.

"This is lovely," Emily comments, a smile stretching across her face.

Sara looks up from her mat and stays silent a moment before responding. "It is, isn't it?" She doesn't look at Emily when she speaks, but she sits back, leaning against her palms and stretching her legs out in front of her. "Gosh, I've been coming here for so many years, I sometimes forget to notice it."

Silence bounces between them until Sara turns to face Emily. "Kinda sad, huh?"

Emily holds her gaze, wondering how on earth she was lucky enough to stumble into this beautiful human again. "No, because now it can be all new to both of us."

Sara bites her lower lip, appearing to temper her grin. "That's a good way to look at it."

·

CHAPTER FIVE

Sara

Sara thinks about asking, then tells herself no, and then asks anyway. "You want to grab a coffee?"

She's worried she may sound needy, but it's been so long since she's felt excited about spending time with another person. Maybe it's her mind's way of battling the loneliness.

"I'd love to." Emily's endearing response puts Sara's questioning to rest.

"There's a great spot just before the bridge. My treat," Sara insists.

"You bought dinner the other night, this is mine."

"Oh, hush." Sara nudges her. "Come on."

Emily orders a black coffee, hot. Sara debates between a few options, eventually settling on a nitro cold brew with lavender foam. The two sit outside under a large floral umbrella. The heaviness of summer hasn't settled in yet. It's seventy-two and sunny. A slight breeze pushes the palm trees side to side.

"Tell me more about your business. How'd you get started?" Emily asks.

"I'll give you the short version." Sara sips her coffee before beginning. "I was working for another firm, here in Wilmington. I had just had Sophie, my first daughter, so this was about eight years ago. I knew I was ready to branch out. Steve had given me his full support. He was doing very well with his real estate firm." She interrupts herself to ask, "You're in real estate too, right?"

"Commercial, yes. Well, I was."

The cheerful expression on Emily's face makes Sara chuckle. "You're that happy, huh?"

"So far, yes."

"Real estate does seem like a bit of a headache," Sara says before continuing, "Anyway, I started advertising around our neighborhood. I was working out of the carriage house on our property at the time, and I was fortunate to land a few home renos, one of which was the owner of the Fire House Cocktail Bar and Eatery. It's in downtown Wilmington, have you been yet?"

"No, I haven't left the beach yet, but I enjoy a dram."

"Dram," Sara chuckles. "I haven't heard that since I was in Ireland."

"Dram or whiskey. Condo or flat. Mind your head or watch out. I don't ever really know what's going to come out of my mouth. The curse of growing up with a well-traveled American father and an English mum."

"I love it." Sara holds Emily's gaze, a spark buzzing between them.

Is she feeling this too?

Sara coughs, an instinctual reaction to distract herself from her ridiculous feelings. "Well." She coughs once more. "They have excellent cocktails and it's right along the water on Front Street. So, the guy who owns it is John. I did a first-floor reno for his home and he loved it so much that when he bought the old fire station, he hired me to convert it into a restaurant."

"It obviously went well?"

"It did. It got a good bit of buzz around town. The local news covered it. The paper covered it. It kicked off my business."

"So where does Jared come in?"

"My knight in shining armor." Sara grins. "We met in design school at NC State. He moved up to Boston after college, married Matthew, and started a whole life there, but we always kept in touch. He's gifted. Really gifted. Especially at design. Fabrics, materials, staging. I knew I wanted to hire him. He'll say it was the cheaper housing that brought him back down, but I know he did it because he believed in me, and he believed in what we could do together." Sara sips her coffee. "And also, Matthew hates the cold." She chuckles. "So that helped. He took a leap of faith and we've been blessed. It's really working out."

"He seems wonderful."

"Salt of the earth."

They both sip their coffee. "Are you looking at getting back into real estate down here?"

"In a different way. I want to bring life back into an old property. I've spent the last few days scouring the area for some cool buildings. Something with a story worth reviving."

"I know a place."

Emily tilts her head. "Yeah?"

Sara stoops her posture a bit. "Well, it's worth noting that it might be a little steep, there's some issue with the back taxes. That's why it's been sitting for so long, but it's in Southport."

"The library?"

Sara raises her eyebrows. "You have been doing your research. Yes, the old library."

"I've got about ten hours under my belt on this specific property alone."

Curiosity and excitement building, Sara says, "Well, tell me everything!"

"In the fifties, it was a library. It's less than six hundred square feet. Sits on half an acre of buildable land. Zoned for mixed-use. The city has it up for three hundred ninety-nine thousand. A steal for the land, but they're asking for the taxes dating back to 1954. Between that and an extensive reno, it'll put me somewhere north of a million five, give or take."

Sara's designer jitters are bubbling through her seams. "I want to see it. Do you want to go see it?" She can barely believe the words that are spilling from her mouth. Asking a near stranger to road trip to see an old, abandoned property.

Emily's eyes light up instantly. "Let's go!"

CHAPTER SIX

Sara

"Tell me what you did again for work in New York?" Sara chokes through the question as she hesitantly climbs into Emily's Mercedes SUV. She knows very little about cars but reckons this one runs upward of a quarter million dollars.

"Hold on just a moment, sorry." Emily answers her phone. "Yes, Mark?" Sara tries not to intrude on Emily's conversation, but the panic she detects in the man's muffled voice tells her he's seeking guidance.

"What's your gut telling you?" Emily asks.

Another pause as Emily listens. Sara peers ahead, impressed by the effortless power that is Emily Brynn.

"Then move forward. Job of this size, put the offer in cash. Short window of acceptance. You walk if they say no. It's a generous proposal from The Brynn Company. A healthy outcome for the client. Everyone wins. What is there left to think about, Mark?"

Sara perks up at the company's name. The Brynn Company. As in Emily Brynn's company?

"Mark, what is there left to think about?" Emily repeats.

"Nothing," Sara hears.

"Right. You know all the answers already. You have a great knack for this. I trust your judgment. Now you need to trust yourself as well."

He rambles a bit more before Sara hears him praise her for the feedback.

"I'm here for you. Now go close the deal, Mark." Emily clicks the phone off. "I'm sorry about that, but to answer your question, that's what I did for work. Answer phone calls. Sign some paperwork."

"More, please."

A grin curls up across Emily's face as she glances over at Sara. They parted ways for a bit after coffee to shower. Sara dabbed her neck with lavender essential oil, thinking Emily might like it while simultaneously wondering why the hell she cares.

"I did real estate."

"I know, but I know there's different segments of the industry. Steve does investment and development. You said commercial, right?" Sara has never really understood Steve's business, but she's hoping the vague description sounds familiar to Emily.

"I know exactly what Steve does. I did similar work. I worked for The Brynn Company."

"I heard that while you were on the phone. Brynn as in your last name? Did you own it?" Sara asks as she shuffles through the very little information she has about Emily.

She knows that Emily is living in the Mayos' beach home, which rents for about six grand a week in the off-season. She knows that in the summer, the rental prices soar to over ten K a week.

Surely, she worked out a nice month-to-month rental agreement with them?

Maybe she inherited a bunch of money from her late father?

Steve does well. Maybe she does better?

A quarter-million-dollar-car better?

"Well, technically," Emily says. "I'm still a co-owner, but my brother, James, runs it. My grandfather started it. We tackle all kinds of avenues within the real estate umbrella. You are probably familiar with the field from Steve, yeah?"

"I don't want to admit this, but his line of work has always been real confusing to me."

Emily chuckles. "We basically research and acquire properties that we think have developmental potential. Then we oversee the construction from the ground up. In some cases we sell the property, in some we keep it, and the company branches out from there. We also started a property management division, and what I'm most proud of is our nonprofit foundation."

Sara's eyes widen. "Did he fire you?" The questions almost sounds defensive.

"What?"

"Did your brother fire you? I don't understand. It sounds like you had a good thing going, so did he fire you?"

"No!" Emily chuckles.

Sara stares blankly, processing everything Emily's told her. "So what did your day-to-day look like?"

"You have a lot of questions."

"Well, if you woulda picked me up in a Honda CR-V, I wouldn't be so curious. But you've got secrets, Emily Brynn, and I've got a right to know if I'm gonna be ending up on the Investigation Discovery Network."

Emily's eyes open wide. "I probably would find that offensive if it weren't for your Southern accent."

"What?" Sara chuckles.

"It makes everything seem so sweet."

Sara can feel her cheeks heat up. "All right, you're distracting from my questions. Spill it, woman."

"I was one of the team members responsible for the initial research and acquisition. A lot of crunching numbers, figuring out what the future city plans were. Lots of negotiations. I also started our property management company, so that required some oversight for some time until we could hire someone proficient enough to take it on."

"Wow." After a long duration of silence, Sara looks over at Emily. "I thought there was something impressive about you."

Emily bites her lip, preventing her smile from stretching.

"So, you were just done with the stress or the people? What was it really?"

"Little bit of everything, I suppose. But when it comes down to it, there's just more I want to do with my life, and I'm very fortunate to be in a position to do it."

"And buying this old library is what you wanna do?"

"Maybe, yes. I want to build something with my own hands, not just hire a general contractor. I want to bring life to something that's been forgotten. And I don't want to spend my evenings managing haughty rich men with seeking hands. I want to sit on the dock behind my rental and fish, or read, or maybe not fish." Emily throws her hand in the air. "I don't know about touching worms and all that." She laughs at herself. "To be frank, I don't even know how to relax, but what I'm saying is that I'd like to try."

Sara hasn't taken her eyes off Emily. She is completely enthralled with her. Her sharp jawline, the way her lips move, and the way she sounds out each and every syllable. "How are you not married?" Sara asks, knowing she's completely switching topics. Before Emily can answer, Sara adds, "This is apparently my new normal, by the way. Abrasive questioning with good but nosy intentions."

Emily cocks her head to the side in a sort of silly confusion. "I guess the honesty makes it okay?"

They both laugh.

"It's the divorce. Just kinda reset my thinking on wasting time. I want the good stuff."

"I like that."

"Now back to the question…"

"Haven't found the one yet, I suppose."

Sara nods. "Okay, then. Well, let's go find you a property to fix up."

Emily laughs, seemingly at the rapid flip-flopping of talking points.

Thirty minutes down Route 17 they pull into the quiet town of Southport, North Carolina. It's dressed in American flags.

Spanish moss drools from every tree. The lawns are manicured, the storefronts charming. "This place is a dream," Emily says, her lustful eyes in awe.

"I want to live here one day," Sara shares as she takes in the Tudor homes, each dressed in a different pastel.

Three blocks back from the waterfront, Emily pulls into a gravel parking lot in front of a red *For Sale* sign. The lot looks as if nature threw a temper tantrum. There is wild brush burying all four sides of the small square brick building, ivy crawling up and through the dilapidated roof. A single push of a finger might cause the whole building to come crashing down.

The two hop out to get a closer look at the few visible areas of the building. "Do you know what's on the other side of this wild maze?" Emily asks.

"It's mostly protected forest beyond the creek. Just over there"—Sara points—"is a memorial for Pirate Stede Bonnet."

"A pirate, yeah?"

"Yep. He's kinda like you. A rich man that left his home for adventure."

"The pirate?"

"Yes! He was filthy rich. Owned a sugar plantation. Left it all for a life of piracy."

Emily tilts her head to the side and grins. "I don't think I'll be stepping into a life of thievery, but I guess we're both just looking for a little adventure, yeah?"

Emily scours the property thoroughly, jotting notes into her phone.

"I can see you're well practiced. You've probably worked on properties twenty-five times this cost, huh?"

"A few. Process is always the same, though. Know the surroundings. Know future city development plans. Determine the quality of the school district. Research the history of the property. Schedule a percolation test. Find out how it's zoned, and if it needs to be changed, can it be changed? The list goes on."

Sara doesn't respond, she's just enjoying being around such an intelligent, driven being.

"It's brilliant," Emily says.

"I knew you would like it." Sara flinches at her reply. She hardly knows this woman, but she did know. She knew that Emily Brynn would like this place. She felt it in her gut.

"I'll have to do some digging, but I'd keep as much of the original material as possible. Typically, any brick building built before the sixties doesn't have an air gap. Just three layers of good solid brick. Might need a little foundation work, but it's small. I'd guess forty to fifty grand to get it stable again. We know that it was a library, and that's all I could find online, but anything before that? I'd imagine it has a steep history. Long before the fifties I'd guess, yeah?"

"I'm not sure."

"I'll do some more research and try to tie in its origin, but I'm thinking books and booze. What do you think, Sar?"

Sara smiles at the way Emily has shortened her name. "Keep going." Of course Sara wants to hear more about Emily's grand idea, but truthfully she'd listen to her speak about pretty much anything.

"White privacy fence," Emily continues. "Around the entire property. I think I'm correct in saying it's about a half an acre."

"I saw the same," Sara confirms.

"Maybe we put a wooden pirate ship playground in the back. Play into the whole Stede Bonnet guy."

Sara gasps in excitement. "I love that! And there's nothing like it around."

"It's always so tough for my brother and his wife to find a place where they can grab a nice drink while the kids entertain themselves. Always thought that was a market I'd like to pursue."

"It's a wonderful idea."

"We'd use every bit of the property. Keep the mature trees but clean it up a bit for outdoor seating. Southport's newest hangout just needs a name."

"The Gentleman Pirate's Hideaway."

Emily sharply turns her head and squints her eyes. "Sounds like a strip club. Explain?"

Sara roars in laughter. "It does, doesn't it? Stede Bonnet was known as the Gentleman Pirate. Maybe we just stick to The Pirate's Hideaway?"

Emily walks up to Sara and gives her a high five. "You are brilliant, Sara Dylan. Now let's get some food."

"I know the perfect spot, but it's no ritzy New York City steakhouse. You gonna be okay, Ms. Emily Brynn?"

Emily doesn't acknowledge the sarcastic dig. She simply spins on her heel and heads to the car. Sara's cheeks flush and her smile stretches. She begs herself silently to hold herself together as she follows Emily to the car.

The two sit on the waterfront at a wooden shack at the edge of town. They drink beer from glass bottles and eat fried shrimp and talk into the late hours over the cawing of the seagulls.

On the drive home, Sara finds herself actively resisting reaching across the console to grab Emily's hand, causing her heart rate to rocket.

Do I like her?

Or do I want to be her?

What in God's name has gotten into me?

A rush of inconsolable thoughts pummel through her.

Is this what happens when husbands leave their wives? Women lose all sense of moral clarity?

I'm losing it.

The thoughts come to a complete halt when Emily pulls in front of Sara's building and reaches her hand across the dash, gently grabbing Sara's wrist. "Thanks for today, Sar. I had a lot of fun."

Sara slowly looks down at Emily's soft hand against her skin. Emily leaves it there. A second passes. Then another. Another. Before Emily pulls her hand back.

"Me too," Sara finally says. She gathers her things and opens the car door. "You'll have to let me know what you decide to do with the property. And if you need a little design help, I know someone." Sara winks, proud of her witty exit despite her mind being in a state of homemade Jell-O.

"You'll be my first call. Have a good night, Sar."

Sara makes her way to the door. Before entering, she looks back and waves goodbye. Emily is still sitting there.

My God, she is gorgeous.

CHAPTER SEVEN

Sara

Sara is rushing around, gathering her tote with all her typical job site essentials: her iPad, her notebook, her catalog of pictures and sketches, samples of countertops and backsplashes, and various fabrics she's assembled over the last few weeks.

"Have you seen my tape measure?"

Jared has plopped himself down in a plush midcentury armchair that sits in the corner of Sara's office. He taps his feet against the woven beige rug like a disappointed parent. "I don't understand how you are always misplacing it."

"Oh, hush. Here it is." She lifts it joyously from her bottom desk drawer. "I've got to run."

"Wait, what did you want to tell me?"

"Oh, remember Emily? The woman that sat next to us for a drink last week?"

"Yes."

"Look at her." She twists her computer around, revealing a picture of Emily Brynn standing on a stage. It's a side shot. She's in a navy silk dress, her shoulders back, her chin up, addressing an audience. Exquisite poise. Commanding attention. "She's a really incredible woman."

"Why are you googling her? Did you run into her again or something?"

"Yes! We did yoga together on Saturday. She might be buying a property in Southport." Sara stops fidgeting for a moment, her brows rising. "And I may have already done some preliminary designs based on the vision she shared with me. I'm crazy, aren't I?"

"Did she say she was going to hire us?"

"No."

"Then yes, you are crazy to be working on a project you may not get for a woman you barely know, given the workload you're already drowning in."

"Oh, hush. We're friends now. I went with her to see the property, so I took the initiative." She leaves out the part about how she hasn't stopped thinking about the way Emily's hand felt against her wrist.

A broad smile curiously unravels along Jared's chiseled face. "What?"

"Nothing." He straightens his posture and replies in a much kinder tone, "I think this might just work out for us, then."

"It will." Sara nods. She knows why he's smiling. She's happy. He sees it. Likely for the first time in months.

"All right, Jare, I gotta get going."

"Good luck at the Food Hall. Take lots of pictures, please. And don't forget to tell Margie to tell Steve he's a dick."

Sara chuckles at his comment, knowing it's a bald-faced lie. Jared adores Steve, he just knows his obligation for humor lies with Sara.

Sara Dylan Design landed the contract for the interior design and decorating of Port City Food Hall two years ago. Steve's real estate company had purchased the property years back for retail development. After numerous hiccups and discussions with the city and surrounding neighborhoods, it turned into Port City Food Hall: the future home of six different cuisines, a coffee bar, a cocktail bar, and two boutiques.

The job was an absolute dream for Sara. Of course, this was before she found out that her husband was having an affair with the twenty-seven-year-old city inspector Margie Filmore. Now every time Sara does job walks, she imagines herself in a reality TV show.

"Hi, Margie." Sara greets her husband's mistress with a forced smile as she enters the north wing of Port City Food Hall.

"Hey, Sara. Everything looks good so far. I was told to get an update on ADA-compliant bathrooms and ensure the gaps between common space seating allows for wheelchair access."

Sara makes eye contact, wondering if this beautiful young woman with the golden hair that looks just like hers—except shinier, and more youthful, and about two inches longer—is still sleeping with the man she is technically still married to. It's not her fault, of course. Who knows if she even knew he was married? But it does make these weekly arrangements awfully awkward and a bit painful to get through.

"We've got an accessibility stall planned for each of the three restrooms. I believe those are set to go in next week." Sara swipes through her iPad until she reaches the schedule. "Yes, next Thursday. Eight to ten days for install. There's a slight delay with the faucets."

"Sounds great," Margie says genuinely.

"There will also be ramp access for all four entrances and plenty of space throughout the building for strollers, wheelchairs, and walkers."

"Excellent. Thank you for the update. I'll see you next week, same time."

At least Margie has always kept their mandatory visits short and professional. She's good at her job. It's not hard to understand how Steve could fall for a woman like her. Beautiful and seemingly intelligent. Similar to Sara, but a decade her junior.

"See you then," Sara says as she pulls out her tape measure and sets to take the dimensions she's missing.

A few footsteps sound before Margie speaks again. "Hey, Sara?"

"Yes?" Sara looks up from her measurements.

"I know this isn't ideal for you." Margie points her finger back and forth between the two of them. "I recognize that, and I want to respect your boundaries. But I...I wanted to let you know that I met Sophie and Joanna this past weekend."

Sara looks at her dumbfounded for a moment, wondering why her girls hadn't said anything. Why they would have kept this secret? Why hadn't Steve said anything? She thinks about answering with neutrality, but her face has already given her away. "I didn't know."

All color drains from Margie's face, perhaps because she realizes she said something that maybe she shouldn't have. "It wasn't planned." She rubs her free hand along her forehead. "I ran into them at the Publix. We didn't...uh...introduce ourselves as anything more than friends, but I just...I just wanted you to know that they seem really great. Really wonderful girls you've raised."

Sara studies Margie's pallid face and worried eyes. This answers her question about their relationship. It's obviously ongoing. Sara exhales before responding. "They are great girls. Thank you for saying that." Sara hastily returns to her to-do list, listening intently to Margie's thirty-three steps out of the swinging glass front door.

Her phone rings. It's Jared. She answers.

"Holy shit, this Emily Brynn is an icon."

The pounding in Sara's head dissolves instantly at Jared's mention of Emily. "Have you been stalking her all morning?"

"No silly, that's ridiculous. I just started."

Sara chuckles. "What have you found? And why are you looking her up?"

"Well, you seem to like her, so I was intrigued," Jared says, as if it's totally normal to do background research on his boss's new friend. "Have you looked up her former company?" he asks.

"Not really, but she's told me a little bit. Why?"

"Well." Jared's long pause tells Sara he is eager to share the breaking news. "She's the part owner of a massive conglomerate. What I'm saying is…she is filthy rich."

"She does drive a really nice car."

Jared stammers, "Why on earth would she move—"

Sara interrupts him. "Tell me what else you found."

"Her father passed away a year ago, and he was honored for his humanitarian efforts at a New York Knicks basketball game." He pauses for a moment, seemingly awaiting a reaction from Sara. "Hello! Are you hearing this? *The* New York Knicks professional basketball team."

"So she's well connected."

"Also, she's a lesbian. She dated Michael Perry's daughter. I'm looking at a picture of them kissing on the red carpet right now."

Sara feels a rush of…something…flurry through her.

"The actor Michael Perry?" she asks.

"Yes."

"Emily likes women?" Heat trickles down her spine.

"I can't be a hundred percent certain, but typically women don't kiss other women on a red carpet unless they're dating."

Silence takes over the line. Sara thinks about Emily Brynn liking women. Kissing a woman. She's known lesbians before. Of course, she has. Well, not many. But the ones she has encountered do not look like Emily Brynn.

Jared breaks the silence. "Gosh, Emily is gorgeous."

The sound of his voice on the phone makes Sara turn red. She's embarrassed by her shallow idea of what a lesbian looks like. "Are you there?" he asks.

"She is pretty," Sara says, reinforcing the obvious. "But I think it's time you stop stalking our potential new client and get back to work."

"Okay, that's fair. You're the boss. This is a lot of fun though, isn't it?"

"Yes, it was. Goodbye."

CHAPTER EIGHT

Emily

May

"All go well with the old library?" James asks.

"We're all settled. I've got the keys."

"Well, that didn't take ya long, yeah?"

"Are you surprised?"

"No, but Mum had me convinced you were going to try and relax there."

Emily hears his silly comment but doesn't feel the need to respond. "I need to find a few contractors that'll work with me. I've never had to start from scratch with connections, but I met a local designer that I think is probably tied in fairly well."

"Name?"

"Sara Dylan."

She hears James typing, and after a few moments, "Whoa."

Emily knows he's just seen Sara Dylan and she knows he thinks what she thinks: Sara Dylan is gorgeous. She wants to tell him all about Sara's Southern drawl, how she elongates her vowels and never pronounces the letter *G* at the end of any word ending in *ing*. She wants to tell James about Sara's soft features and ocean eyes, and the way her skin glows of summer against her mermaid-blond hair.

"You're into her, aren't you?"

He knows.

"No." Emily can't even convince herself. There's no chance her brother will believe her.

"Oh, boy. You are. Is she married?"

"Separated."

"Kids?"

"Two girls."

"Nice! My kids need some cousins."

"Oh, stop it. She's going through a lot."

"I'm sure. Leaving her husband for a woman is a bit much to take in."

They both burst into laughter.

"Stop it, James," Emily begs. "I am not at all, not even a little bit, trying to get involved with a woman going through divorce that I plan to work with. Oh, and by the way, this is a ridiculous conversation because she's not remotely interested in me. She's straight."

"Sure thing, Em." James is well aware of Emily's successful track record with straight women. "By the way, thanks so much for handling the venue paperwork for the gala."

Maya handles nearly everything as their event coordinator. A true professional, but there are certain things that need the Brynn signature, and since Emily bailed on James and the company, she's trying her best to take on some of the fundraiser needs from afar.

"How are the registrations coming along?"

"Amazing. Maya said there's only two tables left. We have room for movement, though. You have a plus-one. Mum said she has a friend from pickleball that she wants to bring. Pretty sure it's a love interest. Roger is his name. Sounds like a dud."

"Oh, James, hush it. I'll follow up with Parker about which painting she plans to donate, but other than that I think we've got what we need. Did you get the Yankees club seats from Joe?"

"Working on it," James says. "Just lock in the art and we're good to go. Speaking of Parker, she could probably be your plus-one, yeah?"

"No."

The mention of Parker does not sting like it once did. It just sort of sails through her these days. Therapy has helped with that.

The two dated for nearly three years in Emily's late twenties. They first met at the grand opening of Parker's art gallery. She was seven years older. Mature. Wildly successful. Quirky. She wasn't big on the flashy parties that most of the other women Emily had dated loved so much, and their fathers knew each other from business dealings. Everything felt right. Meant to be, even. Or at least Emily thought it was. She bought a ring for Parker Anne, but she never proposed. Parker had picked up a part-time teaching position at her alma mater, Parsons, and in a few short weeks it led to a part-time lover to the Professor of Fashion Design. The professor was a man.

Parker apologized profusely, but only after Emily uncovered a string of scandalous text messages.

"Would you ever have told me?" Emily had asked her.

"It was a mistake, Brynny. Just sex," she swore.

But it was over, the fractured trust between them irreparable.

Emily never let on to her sadness under the judging eye of their wealthy circle, but she was embarrassed, broken in a way that her typical easy confidence couldn't overcome in the dark of night.

It was years of small steps. Years of therapy. Relearning how to love, how to be loved, how to give love. Most importantly, how to love herself.

It's been nearly a decade since they split. They found a way to settle into a cordial friendship. A guarded one. A safe one. One that mostly revolves around mutually beneficial work events like The Brynn Foundation Gala that will be held at Parker's gallery.

"Okay, that's fair. She's just so damn cool," James says. "Listen, I've got to run, but I just need to know how you plan on not falling head over heels for this attractive designer you plan to hire."

"Very easy. I'm a professional, James. I'll keep it professional."

"Oh, great plan. Good luck!"

Emily hangs up. "Pshh, luck."

Business first. She pulls up Parker's name and scrolls through the latest messages. The last one is from her, one month back, asking Parker to follow up on the painting she plans to donate.

Emily dials her number. Business is best handled immediately, something her father used to harp on.

It rings twice before Parker answers. "I haven't seen your name come across my screen in years. How are you, Brynny?"

No one calls her Brynny. No one even calls her Brynn. No one except Parker, who even after their breakup wouldn't refer to Emily as anything other than Brynny.

"I'm good. Spending a little time down in North Carolina. I believe James filled you in."

"He did. Are you happy?"

"I am." Emily doesn't have to think about it. Whether she is or isn't, she will tell Parker that she is happy. "Thank you for asking."

"Well, I know you're not calling to ask me to coffee, so out with it."

"That's true. I'm following up about the painting. We're so grateful you've decided to donate one of your pieces again this year. I wanted to know if you've chosen one."

"Enough with the formalities, Brynny. I've got you covered. Trust me. You know that. It'll be here on the night of the gala. Direct your worries elsewhere."

Emily sighs. It's straining gathering donated auction items. She needn't waste her worry on Parker; she's been a loyal supporter since the beginning. But Emily remembers the change of heart Parker had so many years ago, and even if it's silly, she finds herself resurfacing that small truth when Parker says things like *trust me*.

"Thanks, Park. You always come through for us."

"I do. When are you coming back into the city? Would love to catch up over a drink if you can squeeze me in."

Not a chance. "I'm not sure yet. I've got a new project I'm getting started on down here."

"I can take a hint, Brynny. Looking forward to seeing you at the gala. Stay well."

Emily texts Maya and James the update on the painting. Maya writes back instantly.

Parker always pulls through. She wasn't my concern. Can someone get the Yanks tix locked in, please?

James responds: *Just made the call. We're good to go. I'll have them to you by end of day.*

Emily stands up for a stretch before moving on to the only person she wants to talk business with. She sends a text message: *Hi Sara, I settled on the Southport property today. Do you have any availability for a new client consultation?*

Emily had just seen Sara at yoga on Saturday morning, but Sara had to hurry off to the beach with her girls, so Emily didn't get the opportunity to update her on the settlement. Or to have coffee with her, or ogle over her, or listen to the sweet drawl of her words.

Within a minute of sending the message, Emily's phone rings. It's Sara. Emily forces her excitement into composure as she remembers what she literally just told her brother.

I am a professional.

"Hi, Sara."

"Congratulations, Emily!"

"Thank you. So you think you can make space in your workload for an old library?"

"For you, of course."

Emily's cheeks burn crimson. She's thankful that she's alone. "It is appreciated."

"Are you doing anything right now?" Sara continues without giving Emily the chance to answer. "This is gonna sound a little crazy, but I may have been proactively throwing some designs together just for fun and not at all because I really wanted you to hire us for this fun job."

"Sara!" Emily chuckles. "You are awesome. I'll be at your office in thirty."

CHAPTER NINE

Sara

"Em!" Sara just happens to be walking by as Emily tugs open the wooden handle of her oversized glass front door. "That was fast," she says as she leans in for a friendly side hug.

"I need my afternoon pick-me-up. You want a coffee or tea?"

"I'm all caffeinated up. Thank you, though."

Sara pours herself a coffee at the beverage nook to the right of the front door before guiding Emily back to her office. She pulls up a midcentury chair with a high blush-pink back for Emily and puts it inches from her own. "You ready?" Sara says as she scrolls through a list of files.

"I can't believe you've prepared something. What if I never called?"

Sara pauses and looks over at Emily. "Well I knew you would."

The way Emily's lip curls up into a half-grin toward the single freckle under her right eye makes Sara's whole body shiver. She repositions herself, brushing off the reaction before clicking on a file titled *The Pirate's Hideaway*.

"All right," she begins. "So I've got a little design hobby I do on the side. You can hate it. It was just more of a placeholder." She doesn't mean this. She spent hours finagling this design to ensure it was every bit classic, bold, and beautiful. She'd never admit to it, mainly because it would require her to admit why she did it.

On the opening screen of her laptop is a badass logo of a female pirate with a peg leg and long, wavy black hair. A burning cigar hangs from her red lips and both hands are cupping a book. Next to the pirate is the bar's name, *The Pirate's Hideaway*, and beneath that, *books, booze & pirates* in lowercase letters.

Emily's eyes are wide in wonder. "Sara!"

Sara looks over at her again to make eye contact. Emily grabs her forearm. "This is unbelievable. We're using it! We must!"

Sara does her best to ignore the shiver that explodes through her from Emily's touch.

"I'm happy you like it," she says casually, as if Emily's reaction didn't just validate her entire life's work. She scrolls slowly down to the second page, stalling just long enough to think about how odd it is that she feels so drawn to this woman.

"I imagine it looking like a hobbit's home," Sara continues. "A fort feel. Magical for adults and kids." Sara chuckles to herself. "This is so different than my usual clean-cut coastal designs. I had fun with it, clearly."

"I absolutely love it."

There is thrill in Emily's tone. Sara knows she's impressed. She continues, "The front door will be a large rounded wooden door. A heavy handle right in the middle of it. We'll plant jasmine all over the building. It'll be nearly hidden in vines by this time next year."

"My goodness," Emily says.

Sara switches screens and pulls up a 3D rendering of what she's imagined the inside will look like. "Books everywhere. All for purchase. A large selection of pirate books for all ages. Coastal ghost tales. Local fishing guides. I know a bunch of Carolina authors that must be in stock. All things eastern North

Carolina. If we can refurbish the hardwoods, we will. Do you have a GC, by chance? Or are you running the show?"

"I'm doing it, but I'll take any and all contractor references."

"Good idea, it'll save you thousands." She peeks over at Emily and follows up her comment with, "It has nothing to do with the money, does it?"

"No," Emily says with a sly smile, which makes Sara giggle.

"I know some great contractors. I've got a plumber and a floor guy that can do all your tile work too. Not crazy about my electrician, but I'll help you find one."

Sara's electrician is one of those guys that makes snarky, misogynistic comments and then laughs it off with a "just kidding, people are so sensitive these days." He's excellent at his job, so Sara has never hesitated to pass his name and number along, but she doesn't want him around Emily. She'll make some calls and find someone more suitable.

"This is brilliant, Sara. My heart is pounding." Emily presses her hands to her chest. "Haven't felt this excited about a project in years."

"Good," Sara says. "My thought is that we'll stain the floors a dark brown and paint a very faint black treasure map across the entirety of it. Give it a well-worn look." She scrolls further. "Every door will be rounded and here"—she points to the screen, just right of the bar—"will be a tiny little door for the kids that will lead right outside to the pirate ship playground."

There's not a detail Sara missed. From the copper bathroom sink to the ship wheel doorknobs and the golden lights that will shine beneath the whiskey bottles on the bar.

"You are brilliant, Sara Dylan."

"You are," Sara says, looking Emily right in the eyes. "It was your vision, I just brought it to life. I think the concept will do well. A place where adults can have a drink together and watch the kids play. It'll be cozy and fun and clever and full of history."

Sara thinks of the hours she spent designing every little detail from the multitude of hidden storage space to the placement of the wine racks and where the refrigerator will be. The amount of time she spent ensuring that every single inch of the very small interior space gets utilized.

She did it for Emily. And in this moment, it all feels so very worth it.

"I absolutely love it. And get this." Emily shifts her whole body, locking eyes with Sara. "I dug in a bit more. This building was actually part of an old jail in the eighteen hundreds. It held just four cells and a small desk for the officer on duty. Parts of the foundation are original. The rest is obviously newer—early nineteen hundreds based on what I've read. It sat vacant for years, then the city turned it into a library for just three years before they outgrew it and left it to the weeds."

"You think it's haunted?" Sara asks.

"I hope so."

"Me too." A smile curls up on Sara's face. "Have you inquired about a grant to assist with the renovation given the history?"

"Unfortunately, since we're not bringing it back to its original purpose, the answer is no, but they will donate a historical plaque for the entrance explaining its history. It was off the record, but the mayor said she will get it done."

"You've already met the mayor?"

"And made a small donation to a Title 1 school with an underfed PTA." Emily winks.

Sara chuckles. "You are good. We should celebrate. Do you have plans tonight?"

"I started a silly romance novel that was on the bookshelf in the house. I'm in the final chapters, but I can be swayed."

"Good."

A loud shove of the front door tells Sara the girls have arrived. "Mama!" Sophie and Joanna rush down the hallway and into her arms.

Their new summer camp picks them up and drops them off right outside her office in downtown Wilmington. A convenience she's never been more thankful for.

"Girls, I want you to meet Emily."

"Hi, ladies." Emily reaches out to shake each of their little hands.

"I'm Sophie," says the taller of the two.

Sara watched pridefully as her girls introduce themselves. "And I'm Joanna."

"Girls, I just need to power down and then we'll head off to Dad's, okay?" They both nod in understanding. Sara looks over at Emily. "Why don't you hop in with us, Em? I just have to drop the girls off at Steve's office and then we can head out from there?"

"Sure. Sounds wonderful."

CHAPTER TEN

Emily

Before Emily's seat belt is clicked, Joanna starts firing questions in her prepubescent squeaky voice. "Are you married, Emily?"

"No."

"Do you have a boyfriend?"

"I don't."

"Do you have kids?"

"Maybe one day."

"When you find a husband?"

Sara interjects, "Joey! Let's give Ms. Emily a break before we scare her off."

Sara leans toward Emily and whispers, "So sorry." Emily smiles at her in response.

"Well, I hope you find someone, Ms. Emily."

"Me too, Joanna."

Sara pulls into the reserved family parking spot in front of Steve's downtown Wilmington office. In large block print across the glass door is the name of his business: The Wakefield Corporation.

"Can you come in, Ms. Emily?" Joanna asks, clearly a fan of her mother's new friend.

"No, no," Sara hastily interjects. "It's just a quick drop-off, Jo. Let Emily relax, she can meet Dad another time."

"Please, Ms. Emily!" Sophie chimes in now with eyes wide in hope.

Emily looks over to Sara and whispers, "I don't mind," before responding louder, "I'd love to, girls."

Sara and Emily get stuck carrying lunch boxes and water bottles and Sophie's very large art project, while the girls lug their oversized backpacks into Steve's office.

Sara is waved on by Steve's longtime receptionist. "Thanks, Mary," she says as she continues to the back of the building toward Steve's office door. Emily follows close behind.

"There's my girls!" he calls excitedly in his deep manly voice as the girls rush in to hug him.

Holy no way. Emily recognizes him instantly. Steve's thick head of dark hair. The cleanly shaved handsome face and navy-framed round glasses. Exactly the type of man she imagined Sara would marry. Sharp. Tailored.

Sara places the girls' items on a hutch by his front door. Emily follows suit, nervously anticipating the awkward introduction that is about to take place.

"Hey!" Steve hops up from behind his desk when he finally looks up from the girls. "You're Emily Brynn."

Emily looks over at Sara, whose lips are now parted, her eyebrows furrowed in confusion.

"That's me." Emily offers a tight-lipped smile, knowing how absolutely insane this encounter is.

"You're, uh...you're on this, umm..." He's off to the side of his desk, rummaging hurriedly through a thick pile of paperwork. Emily knows what he is about to grab and feels an intense heat race to the tips of her ears.

"You're here."

Steve holds up a magazine titled *INVEST*. The front cover features a stunning Emily and brother, James. Small bold print on the bottom corner reads, "The Brynn Company knows the importance of ethical development and historical preservation."

Emily and James are both dressed in impeccably tailored navy suits. Arms crossed, exuding a distinct air of professionalism. Of power. Of success.

Emily reaches out to grab the magazine from Steve. This isn't the first time she's been on the cover of a magazine. It's always accompanied by a cocktail of emotion: unnerving, humbling, electrifying. She has, of course, already seen this photo. James texted it to her two days ago when it was released online, with a message that read, *Well this is awkward timing, but at least we look good.*

She agreed with James. They do look good.

"I never wanted to do this article," Emily says, examining the sheen copy in her hand. "Really felt like a silly puff piece."

"You look really beautiful in it." Sara's remark is so genuine and unprovoked that it causes Steve to snap his head toward her. Emily, too, finds the comment unexpected and lifts her head gradually to meet Sara's gaze. The two exchange a smile, a moment that Emily finds sweet, distinct, even intimate.

Emily pulls away, catching Steve's curious eyes. Did he notice it too? The energy between her and Sara? The look they shared?

"Well, um." Steve eventually breaks the silence. "I'm sure you two have to get going, but, Emily, about two years ago, I attended one of your seminars at the Marriott Marquis in Times Square. I don't know if you remember me at all, there was a lot of—"

"I remember you, Steve," Emily interjects. "Thank you for what you did that night."

Steve brushes it off with a wave of his hand. "Oh, yes, of course."

"What did you do?" Sara asks, her eyes reverting to a glossy shade of puzzlement.

"Oh, it was nothing, really." He waves it off again, glancing over at the girls to imply that it's not an appropriate conversation to have in front of them. He eagerly changes topic. "So, I guess Sara is helping you with a property you bought down here? She is the best, after all."

"You are right. She is amazing. We're working on something fun."

Sara replaces her look of confusion with a modest tight-lipped grin.

"That's awesome. I look forward to hearing more about it. How long are you in town?" he asks.

"I moved here." Emily knows her reply will throw him off.

"You moved? Are you guys expanding?"

"No, I quit. And now I live here."

Steve shifts his gaze back and forth between Sara and Emily, his expression marked by pure confusion.

"I'm so sorry if I'm being too nosy, you can stop me, but you are the owner of arguably the most successful investment and development company in the United States of America. Definitely in New York City. And you quit?"

"Yes, I quit. I mean, I still own it, technically, but I'm no longer involved in operations."

Steve stares at Emily for a moment and then at Sara.

"Well, hell, Sara. Did you even know the superstar you were working with?"

Sara nods her head, and while stepping toward her daughters, she responds, "I knew there was something special about her." The comment warms Emily's chest. She watches as Sara grabs each of the girls' faces and kisses their cheeks. "I'll see you both on Sunday. Be good," she tells them.

They simultaneously answer, "We will! Love you, Mama."

Sara turns around and says, "Bye Steve" as she walks toward the door to leave.

Steve hastily reaches out his hand and shakes Emily's before she can follow. "You can keep the magazine."

"Oh, thanks," Emily says, still holding it under her arm. "Great seeing you again." She smiles at Steve and then the girls. "Have a good weekend, ladies."

"Keep Mama company!" Joanna exclaims. The comment stops Emily in her tracks. She looks back at Steve, who suddenly looks defeated, then at Joanna. "You don't worry about your mum, we'll have fun." She winks at the girls and swiftly heads out to the car.

Sara already has the car running when Emily exits the building. She hops in, shuts her door, and speaks instantly. "So, I left out some of the small details about my career."

"I see. Can I look at that magazine?"

Emily hands it over, watching as Sara scans the cover diligently before grabbing Emily's eyes. "You really do look beautiful in it."

"Thank you." Emily holds Sara's gaze intently, considering the possibility of something more to this budding friendship.

"Is this your brother?"

"It is."

"He's very handsome."

"He is." *Never mind. Not a chance.*

"I think I'm ready for that drink," Sara says. "How about you?"

Emily huffs out a giggle. "I just bought two bottles of a great tempranillo. I'm up to go out, but if you want, we can go drink them on my dock and then you can walk back to your house?"

"Do you want to just get your car tomorrow?" Sara asks.

"Yeah, that's fine," Emily says, knowing tomorrow is Saturday and that means she gets to hang out with Sara again—if only for a short time to grab her car after yoga.

By the time they settle at the end of the dock with two glasses of red wine in hand, the final few rays of daylight are settling in a pool of orange over the marshland.

"I remember when Steve went to New York," Sara says. "To your seminar. He came back so motivated. Inspired." Sara looks up, her eyes wide with curiosity. "You never mentioned you were a celebrity."

"Well, you didn't ask for a résumé."

Sara chuckles, slapping Emily's knee playfully. "Well, tell me all about the seminar."

"It was all James, my brother. We have a nonprofit called The Brynn Company Foundation that purchases land and develops playgrounds in underprivileged neighborhoods. We do a lot of other things too, like combating student homelessness, protecting historic properties, but the playgrounds are the big driver. It's all in collaboration with local government, but a couple of years back we caught *INVEST* magazine's eye."

"The one you're in, right?"

"Yes, that one."

"They like you." Sara grins.

Emily ignores her comment with a bashful smile and continues, "James asked to partner up with *INVEST* for a networking meeting to talk about ethical development with some of the top executives from around the world: London, Singapore, Dubai, the list goes on." Emily takes a sip of wine, noticing Sara has hardly blinked.

"Am I boring you?" Emily says with a dose of concern.

"No." Sara shakes her head. "On the contrary. I'm fascinated by you."

Emily again finds herself lingering a bit longer than a friend would, drawn to Sara's sweet blue eyes, the single curl of blond hair that's fallen in front of her ear. When Emily feels her face heat up, she carries on. "The problem, of course, was that a conversation around ethical development wasn't going to sell tickets. James thought it would, but sometimes James lets his good-natured passions get in the way of his common sense. And plus, *INVEST* knew it wouldn't and James needed *INVEST* to attract these international bigwigs. So, ethical development turned into one of seven topics discussed during that New York City symposium."

"What was your topic?"

"Sustainable building."

"Should I ask?"

"I'll bore you another day."

"Fair." Sara grins as she sips her wine. "So how on earth did you remember Steve of all the people there?"

"Seeing Steve just now and finding out he's your soon-to-be ex-husband is quite possibly the most bizarre encounter I've ever had."

"Completely bizarre." Sara shrugs her shoulders.

"After the first day of the conference, I went to the hotel bar. Steve was there. Others were there too, but the two of us were near each other when we saw a man try to drug a woman's cocktail. And he would have, successfully, if Steve hadn't intervened. He was as calm and collected as could be. Tried not to make a scene, but the man was so very angry. A total dick. He ended up shoving Steve aggressively, calling him a liar, amongst other names. But I had seen it all as well, so I spoke up. It became a whole cinematic feature. Cops, a crying woman, a bunch of rowdy onlookers. All worth it, of course. The woman thanked Steve profusely."

Sara looks down at her bare feet tapping against the wooden dock.

"I'm surprised Steve never told you. He should have. He should have been proud of himself."

"I wish he would have. I probably didn't ask, though."

Emily doesn't respond immediately, she just watches Sara, the way her eyes flow downstream with the tide. "What happened between the two of you?"

Sara redirects her attention from the water to the wine in her hand. "He cheated on me."

Emily nods, hearing what she says while simultaneously feeling disappointed in her judge of character. She had been certain Steve was one of the good ones. "I'm sorry to hear that."

"It's not all his fault." Sara picks up the bottle between them and pours herself a hefty glass. "We weren't…connecting."

"That happens in relationships. And it's never been a reason to cheat."

"No. It's not. I'm not defending his actions. I just understand them. He was patient for many years." She takes a sip of wine. "Years that I didn't feel close to him. And now that it's all over, I don't think that I ever really did."

"Not ever?"

"No." Sara shakes her head. "I met this wonderful, handsome, polite man. My parents loved him. He was perfect. And I…I loved him too. I do love him." She shrugs her shoulders as she rationalizes the nine years they spent together. "He gave me my girls. The support I needed to kickstart my business. He's a wonderful father. But when he asked to be intimate or even just go out on a date, I just…I couldn't. And he didn't push. Never did, but then he asked for therapy. Again. And again, and again, and I was always too busy starting up my new business, or too busy doing something for the kids, or too busy making up some ridiculous reason to be too busy for him." Her eyes fill with tears. "I wasn't a good wife. And I think he was just tired of waiting around for me to not be so busy."

Emily reaches her arm across the gap between them and wraps her hand tightly around Sara's. Sara gazes at Emily and then at her hand. Emily notices the way her eyes scan their interlocked fingers. She notices her long, manicured fingers, how soft her palm feels against her skin. She reaches over instinctively to offer comfort, safety, warmth. And she's finding all of that for own self as well. Sara inhales loud enough for Emily to take a hint. She pushes back, releasing her grip.

"Enough about me," Sara says. "Gosh, I'm a mess. Tell me about you. How on earth have you not been swept away by some perfect human?"

Emily leans back into her Adirondack chair, folding her hands into her lap with a curious grin. She wonders why Sara used "human" instead of "man." Does she know?

"Ah, well…it's been months since my last girlfriend and I broke up."

Emily looks at Sara briefly, waiting for a change of expression, but Sara simply asks, "What happened?"

"I had a pretty glamorous social life in New York." She chuckles. "It really sounds silly saying that, but it all revolved around work. Parties with celebrities. Courtside tickets for the Knicks and Nets games. And the girl I was last dating, Romi was her name, was very, very much into that life. It wasn't just her, though. It was most everyone before her as well. And don't get me wrong, there were times that I very much enjoyed the lifestyle too, but it was always work. And for Romi, it didn't feel like work. She loved it. It was go, go, go. Never any time for just the two of us. To talk, to relax together. At the end of the day, we just wanted different things."

"Grew in different directions. That happens."

"Yeah. I guess so." Emily picks up the bottle, pours herself a second glass, and tops off Sara's. "So, I get mixed responses on the dating women thing. Did you know?"

Sara chuckles. "No, not at first. But Jared and I did a little stalking. Did you actually date Michael Perry's daughter?"

Emily grins with wide eyes. "You stalked me?"

Sara gently slaps Emily's knee. "I had to know more about my new friend."

Emily finds it slightly peculiar, but mostly sweet, that Sara stalked her.

"So did you?" Sara asks again. "Date her?"

"It didn't last long."

"Hmm." Sara looks back to her wine and starts to spin it in circles again. A stalling tactic, Emily thinks. "If I'm being honest, you're the first lesbian I've ever been friends with."

"The first!" Emily's eyes bulge in amusement. "I guess I've been spoiled up in New York. Dating women is just…well, it's not really seen as anything different from dating men."

"It's pathetic, huh?"

"No! No, of course not. A little. Yes."

They both chuckle.

"That's the South for ya." Sara shrugs her shoulders. "It wasn't an option to dress in Lilly Pulitzer and be a lesbian. It actually wasn't an option to be a lesbian"—her brows furrow in realization—"regardless of how you dressed."

Emily thanks God silently for growing up in the more accepting cities of London and New York. For having two supportive parents that wouldn't have cared who she loved regardless of where she lived.

"You want to know something crazy?" Sara asks.

"I do."

"Jared was my first gay friend and that was in college. My only, really…until you." She looks at Emily, not waiting for a response before she continues, "Gosh, I would have never been able to…to…"

"To?"

Sara huffs out a laugh. "I'm just glad times are changing."

Emily notices the blood that's rushed to Sara's cheeks. She watches her sip her wine and go back to spinning it around in her glass. She feels a knot in her throat, wondering if Sara is feeling what she's feeling right now. The draw, the desire, the need to touch her, to kiss her.

She shoves the thoughts out as quickly as she let them in when Sara speaks again. "It's nice that you had a positive experience with your sexuality. I've heard horror stories."

"I'm fortunate." Emily nods. "Accepting neighborhoods. Two accepting parents. I'm very fortunate. Definitely."

Sara opens the second bottle of wine and pours each of them a glass. "Let's fish."

"Fish?"

"Yes, I saw some fishing poles back against the house."

Emily laughs, sensing this shift in subjects is one Sara desperately needs right now. "Okay, but we don't have any bait."

"Oh, I won't touch the bait anyway. Casting is what makes it fun."

Emily chuckles at their similarities. Too impatient to await a fish, too squeamish to hook bait.

Sara scurries up the dock and returns with two red fishing poles. Their old lines are tied to rusted hooks. The two cast out and reel in on repeat until the second bottle of wine is long empty.

"I can't believe this," Sara says, straight-faced. "But I've caught nothing and it's nearly midnight."

"Shocked." Emily mimics her appearance.

"I should head out," Sara declares. "I don't really want to."

"Then don't."

Sara stares for a long moment at Emily, eventually choosing not to respond. "Yoga tomorrow?" she says instead.

"I'll be there," Emily confirms.

"We can grab your car after," Sara says as she wraps her arms around Emily for a hug. Emily feels her relax against her body. She nuzzles her head into Emily's neck, her lips just an inch from Emily's skin. She can feel her breath.

"You smell like jasmine…and salt water."

It takes every bit of Emily's drunken being to resist bringing her lips up to hers. Instead, she gulps down the lump at the base of throat.

"I'm glad you moved here," Sara whispers.

"Me too."

When Sara departs and Emily is sure she's out of sight, she spins around in enthusiastic circles until she settles herself back on the dock under the star-splattered night.

"How could she not feel like I feel?" Emily giggles to herself, sensing there was something more in their hug. Something pure, real.

Something a lot like love.

CHAPTER ELEVEN

Sara

Morning yoga turns into coffee, which turns into a walk along the sand for mango smoothies.

Sara's had a tickle in her belly since the moment she met Emily.

"Do you want to go on an adventure?" Sara asks, slurping down her final icy sips. She doesn't want to go get Emily's car yet, or go home to her quiet house, or bury herself in piles of design.

The question makes Emily laugh out loud. "An adventure? Where to?"

They are like two children. Young and free and full of joy.

"To hunt for Venus flytraps!" Sara offers a jovial expression.

Emily's eyebrows raise in interest. "Do those exist here?"

"Yes, one of the only places in the entire United States."

"Really?"

"Really. Did I just teach you something, Ms. Emily?"

"You did."

Sara starts the walk back to Emily's where her Jeep is still parked from the night before.

"They're in the Carolina Bay. You can find 'em in Pender County and Bladen County and Brunswick County, which is where we'll go today. All the way down to the very southern tip of Pleasure Island."

When the two arrive at Emily's, Emily runs in for a small stick of sunscreen and a refill of their water bottles. The two drive past Carolina Beach, then Kure Beach, and finally, after about thirty minutes, they reach Fort Fisher State Park.

"This is an old civil war fort," Sara says. "A key port for the blockade runners to bring supplies in for the Confederate army." It's seventy-eight degrees. Not a cloud in the May sky. A soft salty breeze blowing in off the coast.

"Are you a history buff?" Emily asks.

"Hardly." Sara leads them to the manmade path that circles the park. There are large boulders on their right. Foamy waves coddle the shore on their left. "We did a library reno for the city last year. Jare and I did a bunch of research on the state with the intention to incorporate local touches. We learned a ton."

"My own personal guide."

Sara winks at her before looking around to ensure there's no one in the near vicinity. "Okay, listen. We're gonna break the law here."

Emily shakes her head.

"Yes, we are. Follow me. Don't touch anything."

Sara takes long, careful steps through the boggy wetland, down a small hill that leads them closer to the edge of the ocean. Emily follows. "I feel like we're pirates, hunting for gold."

Sara stops and turns around to face Emily. "Well, if you're into that sorta thing, I'll fill you in on a man name Edward Teach another day."

"As long as I don't have to break the law to hear it."

Sara ignores her. "Look here, Em." She points to a single, small Venus flytrap.

Emily steps in beside Sara, the two staggering in the thin marshland between the plant and the ocean.

"How on earth did you know this was here?"

"The girls and I have done this a time or two." Sara grins proudly as she holds her finger to her lips. "Shh."

"It's smaller than I thought it would be."

"Did you think it was gonna be like a *Goosebumps* story? 'Carnivorous plant eats entire woman'?"

"Well, yes. Duh."

The two lose it in laughter, so much so that Sara nearly falls back, but Emily grabs her arm and heists her upright, which only makes the two of them laugh more. They trek back up the small hill, careful not to disrupt any of the habitat along the way.

"Now listen," Sara says. "Don't tell a soul about this. I have a reputation to upkeep 'round here."

"It's not really illegal, is it?"

"Oh, it is, but there are worse things than going off-path to admire a Venus flytrap. It's not like we dug it up and stole it."

"People do that?"

"People do all kinds of crazy things."

Like fall in love with women they hardly know. The thought slips in and out, leaving Sara's face in a flush of rose red.

As the two approach the car, Emily asks, "Now what?"

Joy rushes up Sara's toes and through an uncontrolled smile.

Sara spent all last night thinking about Emily. Her voice, the shape of her face, the way her lips move. She thought about her when she woke this morning. She wondered why she was thinking so much about her, about a woman. She attempted to convince herself that it was best to just not worry too much about it at all. It wasn't like she was ever going to pursue anything. What would she even pursue?

And now, in this moment, her face flushed with gobs of admiration, she tells herself again that it's best not to worry too much.

Emily wants to continue hanging out and so do I. This isn't complicated.

"Let's go ride the ferry to Southport and grab an early dinner. Check out your new property again."

"Somewhere casual for dinner, I hope," Emily says, looking down at her athletic wear.

"Everywhere is casual when you live in a beach town."

Sara pulls up to the very end of Pleasure Island and drives her Jeep atop the ferry alongside a few other dozen cars. When a large horn blares, declaring it's safe to move about the ship, Emily and Sara step outside onto the gray beaded floor and walk up to the top of the ferry.

There are osprey perched on wooden markers. The air is soothing and smells of salt.

"I think I mentioned that I'd like to live here one day," Sara says as she leans against a red metal banister.

"You did."

"So, my ultimate dream is to purchase a property right in town. Build out a custom bungalow with a quaint front porch. Paint it pink." She grins. "I've always wanted a pink home. Keep a nice garden in the backyard with azalea bushes and a saltwater pool. Wallpaper and wicker furniture. Local art only."

Sara finds herself dreaming of an afternoon sipping lemon-infused sun tea. She and Emily swaying on front porch rocking chairs.

"What's holding you back?" Emily asks.

Sara shoves the fantasy aside. "Financially, it's a big undertaking. But once Steve and I settle the divorce, I'll be on the hunt. It's actually more of a possibility now than it ever has been. I don't think there is a thing in the world that could convince Steve to live in a pink home." She chuckles.

"Well, I can't wait to enjoy that front porch."

Sara smiles, leaning over to nudge Emily. Her desire to touch her makes it nearly impossible to ignore.

"So, what's your dream in this silly little life, Em?"

Emily huffs out a chuckle. "Tough question. Never really thought about it until moving here."

"How come?"

"I don't know. Made myself busy enough to ignore it?"

Sara nods.

"I'd like to find someone. To spend my life with."

Sara's heart picks up pace at the raw sentiment. She tries to consciously slow her breathing, forcing away thoughts about grabbing Emily's hand, pulling her close, kissing her face, shouting something insane like, *Pick me. I want to be the one you spend your life with.*

Fortunately, Emily continues without noticing Sara's beet-red face. "I want to keep expanding our foundation. We run into quite a few zoning issues with the city, so I'd like to streamline that a bit. And I'm really excited about this new project, The Pirate's Hideaway. I thought I'd hire a manager to run the place, but I think I'd like to run it myself. At least for a bit. See what happens from there. I ordered a few books about managing a bar." She looks over at Sara with excitement. "And I just signed up for a bartending course in downtown Wilmington. Thought I'd learn a few things about making a cocktail."

Emily carrying on gave Sara the time her heart needed to settle. "Well, I think that's a great idea. That means we get to keep you down South a while longer, huh?"

"Yes. I suppose so."

The ferry horn beeps loudly, indicating that the travelers should return to their vehicles and prepare for docking.

Sara drives off the boat and maneuvers her way through the quiet old city to Emily's newly purchased plot of bamboo and rotting wood. Before they leave the car, Sara pulls up her Spotify and presses play on James Brown and The Famous Flames's "I Got You." She turns the dial up as loud as it'll go and shouts over to Emily, "Let's do a celebratory dance!"

Sara hops out of the car and hurries over to grab both of Emily's hands, dragging her onto the sandy unmanicured grass, where she spins her round and round. Emily's hazel eyes are glistening in the late afternoon sun, and Sara thinks to herself that this is what falling in love must feel like.

"This is what motherhood has done to me," she says as the song comes to a close. "Dancing like an idiot to celebrate everything. Tying shoes, eating broccoli, buying new investments. All deserving of its own little party."

Emily is laughing boisterously.

After a stroll around the lot, they walk into town, past the long fishing pier and around a bend to a small seafood restaurant built over the water. They order grilled grouper on spinach salad and two glass bottles of Pacifico.

"This is sad," Emily says. "But I haven't had this much fun in a really long time."

"Well, I'll be sad with you." Sara nods, gulping down a swig of icy beer. "Because I feel the same."

"No, can't be. You are so outgoing. Adventurous. You dance!"

"Me?" Sara's eyes widen. "I'm boring. You're the adventurous one! Moving your whole life to a small beach town where you don't know a soul."

Emily shakes her head in denial.

Sara chuckles, reflecting on her short time with Emily. She is more alive, more adventurous, more fun than she was just a few months ago. "It's you, Em. You bring it out of me. The fun." She smiles softly, gazing at Emily as a similar twist of her lips unravel across her face.

I could kiss you.

As they finish up, heavy rain clouds send them scurrying hand in hand all the way back to The Pirate's Hideaway where Sara's Jeep is still parked on the unpaved pad. With bellyaching laughter, they slam their doors shut at the same time.

"That was entertaining." Strings of Emily's dark hair are matted to the side of her face.

Sara wrings out her shirt over the rubber floor mat. "Agreed, and now I need a shower."

By the time they reach Emily's house, the rain has passed. Sara thinks about leaning over and kissing Emily on the cheek, as she would do when saying goodbye to most of her friends, but she stops herself because she's not sure she could touch her lips to Emily's cheek and stop there.

Emily doesn't appear to contemplate a thing. She hops out quickly, briefly looking back to say goodbye, and heads into her home.

Sara shouts, "I'll see you tomorrow, Em."

Sara didn't want Emily to get out of the car, but there wasn't a way she could possibly prolong this night any further. She pulls away reluctantly and into her condo parking lot with her thoughts buzzing annoyingly in and out of sanity. She heads up the stairs to her third-floor condo and goes directly into her bathroom. She strips off her clothes and steps into a warm shower, letting the high-pressure water wash over her.

She finds herself replaying the way Emily calls her "Sar."

Hi, Sar.

Thanks, Sar.

Let's go home, Sar.

How Emily's smile favors the right side of her face. Her dimples, her perfect lips. Her lips. Sara closes her eyes and imagines kissing her. Soft and sweet and warm. A fire runs up her thighs and swirls inside her. She leans one hand against the glass shower door and slides her other hand down her belly and between her legs. She gasps softly as she touches herself. Imagining Emily inside of her. Emily's body, bare against hers. Sara moves her fingers back and forth, back and forth, the water rushing heavily down atop her.

I want her lips, her skin, her body. I want her. I want her. I want her.

"Ahh!" She screams out passion and inhales shame. "What in the hell am I doing?"

CHAPTER TWELVE

Sara

Hey Em, I'm so sorry to do this, but my parents just let me know that they are making their monthly unannounced visit to town today. Do you mind getting an Uber over to your car?

Sara sends the text and puts down her phone, feeling oddly thankful for the surprise visit. A mass of confusion has planted itself deep in her gut and she's struggling to settle her thoughts. Though she's told herself repeatedly that she's not at all interested in women, she's just overwhelmed by life.

Her phone buzzes. It's Emily. *I'll grab an Uber, no worries at all. Have fun with your parents.*

Sara slides open the balcony door and lets the cool air filter in. She sits cross-legged on the floor and takes a series of calculated breaths, guided by the sound of rolling waves.

Inhale for four.

Hold for four.

Exhale for four.

This is her attempt at recentering herself. Not just from Emily, but for the onslaught of premeditated questions her mother will surely fire her way. Sara gives herself enough time to feel relatively sane before pulling herself up from the floor. She meticulously cleans the condo, despite it already being, by most standards, immaculate. She lights a lemon and sea salt candle and puts on a pot of coffee before the familiar five knocks on the door arrive.

"Hi, Mom. Hi, Dad." She wraps her arms around each of them. They drive her nutty, but their touch is still home. She needs that right now.

"Hi, sweetie, I made us a lunch reservation at the country club."

Predictable.

Linda and Robert are part-time members of the prestigious Forest Hills Country Club, a lavish status-buy that they use on their monthly visits out to the coast. "Your father will play golf while we eat."

"You're not joining us, Dad?" Robert is the barrier that Sara needs when her mother is hammering her with questions. Not that he ever says much.

"You ladies get your gossip in. My buddy Chris is in town, and I told him I'd meet him for nine."

The name Chris doesn't ring a bell, but Robert has a long list of golfing buddies that Sara has never been able to keep straight. "All right." She tries to sound upbeat. "Well, let me go put on something nicer to wear. Feel free to grab a coffee while you guys wait."

"You know I love a fresh cup of coffee. Do you have the cream I like?"

"In the fridge, Mom." Sara always keeps her mother's favorite heavy whipping cream in stock for random visits like this.

Sara throws on a blue-and-white seersucker dress that sits just above her knees. She purposely puts on the pearl earrings that her mother loves and slides on a pair of braided tan sandals.

"You look beautiful, darling." Even though it's from her mom, the compliment is nice to hear.

"Thanks, Mom."

The three of them drive off Wrightsville Beach and into the Forest Hills neighborhood. The neighborhood that she spent nearly a decade in with her soon-to-be ex-husband and their two beautiful daughters.

"Have you been to the house recently?" Sara's mother asks.

"Just to pick up or drop off the girls a few times."

"Do you miss it? It's a lovely home. I'm sure Steve is taking great care of it."

Of course Sara misses it. She loves that home. The home she brought her babies home to. The home she spent Christmas mornings in and cooked up lavish Thanksgiving spreads. The home she planted peas and tomatoes and pumpkins in. The home she poured her heart into designing and then decorating.

"Yes, I'm sure he is taking good care of it."

"Do you miss it?" her mother asks again.

"I'm happy where I am." She is happy. She can feel two things at once. She misses her home in Forest Hills and she's also happy where she is. It feels good to say it and also mean it.

Her mind drifts off to a few weeks ago when she caught sight of Emily running by. Her toned legs, her jet-black hair shimmering in the spring sun. It makes Sara feel warm inside.

Her mother looks into the back seat. "You seem like you're doing a lot better, sweetie."

Sara realizes a smile had overtaken her face during the memory. "I am."

"Good." Her mother turns her head back toward the windshield.

After a hearty cobb salad and a slice of raspberry pie, Sara and her mother take their iced teas out to the back deck where they plan to sit on white rocking chairs in the warm sun until Robert finishes up his nine holes of golf.

"Did you ever ask Steve to go to therapy?"

"Mom, not today." Sara knows her mother has been trying to squeeze in this question since the beginning of lunch.

"Honey, I'm just curious. You know, no papers have been signed yet. There's still time to reconcile. You two were so perfect together."

"He cheated on me, Mom. I have the divorce papers at home. I'll be signing them this evening and dropping them off at the lawyer's office before work tomorrow."

"Well, Sara, honey, you've said it yourself, you were too busy for him. Maybe you just need to make more time."

Sara wants to reach over and strangle the words back into her mom's throat. It's as if she's just heard nothing Sara said. She is signing the papers tonight. It's over.

Inhale for four.

Hold for four.

Exhale for four.

"Mom." Sara looks at her mother firmly. "I need you to listen to me. I didn't make time for him. You are right about that. He wasn't happy. I wasn't happy. But I don't love him. Not in the way I should." Sara is speaking decisively, and her mother's eyes are open wide, intently listening.

"I have spent night after night after night thinking about this and sadly, I don't think I ever did love him. Not in the way that someone is supposed to love the person they are married to." Sara's heart speeds up a beat. She's never shared these feelings with her mother, and rarely has she been so forthright with her. "I loved the idea of Steve. I loved that you and Daddy loved him. I love that we had two beautiful babies together, that we were able to help each other launch our businesses, but now I need to love myself and I need to focus on the girls and my business and my life moving forward. Steve and I are over. We are not ever, ever going to get back together. I do not want to talk about him for the rest of your visit."

Her mother's eyes are still wide. She hasn't blinked. She's heard Sara. Maybe for the first time in Sara's forty-two years of life. At least it feels that way. A few long moments skip by before her mother replies, "Okay, I hear you."

Linda leans back into her rocking chair, and then, as if the conversation never happened at all, she completely changes the subject. "How's your tea? It could use a bit more lemon, don't you think?" Sara chuckles softly to herself as her mother continues, "You know your father has been complaining about his knee for months now."

Her mother's voice hums out as Sara acknowledges the newfound lightness in her chest. She takes a sip of her iced tea and places her hand over her mother's. She hasn't heard a word Linda has said, but as soon as she quiets, Sara speaks up. "Thanks for coming today, Mama."

Her mother squeezes her hand. "Of course, honey."

CHAPTER THIRTEEN

Emily

June

Emily's been working day in and out alongside a group of contractors largely recommended by Sara and Jared. The entire first three weeks of construction was spent pulling shrubs and trimming trees and cutting down gaggles of fifteen-foot bamboo stalks. From there, they got started on the foundation issues. She's determined to keep as much of the original construction materials as possible, but it's basically a demo and rebuild to allow for new window framing and foundational support. It feels as if she's gotten nowhere and so far all at the same time.

"I can't wait to see what all you've done," Sara tells her as she pulls open the door at Thursday's Coffee House. A bell rings as they enter, grabbing the barista's attention.

"Hi, Ang!" Sara shouts. Angie is one of Sara's best friends. She explained to Emily that the two went to grade school together.

"The regular?" Angie asks Sara.

"Yes, please. And whatever Em wants."

Emily orders a black coffee before Sara extends a formal introduction.

"Ang, this is my friend Emily."

"Hi, Emily." Angie offers a perky grin. "What are you ladies up to today?"

"Em's got a fun little project I'm helping her with in Southport."

"Ooh." Angie's eyes raise. "I can't wait to hear more about it."

Sara and Angie move toward the other end of the counter as they chitchat about their Tuesday evening tennis league. Emily steps toward the high-top tables against the front window, where she spots a familiar young woman with a tattoo sleeve on her left arm.

"Hey," Emily says. The woman is enrolled in the same Monday night mixology course as Emily, where they're delving into fine liquors and mastering the craft of classic cocktails.

The woman looks up from her sketch pad. Her hair is in mounds of dark curls, her eyes a feline green. "Hi." Her voice is soft, unfitting for the boldness she emanates. So soft and so uncommanding that upon hearing it for the first time during their class introductions, Emily specifically recalls thinking that this woman would get eaten alive if she were living in New York City.

"It's Aly, yeah?" Emily confirms. "We're in the same mixology course, I believe."

"Yeah, we are." Aly holds out her hand. "Emily?"

Emily grins with delight that Aly remembers her.

"Your drawing has come a long way in twenty-four hours. I saw you working on it before class yesterday. It looks great. What's it for?"

Emily looks her over. She's younger. Mid-twenties, if she had to guess. She's wearing a thin rainbow bracelet amongst a dozen others that are weaved up her wrist. Emily watches her sit back with a casual ease, a thin smile unraveling along her cheery face.

"High Dive Brewing," Aly tells her. "I'm doing an outdoor mural for their new spot. I've been working on this all weekend. I think I'm finally getting it right." She spins her book around so Emily can get a better look. "What do ya think?"

The sketch features a flamingo in sunglasses plunging off a high dive into a sea of ocean animals. Sharks, a bright-pink jellyfish, a clownfish, and a smiling neon-green alligator in a lawn chair. It's fun. Colorful.

"Brilliant."

Aly flips the drawing back around. "Thanks. Have you been to High Dive?"

"No. I haven't been many places yet. Still pretty new here."

"You're from New York. I remember."

Emily offers a half-grin. "Yeah. That's right."

"Well, maybe we can grab a drink there sometime?"

Emily assumed Aly's quiet tone would be accompanied by shyness, but that doesn't seem to be the case.

"Yes." Emily nods her head, wondering if this is just a friendly invitation or something more. "Sure, I'd love that."

Aly writes her number on a piece of sketch paper as Sara walks up to the two ladies.

"Wow," Sara says as she hands Emily her coffee. "That drawing is unbelievable."

"Thank you," Aly says before quickly redirecting her attention back to Emily. "I'm sorry, I didn't know…"

Emily's eyes widen with this new confirmation that Aly was indeed insinuating something more than a friendly invite. "No, no, we're not…" Emily motions her hand awkwardly between herself and Sara. "This is just my friend Sara."

Sara is profoundly confused—it's evident in her wide eyes—and Emily, who is typically so sure of herself, feels her face redden.

Aly giggles. "Sorry," she says in a near whisper.

Emily holds up the scrap piece of paper with Aly's phone number on it and in a similar decibel replies, "I'll call you."

As Emily and Sara are shuffling out, Angie shouts, "Don't forget the double date, Sara!"

Sara doesn't respond. The door swings shut behind them and Sara asks instantly, "Was she hitting on you?"

"She didn't hit on me. She asked if I wanted to get a drink. She knows I'm new here."

"She hit on you," Sara repeats. "And she's really hot."

Emily chuckles. Sara is always so proper. Hearing her say "hot" sounds funny.

"What's funny? Are you going to call her? You should."

Emily steals a glance over at Sara, wondering if she really means what she's saying.

There have been countless moments since they first met where their gazes lingered, or their hands lingered, or the hugs lingered, and in these moments Emily finds herself entertaining the idea that there may be something more than just friendship blossoming between them. How could there not be?

However, just as quickly as the fanciful daydreams arrive, she always finds herself dismissing them because Sara inevitably does or says something that jolts Emily back into reality.

This is one of those moments.

Emily is a lesbian.

Sara is straight.

They are just friends.

"Probably," Emily says as she approaches her car. "Yeah. I'll call her."

Emily lets the conversation sink in as she buckles her seat belt. Finding a girlfriend would be wonderful. She deserves a nice person to spend her time with. This is best. Emily can shove down her feelings for Sara, knowing that the world is operating as it should. Sara is straight. Emily is a lesbian. And they are just friends.

Emily pulls out of the parking lot and flips the conversation on to Sara. "I heard 'double date' back there? Sounds like you might have someone to call as well?"

"Ang has been trying to introduce me to one of her husband's friends for months now, and since the divorce is finalized, she won't let it go. I have no interest in meeting him."

"The divorce is finalized? I'm sorry, I didn't know. How are you doing?"

"I didn't mention it to anyone, really. I feel fine. Honestly. The chapter is closed."

Emily reaches over, placing her hand softly on Sara's wrist. "I'm here for you if you want to talk."

Emily glances over at her. The early afternoon sun is stretching in through the passenger side window, causing a halo effect around Sara's flawless skin. She looks like an angel.

"Wow!" Sara is clearly impressed with the progress at The Pirate's Hideaway. Emily knew she would be. Most of the overgrown shrubbery has been removed. The sole structure is starting to look like a building rather than a pile of wobbly bricks, and around back, the future beer garden and playground has been leveled out.

"I noticed your arm muscles looking chiseled." Sara isn't looking at Emily, but Emily sees that her smile is stretched ear to ear. "And your tan is looking good too. I see why now. All those hours out here have paid off."

Emily laughs, brushing off the compliment, but she's overwhelmingly pleased that Sara has noticed her body in any capacity. "Okay, okay, I'm blushing. Come here, come here." She waves. "I've got to show you this."

The two walk in through the gaping hole that will eventually be secured by a front door. Just to the right, Emily shimmies out a brick. Behind it is a wooden matchbox, smaller than her palm. She flicks its tiny latch open to reveal a rolled-up piece of parchment. Carefully, she unfolds it as Sara steps beside her. "Look," Emily says as she directs Sara's vision to the single black-inked sentence that reads, *We were bigger than the ocean.*

Sara looks over at Emily, pressing her hand against her heart. "A love letter?"

"I think so." Emily rolls it back up, returns it to its matchbox home, and slides it back behind the brick.

Sara's eyes dart around, seeking clarity. "You're going to leave it there?"

"If I find anything historical, I'm supposed to turn it in to the city, so I'd like to propose a change order."

Sara nods, urging her onward.

"Let's leave this wall as exposed brick, and when we repoint we'll skip this one single brick. That way we can continue to shimmy it in and out. A small secret so this love note can live on in the walls."

Sara's admiration is evident in her gaze, clearly approving of the idea. "Your secret is safe with me."

Emily can't help but smile. There's something romantic about it all. The two of them sharing this secret of a love greater than the whole damn ocean. She wants to ask, *Is there something more here, Sar?* But instead, she blinks away from their eye contact.

"Great."

"How old do you think that note is?" Sara asks as the two step out the back door.

"I looked up the design on the matchbox and I'm thinking that it's late eighteen hundreds, but I don't think the note is that old. Who knows, though. Not sure how it would have made it through the renovations in the early nineteen hundreds, so maybe it's from then."

"A mystery." Emily catches Sara's sweet smile as they reach the back of the lot.

"All right, so let's get to the real reason for me dragging you out here. You see that tree right there?" Emily points.

"Yep."

"I want to build a fully operational tree fort for short-term rentals."

"There is no way the city will allow it."

"It's already done."

Sara's jaw drops. Literally drops.

Emily beams. "So, this location is actually just outside the official city limits, so they were willing to budge on the zoning laws."

"Budge?"

"I also made a very hefty donation to the city's Parks and Recreation Department."

Sara's eyes widen with her smile. "My goodness, Emily Brynn. You really do know what you're doing."

"I do," Emily confidently agrees. "Now, here's where you come in. I want it to be magical and romantic. Enough space for a family of four, but ideal for a couple's getaway. What do you think?"

"Running water? Electricity?"

"I know both are doable, and the answer is yes."

"Wow, how fun. Consider it done."

CHAPTER FOURTEEN

Emily

July

"The Pirate's Hideaway is so much cooler than I expected, Mum."

"James was telling me. He said it was an old jail?"

"A jail and then a library. It's been a fun project."

"Is it haunted?"

Emily chuckles. "That's what my friend Sara asked. But no signs yet. I do hope, though."

"Sara, the designer you hired?"

"Yes, Mum. We're just friends."

Charlotte chuckles. "I didn't ask."

"Mm-hmm." Emily hasn't dare made mention of Aly. Not that there's much to say. They've hung out a handful of times, a dinner one night and a couple of cocktails on another. One kiss in the car led to a steamy evening, but it ended with Emily lying on her back thinking of how nice it would be to have Sara beside her.

"If you haven't found a date for the fundraiser, maybe Sara would like to join you. It sounds like you two are good friends."

Emily allows the idea to settle in as a ball of nerves tingles down the back of her neck.

"Probably not, Mum." It would be tough to hide her feelings from Sara. She can barely keep herself together now. The two of them sharing her New York City flat would make it near impossible.

"Well, I can't wait to see you at the gala, darling. I'm bringing Roger from pickleball. He's very nice. He's not my boyfriend either, but you'll like him."

The very mention of "boyfriend" has Emily rolling her eyes. According to James, Mum had Roger accompany her to last Sunday's brunch at James and Lilly's house. James shared that Roger is a nice man but he talks too much about cable news and all the stairs he has at his home in the Hamptons.

"These are things retirees must talk about," James had told her.

"I'm looking forward to meeting him, Mum."

"I saw Maya at the Greenbergs' holiday party. She said that she's coming to visit you this weekend."

"She is. I can't wait to see her. It's a quick trip. She is taking a direct from LaGuardia on Friday afternoon and going home Saturday afternoon. It's for a hug, she tells me." Emily chuckles.

"She's the best. Have fun with her."

"We will, I'm sure. Give my nephews and niece a kiss please."

"I will. Chat with you soon, darling."

Sara's ears must have been ringing, because she's calling. Emily answers, "I was literally just talking about you."

"Good things, I know."

"Of course."

"Any interest in joining Jared and me for a drink on this beautiful Thursday afternoon?"

The two have been spending every other Saturday together. If her girls are with Steve, Sara is with Emily. If the girls are with Sara, Emily is working at The Pirate's Hideaway. But today is Thursday, and despite already having plans with Aly, Emily knows instantly she wants to get a drink with Sara.

"I'd love to. Do you mind if Aly tags along? We were supposed to grab a drink this evening."

"Bring her! She's welcome, of course. Matthew is joining as well."

"Brilliant."

Shortly after 5:00 p.m., Sara stops by Emily's so they can take the stroll to the Shark Tooth Tavern together. "You look cute," Emily tells her, unable to resist. Sara is wearing wide-legged jeans, a crop top tee, and slides. Her skin is tanned from the early summer sun, her blond hair thrown into a messy bun. Looking easy as grace on Sunday.

"Thanks, Em," Sara says, nudging her arm as they step in line. "How's it been going with Aly?"

Emily finds herself defeated by the question. A sort of placeholder in her actual wishes for companionship with Sara.

"It's fine. She's fun. I don't think it's anything too serious. I also don't think I'm the only one she's seeing."

"Really?" Sara stops and grabs Emily to face her, demanding eye contact. "Why on earth would she want anyone else if she's already got you?"

Emily feels a rush of heat down her back, unable to formulate a response. Sara's stare is wide but untelling. *What is happening?*

"She seemed so shy. Guess not."

"Her voice is a little deceiving. She's quite confident," Emily says, still processing the look they've just shared.

Jared and Matthew are already seated. They all exchange hugs and sit before Aly walks in.

"Hi, Aly." Emily waves her over to their high-top table in the back.

"Hi, Emily," Aly says, kissing her cheek. She shakes everyone's hand around the table, repeating each of their names as they say them.

Aly is not only the outsider in the group, she's younger by over a decade. Nearly two decades in the case of Sara and Jared. Emily has learned that Aly still likes to smoke weed at midnight and eat cereal on the kitchen floor. She shares an apartment in the Cargo District and spends all her money on soy lattes and all her evenings on TikTok. These are things that physical and mental metabolism no longer allows once one hits the age of thirty-five.

"I brought us special magic chocolates, my friends," Aly says as she takes her seat.

"Yes!" Jared shouts gleefully. "Aly, you are welcome at this table anytime." She hands him a square and he pops it right in, relaxing his shoulders in a dramatic manner as if the high hit him instantly.

"I'll pass," Emily says. She's never been one for marijuana. It makes her hands tingle nervously.

"I'll have a piece." The whole table spins to look at Ms. Buttoned-Up Sara Dylan.

"What?" She grins slyly. "I'm fun."

Jared rolls his eyes and Emily chuckles.

"Here ya go, my lady." Aly hands Sara a square and she pops it right in.

Within thirty minutes, the table is roaring in laughter and all prim and proper appearances have dissipated. They order chicken wings and a hummus platter. Sara is licking her fingers after each bite, which Emily notices because it is so entirely out of character. It's oddly enticing watching her rebel against manners.

Matthew pulls out a stack of playing cards titled "Table Talk," and happy hour has now turned into another round of regularly priced beers.

"I'll pull first," Sara volunteers. She lifts a card from the stack and reads, "Have the table tell you what color your eyes are." She instantly shuts them so the table can't see.

"Uhh, I should know this," Jared mumbles.

"You should know this, Jare!" Sara says, her eyes still clenched shut.

"They're blue," Emily says calmly. *Blue as the sea.*

Sara opens her eyes, finding Emily's from across the table. "Yes," she says warmly. "Your turn." She slides the deck over.

Emily reads, "What is your favorite recent memory with someone at this table?" Emily puts the card down. It's an easy question. She immediately recalls Sara leaning against the red balcony of the large ferry. She remembers the way her wet hair felt against her skin on the car ride home from dinner. How she wanted to reach over and pull her in for a kiss but instead hopped out of the car to save her from any further agony. "The ferry ride to Southport with you, Sar."

Emily avoids Sara's eyes. She knows the way the comment came off.

"Not meeting Aly or anything?" Jared chimes in, seemingly more for the reaction than the truth, because Emily knows by the look in his curious eyes that he feels what she feels.

Chemistry.

"Of course." Emily smiles softly. "That's been really great too." Emily leans over and kisses Aly's youthful cheek.

"Mm-hmm." Aly nods. "All right, my turn."

It's nearly ten when Emily feels the tug from Aly. She wants to leave. Emily doesn't, but she can't say that. Aly is her guest, after all. "All right, guys, me and Aly are going to head out."

"Boo," Jared and Matthew simultaneously shout.

Emily chuckles at them. "See you Saturday at yoga, Sar?"

"Yep, the girls are coming with me this weekend."

"How nice. My friend Maya is flying in from New York for the night, so she'll be here as well."

Sara's eyes perk up. "I look forward to meeting her."

Emily touches the top of Sara's hand. "See you Saturday." She looks up and redirects her attention to the guys. "See you both soon."

CHAPTER FIFTEEN

Sara

Without a blink, Sara watches Emily and Aly leave the tavern and Jared watches Sara in disbelief. She knows this because she sees his dumbfounded look in her peripheral vision.

"Sar."

"Yes?" Sara responds, still looking at the door.

"I am so sorry if I'm overstepping here, but am I missing something between you and Emily?"

"What?" Sara snaps from her trance. She didn't think he'd actually ask.

Jared's eyes widen. "You are!"

"I am what?"

"Sweetie, you didn't take your eyes off her all night."

Matthew chimes in. "You knew that she wants her wedding walk-out song to be Sara Bareilles's 'I Choose You.'"

"Yes!" Jared shouts. "When did you even have time to talk about that?"

Sara's eyes frantically search the room, ensuring no one is hearing this conversation. "Friends talk about things, Jared."

She shrugs her shoulders, realizing for the first time tonight how high and tipsy she is.

"Of course they do." Jared has lowered his voice, likely sensing Sara's nerves. "But you also knew that she eats the outside of the Reese's Peanut Butter Cup before the center. And you were able to answer her middle name before the girl she's sleeping with answered it."

"You think they're sleeping together?"

Jared rolls his eyes. "Honey, you've got a crush on Emily. Friends don't make eyes the way you two did."

"Make eyes?" Sara's concerned glossy glare turns into a grin. "What on earth does that even mean?"

"Tell me something. You can't lie to me when you're high." He furrows his brows. "Though it has been about fifteen years since we were high together. Do you get high often these days? Are you holding back on me?"

She looks at him, confused, and he continues, ignoring his own questions. "Did you have feelings for Jenna from our architectural drafting class?"

Sara thinks back for a moment, her eyes locked on Jared. "Maybe."

The weed has altered her inhibitions. Maybe she did have feelings. Maybe she's had feelings for women her whole life, but she's shut them all down because a blond-haired, blue-eyed girl from Wilmington, North Carolina can't attend NC State and become an interior designer and have two babies and build the house with the white picket fence and also be a lesbian.

Jared and Matthew gasp at her response. "Aww, come here, hun." Jared pulls Sara in for a side hug. "I knew you did."

"What do you mean you knew? Why didn't you ask then?"

"Wasn't my place. You joined the sorority and started talking to that Anthony guy, remember?"

Sara looks blankly for a moment before shaking the high from her head. "Oh, this is silly. I don't like women. Are you kidding me, Jared? I was married to Steve for nine years. I have two daughters."

Sara ponders her thoughts for a moment.

"I mean…I didn't mean a woman with children can't be interested in women. I'm just not one of those women."

"Okay, sweetie. Time to call it a night."

He's disappointed in her. She knows. She's disappointed in herself. The table sits still for a very, very long antagonizing moment before Sara speaks again. "What if I did like a woman?" She looks at Jared. "What if I like Emily?"

A heavy exhale falls from Jared's smiling lips. "You tell her."

CHAPTER SIXTEEN

Emily

"This is delicious," Emily says with a mouth full of red sauce and cheese.

"Agreed. I can't remember the last time I ate pepperoni pizza."

"Could you pass me one of those beers, Maya?"

Maya, in her classic coordinator ways, had found an oversized silver bucket in Emily's kitchen and neatly placed a twelve-pack of beer in it before icing it down. Emily asked if she was planning a party for her, to which Maya replied, "We are the party and we deserve to feel like it." Then she lugged it down to the dock.

Maya cracks one open for Emily, wraps a napkin around it, and says, "Sara seems sweet," as she passes it over to her dear friend.

Emily has been preparing for the questions. When Maya landed earlier this morning, she had two requests: see Emily's new project in Southport and enjoy a sunset on the dock.

What Emily didn't expect was to see Sara at The Pirate's Hideaway. Sara had popped over after work to meet with the architect of record on site.

Hearing Sara's name from Maya's lips instantly draws in Emily. She sees a mischievous smile curl up on Maya's face.

"Oh, stop it," Emily says.

"I've said nothing!"

Emily looks at her, slouching her shoulders with a knowingly flushed grin. "She's beautiful, isn't she?"

Only the midnight hour knows of Emily's crush. She's bottled up her feelings and distracted herself with Aly for nearly two months now.

"Gorgeous. You never mentioned that you had a crush on her."

Emily takes a gulp of her crispy cold drink. "Is it that noticeable?"

"You were so giddy around her. Adorable." Maya chuckles as Emily slaps her knee.

"She's recently separated."

"Kids?"

"Two."

"Fun!" Sparkles explode in Maya's eyes. "Has she ever been with a woman?"

"Not a chance. We've never talked about it, but she definitely has an image to upkeep, and I can't imagine it includes a woman."

"Ooh, one of those. You don't know for sure, though." Maya pops open her own beer, fueling up to assuredly spit out a list of risky questions. "Have you tried to make a move?"

"No, no. But there have been some interesting moments. I don't know. She's tough to read. And we have such a nice friendship, I'd hate to cross a line I couldn't come back from."

"Cross it!"

"We'll see. I've told you about Aly, yeah?"

Maya nods.

"She's still around. Though maybe not after last night." Emily furrows her eyebrows in thought.

"What happened?"

She grimaces in embarrassment. "She wanted to hook up."

"You haven't had sex?"

"Of course we have, but not last night."

"Why not? She's hot and young, so probably a lot more fun than us." Maya's tone changes from accusatory to thoughtful. "Maybe that's what you need to gain a little confidence to pursue Sara." She winks.

"I couldn't! I wasn't into it. I'm getting old, I think. I just don't have the same desire I once had to have these futile relations without feeling…sad."

"Oh boy." Maya's eyes are wide.

"I keep thinking that maybe we'll find some deeper connection, but it's really a lie I'm telling myself. She sort of just feels like a distraction from Sara."

Maya slurps down her beer. "Just end it with Aly. You've got a real woman to pursue."

Emily holds up her beer for a toast. "To you, for such sage dating advice, my dear married friend."

"Well, I've got one more for you, while we're scrolling through your women. I was working a bat mitzvah at Parker's gallery last weekend, and she brought you up to me. Have you two spoken?"

"Not beyond our discussion about her gala donation."

Maya cocks one eye up. She and Parker maintained their friendship after Parker and Emily split. Maya had told Emily, "I love you. I know you are hurt. What Parker did was wrong, but Parker is a work acquaintance that I intend to keep. I just need you to know that I'm not one of those friends that will cut off all ties to show my loyalty. I'm loyal and I'm keeping my ties."

Emily had understood. The breakup didn't warrant any allegiance. Things happen. People part ways. Life goes on. And Maya was there for her every step of her grieving process, making it undoubtedly clear how much she valued Emily.

"It was so interesting," Maya continues. "She asked if you were seeing anyone. Asked if your move to North Carolina was for a woman. It felt…odd. She told me she was excited to see you at the gala in August."

"No, she didn't."

"I swear it. I'm telling you, Em. She never brings you up to me, but she was pushing."

"You know how she is. Talking just to talk."

"Not true. Not when it comes to you. When did you two break up? Seven, eight years ago?"

"Seven."

"Not in seven whole years has she brought you up to me. Until now." Maya throws back a big gulp of her light beer. "My guess is she saw the magazine article in *INVEST* and got the hots for you again." She winks a conspiratorial grin on her face.

"That's ridiculous."

Maya rolls her eyes. "We'll see."

CHAPTER SEVENTEEN

Emily

"Hey, Sara, you and the girls should join us," Maya says as she rolls up her yoga mat. "We were going to ride over to the farmers' market and then hit the beach."

Emily's jaw clenches, knowing the motive of Maya's question. She avoids eye contact with her, knowing it will only lead to hysterics, and instead turns to Sara with an approving nod.

"You sure?" Sara's eyes are wide in question.

"Yes," Maya says before Emily can respond, which makes Emily smirk.

"Yes, please join us," she says.

Sophie answers first. "Only if we can ride in Emily's car."

They all chuckle. "Okay," Sara says. We'd love to join y'all. Looks like you'll be driving, Em."

The group parts ways to freshen up, and Emily and Maya make a quick coffee run before swinging by to grab Sara and the girls.

"I'll sit in the back." Maya hops up and crawls over the center console. Emily tries to grab her leg but stops a scene from unraveling when she sees the girls hurry toward the car.

"I don't want to miss any subtle flirting. I can see it all from back here."

There's no time for Emily to respond. "We've got drinks, ladies!" she instead shouts as the girls swing open the car doors.

"Sophie," Emily says as she hands her a tall clear cup filled to the brim with ice. "I understand you're a lavender latte lover like your mum. Decaf, of course. And, Joanna, this is yours. Hot chocolate, despite it being eighty-eight degrees outside."

"Thanks, Emily!" the girls reply in unison.

"We just love your car so much."

"Thank you, Sophie. I like it too."

"Don't spill. You hear me, ladies?"

"Yes, Mom."

Emily chuckles and hands Sara her coffee.

"Thank you, Em. And Maya, you didn't have to sit back there." Sara spins around to make eye contact.

"I'll never be able to afford one of these, so I wanted to embrace as much of it as I can while down here."

"Maya!" Emily shouts.

Sara chuckles before adding, "Well, me either, so I'll hop back there for the ride home."

The morning flies by. Emily buys a woven basket from a vendor. She walks beside Sara like a couple would, nearly touching, talking softly, laughing boisterously. They fill the basket with carefully chosen vegetables and fruits. They eat eggs and bacon and stacks of blueberry pancakes from a food truck, and the girls somehow save room for soft-serve ice cream. They listen as Maya tells Sophie all about her ten-year-old son, Ben, and Sophie goes on and on about how funny it is that Ben likes the graphic novel *Ghosts* as much as she does.

"Can you bring him next time, Maya?" she asks.

"I absolutely will, Sophie."

It's after two by the time they pull back into Wrightsville Beach. There's no time for digging their toes in the sand this trip. Maya and Emily drop Sara and the girls off, hurrying back to Emily's to gather Maya's things.

"I just called for an Uber, Em. I want you to go put your bathing suit on and meet Sara and the girls at the beach."

"Maya, why would you do that?" Emily whines. "I wanted to take you to the airport."

"Nope. You've only got a few weeks left before the gala, and I want you to invite Sara. I demand it. She's wonderful and I see something in you two." Maya smiles her perfect white-toothed grin.

Emily props her hand on her hip. "Are you in cahoots with my mum?"

"We're all in cahoots for you, Em." Maya leans in for a kiss on the cheek and hurries out the front door. "See you in August!"

Within a single minute, Emily texts Maya: *You think she likes me?*

The reply is almost instant: *I am absolutely certain.*

A grin stretches across Emily's face as she hurriedly tugs up her swimsuit. There is something between them.

Of course there is.

CHAPTER EIGHTEEN

Sara

"Can I join you?"

Emily's eyes are lit up in a way that makes Sara feel as warm as the late July sun. She and the girls had slipped on their suits, propped up a teal umbrella, and settled down at the beach.

"Sit, sit." Sara readjusts her chair to make room for Emily's under the shade. "You didn't take Maya to the airport?"

"She called a lift." Emily rolls her eyes.

"Well, I'm glad you're here. You want a, uh…" Sara reaches in her small cooler. "A coconut-flavored sparkling water, or key lime?"

"Key lime, please." Sara hands her the can, their fingers brush, and Sara feels a pulse vibrate right to her heart. "Maya seems cool," she says, trying not to make too much of a moment.

"She's the best, isn't she?"

"Sophie is a big fan. She can't wait to meet her son, now." Sara giggles as she opens her own sparkling water.

Before the two can pursue any further conversation, the girls are sprinting up toward them, pink skimboards in hand, shouting in jubilation for Emily.

"Let's play paddleball!" Joanna insists.

The four of them play paddleball, and they take a long walk down to the fishing pier. They argue about whether soccer is football, or football is soccer, and which Disney princess is their favorite.

Sara notices a spark within herself. A whole afternoon with her daughters and Emily. A joy she couldn't possibly put into words.

Around dinnertime, the girls hug Emily tightly goodbye. Sara squeezes her hand and there is something so dynamic about the feel of her skin that it tingles her to her core. If only she could muster up the courage to tell Emily. Tell her that she's feeling something she hasn't felt before. It's powerful and wonderful and she wants desperately to talk about it.

When Emily walks away, the girls tell their mom how much they love her and how happy they are that she's their neighbor.

"I have an idea, girls. It's gonna rain all day tomorrow, so let's go to the store so we can bake and watch movies all day."

"Can Emily come over too?"

"Let's ask her, but first I want to grab her a little surprise at the Surf and Tackle shop before we head to the grocery store."

Long after nightfall, Sara lies under her covers and dreams up an entire life with Emily Brynn. One where she is proud to love her. One where they wake up next to each other and walk out the same front door for Saturday morning yoga. One where they plant vegetables together and take sunset walks along the beach and buy new fishing poles to cast and reel and plan autumn vacations to the mountains of western North Carolina with Sophie and Joanna.

One where she could kiss Emily.

Touch her.

Make love to her.

Ugh.

She presses her hands against her eyes, wishing the whole fantasy away. *I cannot be the woman that loves another woman.* Anxiety overtakes her. The conversation she had at Shark Tooth Tavern with Jared and Matthew about potentially liking Emily as more than a friend barges in and sits on her chest like a heavy brick.

Would Jared ever bring it up?

He hasn't texted me about it—maybe he'll let it be?

He wouldn't tell Emily, would he?

No, not a chance, but he knows. He will never not know.

Sara finally drifts off to sleep, committed to repressing her desires for Emily. But just hours later, her eyelids fly open. Long before the sun. Long before the Carolina wrens and mockingbirds.

She quietly throws on a rain jacket and hurries down the street to Emily's to leave a pair of yellow boots by her front door. She sprints home, careful not to wake the girls, straightens the house, brews a pot of coffee, and waits until six in the morning to text Emily.

This isn't something friends do. She knows that.

CHAPTER NINETEEN

Emily

Emily rolls over to find a message from Sara. Her heart nearly leaps from her chest at the sight of her name on her phone.

Last night, when she lay in her lonely bed in her quiet bedroom, she scrolled through messages from Aly.

Do you wanna hang tonight?

You there?

Never mind, I'm going out with my friend, Shaun. Let's catch up tomorrow!

She never texted back. Why would she, now that she knows for certain that Sara is who she wants? She's known, of course, but it's really easy to suppress love into thinking it's nothing more than friendship. Until it explodes. On a beach, on a Saturday afternoon, while building sandcastles.

Emily thought about Sara all night long, tossing and turning, wondering how in the world she could express her feelings. Wondering if Sara might be feeling the same. How could she not? Taking note of every time their eyes locked a moment too long, their hands lingered, their knees touched.

She slides open the message: *I left you a little something by your front door.*

The sky is middle-of-the-night dark, heavy with clouds and noisy with rain, but Emily hops out of bed like a child on Christmas morning. Just outside her front door, protected under her awning from the chaotic wind, she finds a pair of bright yellow rain boots and a wiry bouquet of purple wildflowers tied together with a note. Emily brings the boots and flowers in and sits down immediately on the wooden bench beside her front door, not able to wait a single moment more to read the note.

Yellow boots brought you here, hope these will make you stay. We've got plans to bake cookies and binge movies. Slip these on and join us if you're up for it. I have wine. –Sar, Sophie, and Jo

Emily presses the note against her chest, letting herself bask in the thoughtfulness. This isn't something friends do, and she knows this. She looks at the clock on the wall. It's not even 7:00 a.m., but after spending an entire night dreaming about touching Sara's skin, she's feeling brave.

"What the hell, I'm going over."

Emily sends her mother and brother a "missing you" text because it's Sunday, and Sunday always make her miss her family. She packs up a bag of the fresh fruit she purchased at the market yesterday and slips on her new yellow rain boots.

It's downpouring. The wind is roaring and her weather app says it will be like this until late this evening, so Emily zips up her rain jacket, opens her personal-sized polka-dot umbrella, and makes a run for Sara's condo.

She silently prays that Sara is awake before she knocks softly on the condo door. Only a breath passes before Sara opens it. It's as if she's been waiting for her.

"Good morning, sunshine." Sara smiles wide and grabs the bag of groceries from a drenched Emily. Water is dripping from the ends of her spiraled hair and her umbrella is inside out. "Come in, come in." Sara presses her hand against Emily's back, guiding her inside. She helps her take off her drooling coat and hangs it on the hook by the front door.

"Boots held up great." Emily peers down at her dry socks. "The rest of me, not so much." The driving rain had managed to soak between the buttons on her jacket. "Can I borrow a shirt?"

"Come on back." Sara's home smells like hazelnut coffee. It's quiet, other than the heavy sound of rain against the glass slider that leads out to a broad view of a very angry ocean.

"You're gonna have to wear pajamas, since I'm still in mine." Sara is talking softly, careful not to wake the girls.

She tosses Emily a similar outfit to the one she's wearing: flannel pants and a well-worn oversized shirt.

Emily starts to undress right in front of her. She's never been the modest type. She shimmies off her glued-on pants and peels off her shirt before clothing herself in Sara's lavender-scented laundry. She doesn't think twice about it until she looks over to thank Sara and finds her eyes on her.

"Fit all right?" Sara says hastily.

"Perfect," Emily says as she walks toward Sara, thinking Sara will head back toward the living room. But Sara just stands, so Emily stops.

"You look cute." Sara smiles sweetly as her posture relaxes.

Emily feels her cheeks tinge with nervousness. If she leaned in and kissed her, would Sara kiss her back? The thought pulsates through her.

"I'll take those," Sara says as she grabs the wet clothes from Emily. "I'll toss these in the dryer."

Duh, she wanted the clothes. Not me.

Sara starts up the dryer and nods her head toward the living room. "Let's go drink coffee before the girls wake up."

The two cuddle up under creamy knit blankets on opposite ends of the couch, steaming cups of freshly brewed coffee in each of their hands.

"How's Aly? I enjoyed hanging out with her the other night."

"Ah, I'm not really sure."

However insincere, Emily can't find it in her to care. Sara is just an arm's length away from her. Sara with her lightly freckled cheeks and her sea-blue eyes and her sweet Southern concern.

"I thought you guys had a good thing going?"

Emily shrugs her shoulders. "It's not going anywhere."

"Oh," Sara says, filling the silence.

"Hey, this is last minute," Emily says, eager to change topics. "But our foundation's gala is in a couple of weeks. Would you want to come with me?"

"Oh, you're serious about you and Aly really not making it, huh?"

Emily grins at her innocent probing. "We're over...and if it helps to convince you, it's free drinks." Emily raises her eyebrows.

"What do I have to wear?"

"Black tie, but you do not need to worry about that. I've got plenty of options for you."

Sara's furrowed brows conveys the question: What kind of woman has loads of black-tie options lying around? But it doesn't stop her from committing. "I'll come with you. I want to."

Emily can hardly contain her excitement, and it's showing in her toothy grin.

"I've actually got a dress from a wedding last year that I can wear."

"Brilliant."

"Will we be back Sunday?"

"Yes, late evening," Emily tells her, hoping it won't sway her decision.

"Steve can take the girls, I'm sure. I'll just need to make sure he can keep them through Monday. He'll be by later today to grab them. I can ask then."

"I'm excited." More than Sara could possibly know. The two of them alone. In New York City.

Sara cups her coffee in both hands. "Me too."

"Hi, Emily," Sophie whispers sleepily, hurrying into the living room to squeeze herself between them on the couch. "Did you like your yellow boots?"

"I adore them, Sophie. That was really, really thoughtful of you three."

Joanna runs past Sophie and into Emily's arms. She makes herself comfortable on her lap. "Mama, can you make us pancakes?"

Sara looks at her girls snuggled up next to Emily. "I would love to make you pancakes, my girls."

By 4:00 p.m., the four of them have played two rounds of Yahtzee, baked chocolate chip cookies, and watched a National Geographic special on shark tooth hunting along the Carolina shore. Sophie was invested in the multitude of megalodon teeth discovered just thirty miles off the Topsail Island shore. Joanna couldn't have cared less and buried herself in a pile of Magna-Tiles.

CHAPTER TWENTY

Sara

"Dad's on the way, ladies. Go get out of those pajamas." The girls hustle back to their rooms to freshen up. Sara pours two hefty glasses of red wine.

The doorbell rings. "Hi, Steve." With each passing month, it gets easier to carry on around him. She's grieved the departure of her picturesque Southern existence but hasn't quite gotten over why he didn't just leave her before sleeping with another woman. A much younger and youthful and gorgeous woman.

It's her ego that's still mourning.

"Hey, Sara." His voice picks up a notch when he sees Emily, in what he probably realizes are Sara's pajamas. "Hi…Emily. Did you…sleep over?"

Emily appears to have forgotten she is still wearing Sara's pajamas. She glances down at herself. "Oh, no, no, just having a lazy day with the neighbors."

"You live in this building, too?"

"Just down the street."

"In the Mayos' house," Sara adds.

"Ah, the sailboat house. Beautiful, huh? How funny."

He and Emily share a genuine smile that Sara notices before he continues to speak. "That's great. The girls have told me they love hanging out with you but never mentioned you were a neighbor."

Emily nods. "Yup."

"Hey, you can say no, but I've got a question about a new market segment I've been contemplating jumping into. I'd love to pay you for your time if you can sit down with me for an hour in the next couple of weeks." Sara busies herself with the dishes, careful not to seem too interested in his ask, though she is.

She's interested in all things Emily.

Emily appears unfazed. "Of course. I'll get your number from Sara. I would love to help if I can."

"I'm sure you saw the newspaper today?"

Sara stops the dishes and turns to hear the scoop. "No," Emily says.

"Article about you." Steve reaches in his back pocket and tosses the rolled-up paper onto the kitchen island. "I wouldn't let it get to ya. The old Southern hospitality was always a bit exaggerated. I'll bet the comment section online is mostly positive."

"Fun." Emily hops up from the couch as the girls emerge from packing.

"Daddy!" Joanna sprints down the hallway.

"Hi, Joey girl!" He lifts her in a big bear hug and kisses both her cheeks.

Sophie follows. "Hi, Dad."

"Hi, baby. You girls have a good day?"

"Yes," they reply, instantly listing off the activities they did. Steve chuckles at their energy.

"Is it clearing up out there?" Sara asks, wanting to shove them out so she can read the article alongside Emily, who's already at least a few paragraphs deep.

"Eh, still pretty gloomy, but not so windy and the rain's slowed down. Roads are totally fine. A few branches down in the neighborhood, but didn't see anything on the way out here."

"Good." Sara kisses both girls and then looks at Steve. "Hey, in a few weeks, Em's invited me to a fundraiser that her family does in New York."

"The Brynn Foundation. For playgrounds, right?"

Emily smiles. "That's it."

"I read about it in that magazine article."

Sara is weirdly happy that Steve read the article and has a small glimpse into how wonderful Emily is. "Think you can keep the girls for me?"

"Of course." Steve looks at Sara, then Emily. A slight smile forms. "All right, ladies, you two have fun. Let's go, girls. Just text me the dates, Sara, so I can put it in my calendar."

Sara locks the door behind him and exhales deeply. The familiar bout of sadness rushes her like it does every time she parts ways with her daughters. She knows Steve feels the same, though. Splitting time is not easy on anyone.

Emily mistakes the look. "Are you mad I agreed to help him?" she asks with genuine concern.

"Oh, no. No, not at all. I'm long past the angry stage. Lord knows he needs the help."

Sara's comment brings out a chuckle from Emily.

"So, what's the article say?" Sara says calmly, though her insides are exploding with curiosity.

"I think Steve was wrong about the Southern hospitality. This is actually quite nice on the scale of slander I've seen. It's a brief smear on my late father and a public awareness announcement that a lesbian has moved south."

Sara gulps, taking the paper from Emily. She sits at the kitchen island, her back to Emily so she doesn't have to alter her reactions.

She reads the title: *Daughter of late disgraced billionaire buys up property in Southport.*

Her heart picks up pace as she continues speed-reading the article.

Brynn is known for flaunting around with various women of stature, from professional athletes to the daughters of movie stars, none staying around too long. Still, her lengthy dating profile doesn't overshadow the endless scandals of family business.

Brynn's brother, James, let his younger sister go earlier this year after settling a yearslong battle with tax evasion that troubled their father until his final days.

Sara can't read another sentence. She feels a small bead of sweat build up on her temple. "How much of it is true?" she asks as she slowly turns around.

"Well, I suppose it's all sort of true, just depends on what lens you look through."

Sara watches Emily prop her feet up on the ottoman, seemingly unfazed by the 500 or so words disgracing her private life, her family, and her business. She firms up a bit and asks again, "I need an explanation. This doesn't exactly show you in the shiniest light."

"Oh." Emily removes her feet from the ottoman and straightens up. "You're worried you're in the presence of a serial dater and a felon."

Sara senses the humor and lets her shoulders relax. Emily smiles at her and joins her on a stool at the island.

"Let me see." Emily grabs the paper and starts scanning. "Did I date women? Yes."

Sara feels her body inflame as she watches Emily move her finger down the article.

"Did my brother let me go? Of course not. Pure clickbait. And the tax evasion stuff is nonsense. I don't even like to talk about it, really. We're innocent. My father was innocent. It's defamation. See, this article was picked up by the local newspaper from the Associated Press. This was written by some thirsty New York City journalist trying to stir up a riot. God forbid they let me escape the ruthless bubble. They probably called this..." She flips to the cover. "This *Port City Daily* and told them to run it. This is what the media does. Anything for clicks, Sar."

Sara looks over with a sweet smile, sort of flustered by the article but entranced with Emily's passion. "I like the way you say my name." Sara can't believe what just came out of her mouth, but it's like she can't control herself around Emily, and, in this moment, in the security of her home, just the two of them, she doesn't try. "I believe you. Come on back to my bedroom. I wanna try on this dress for the fundraiser."

Sara walks, noticing a long quiet pause before Emily finally gets up from her stool and follows her back.

Once in her bedroom, Sara pulls out a champagne beaded floor-length dress from the closet. "I sure hope this still fits."

"I'll help you zip it up."

CHAPTER TWENTY-ONE

Emily

Now that the thoughts of intimacy with Sara have flooded her, it doesn't seem plausible to pull back. Emily breathes deeply, conjuring a dose of composure as Sara steps into the walk-in closet, shielding herself from Emily as she changes. Emily sits on the bed and anxiously plays an imaginary piano against the olive-green linen comforter until Sara reemerges.

"Wow." Emily is motionless when Sara walks out. The sleeveless dress fits her snugly from the high neckline down to her knees where it flares out just slightly. Striking. "You look stunning, Sara."

"Thank you. Can you help me zip it?"

Sara stands in front of her woven rattan, floor-length mirror. Emily hops up and stands behind her. The wood floor creaks beneath her bare feet as she tugs softly on the zipper and begins to trace it up the curve of Sara's spine to the base of her neck.

"How many women?" Sara asks.

Emily doesn't answer. She notices Sara's arms fill with goose bumps and she steps back just slightly.

Was that from my touch?

Emily desperately wants to make a move but she's fearful to overstep. What if she's reading this all wrong? "A few."

Sara turns around, a half-smile on her face.

"So, what do you think?"

Emily grabs Sara's eyes and tells her with every bit of truth in her bones, "You are lovely, Sara Dylan."

Everything goes still. Silent. The air between them lingering between desire and confusion. Yearning and fear. Neither has blinked. Emily, with her breath tied up in her throat, takes a small, daring step toward her and slowly inches her face close to Sara's. Just a breath away, Sara hastily lowers her head and spins back around. "Can you unzip me?"

"Ye…yes," Emily stutters in a near whisper, her heart beating wildly. "Of course." She tries to recover with more words. "It's perfect for the fundraiser. I really like it. I think I should probably change out of these pajamas now too, yeah? Head on back to my place and get some things done before work tomorrow."

Two deep breaths pass before Sara heads toward the closet. "Yeah, okay."

CHAPTER TWENTY-TWO

Sara

August

Sara plops down in Jared's office with a short list of to-dos numbered on a pad of personalized Sara Dylan Design paper.

Jared reaches for it and ensures, without reading it, that it'll be done. She knows this is true.

"Now, are you excited to get all fancy this weekend?" he asks.

"The architect for The Pirate's Hideaway just quit."

Jared's head jerks upward. "Why?"

"She said she read the article in the *Port City Daily* and Emily doesn't align with her Christian values."

"Christian values?" A look of disgust unravels on Jared's face. Sara doesn't flinch; she hasn't quite digested the conversation.

"I asked what she meant...specifically what part of the article didn't sit well with her, and she said, 'I think you know.'

"I told her I know Emily personally and she's wonderful and her family is innocent of the offenses the article talks about, and, in fact, they donate millions each year through their foundation."

"And her response?"

"'I've seen just about enough of these Northerners bringing their lifestyles down here to our quiet little towns.'"

Jared's eyes raise in fury of fire. "And what did you say?"

"Nothing. She said, 'I hope to work with you again, Sara, just not on this one.' I couldn't believe it. You know it's Carrie Mae's firm? We've done dozens of jobs together."

Jared rolls his eyes. "Wow. This makes even more sense now. Bitch has never once looked me in the eyes. Did she close with her infamous, 'I hope you have a blessed day'?"

She did, of course, but Sara ignores Jared's comment. "It's because Emily's a lesbian, isn't it?"

"Yes. And it's not just because she's a lesbian. It's because she is a proud lesbian, one that hasn't denied the article, one that's not afraid to be photographed with another woman on red carpets. It's that Emily might put a rainbow sticker on a front window to project that all love is good love and Carrie Mae can't have a rainbow sticker on her projects. Carrie Mae would be fine helping a quiet, closeted lesbian, but God forbid a happy one inquires. Good riddance." Jared flips his hand aggressively in the air.

"I can't believe it."

Jared sits back in his seat, releasing the huskiness from his angered tone. "We're in the South, Sara. Believe it."

The two sit in silence for a few moments before Jared begins to write himself a note. "I'll call Michael from Coastal Home Architects. He did a great job on the Figure Eight Island job. And he doesn't mind a happy homosexual."

The comment raises Sara's eyebrows and the corners of her lips. Jared mimics her.

"Thank you."

"I'm thrilled to do it. Now tell me, are you excited?"

"I am. I'm excited. We're staying at her condo in the city. Her 'flat,' as she calls it." Sara feels tension jitter through her spine at the thought of Jared bringing up the conversation they had about Emily at Shark Tooth Tavern. He knows she's excited because he knows she likes her, but she can't bring herself to expand on her feelings.

"Well, let yourself loose, Sara. You deserve it." His warm eyes tell her that she's welcome to spill it all. She considers it, just for a moment. She considers spilling it all out.

Telling him how she can't wait to have Emily alone for a whole weekend in a place where no one in the world knows her. Where she has no reputation, or family, or career to worry about.

Telling him about how the cruel article in the *Port City Daily* sits like a heavy brick on her chest.

Telling him about how she desperately wants to kiss Emily. How Emily has somehow caused her to have a sexual awakening that's been pulled from the depths of her suppression and it's impossible to turn back now.

She wants to express her concern that other people might see her with Emily and…think things. Other prospective clients might find out she's working with Emily and think things.

She wants to tell Jared that she likes Emily so much that she thinks about a life with her. Waking up next to her. Coming home to her.

She wants to chat more about the repercussions of Carrie Mae quitting likely because she doesn't approve of a woman dating another woman, and how many other people in their small little city feel that way?

But instead, she stands and rests her hand on his. "Thanks, Jare. Have a great weekend. I'll see you Monday."

CHAPTER TWENTY-THREE

Emily

"I'm one of those people that gets excited about airport food," Sara admits as they walk into the terminal.

Emily chuckles.

"What?" Sara whines. "I don't get out much."

"Well, it's basically holiday, yes?"

"For me, yes, it's vacation." Sara grins, seemingly pleased with the excuse Emily's provided her.

Once seated in their first-class chairs, Sara pulls out the goodies she purchased from the Port City Java airport vendor. A bag of granola, a ripe banana, one organic dark chocolate bar, a yogurt cup, and a black coffee.

"This should get me through the flight."

"I would hope, since it's just over an hour."

"Are you gonna want some?"

"No, no. Don't worry, I'm good with my tea." Emily holds up her own cardboard cup.

Sara winks, acknowledging that Emily gave the right answer.

A text message buzzes in from Emily's mother. *Are you doing okay? Are you and Sara on the flight?*

The thought of hugging her mother makes her smile. Prior to her move south, they spent every single Sunday together since the passing of her father, and it's hitting her in this moment that it's been entirely too long since she buried herself in her loving arms.

"What's funny?" Sara asks.

"Oh, nothing. It's my mum just checking in."

"Aw." Sara hasn't looked up from her lap of treats. "Did you tell her that we're sitting first class?"

Emily's mother wouldn't dare sit anywhere but first class. In fact, she has been asking Emily and James to make an exception so she would be allowed to fly private when she travels, but The Brynn Company policy is clear: in no case at all is a private jet—or even tickets on a charter—to be purchased. Not for personal use or for company needs. Fly commercial. Make it work. End of story.

When Charlotte explains that she doesn't work for the company, Emily and James have to inform her that she's guilty by blood and The Brynn Company has made a commitment to lowering their carbon footprint when possible.

"I told her. She's excited to see us."

"I'm excited to meet her."

"She's lovely."

"She made you. I have no doubt."

The comment has Emily blushing. She avoids eye contact and texts her mother back. *All good, Mum. We just boarded. See you tomorrow. I love you!*

It's right around dinner when they land. Down at baggage claim they meet Eric. Eric's been a longtime driver for the Brynn family. He's just turned sixty. Shiny bald head. Strong as an ox.

"Hi, Ms. Emily." He pulls her in for a side hug.

Emily squeezes him back. "Been a while, old friend."

"Still got a few muscles, though." He flexes before insisting, "Let me grab those bags." Without awaiting an answer, he flings Sara's duffel over his shoulder and grabs the rolling bag from Emily.

"Thanks, Eric. This is my dear friend Sara."

"Hi, Ms. Sara."

Sara shoves her last plane snack into her mouth so she can shake his hand with a full smile.

"Follow me, ladies. Clock's ticking, Ms. Emily. I can only weave through so many bumpers."

Emily looks over at a questioning Sara and smiles at her before saying, "Let's get to it!"

Emily and Sara are in a near jog trying to keep up with Eric. They hastily hop into his black Escalade. It's spotless, just as Emily expected.

"I saw your brother this morning, Ms. Emily. He was telling me all about the big night." Eric peers through the rearview. For a man with no hair on his head, his bushy eyebrows dominate his reflection.

"How was his mood? You know how he gets a little high-strung before these things."

"He seemed good. He was very excited to see you."

"I'm excited to see him too."

Sara nudges Emily and whispers, "Where are we going?"

"A surprise."

Thirty minutes fly by and then Eric whips up to a curb. "Looks like we made it in time, Ms. Emily."

"Brilliant. Thank you so much, Eric."

"Mike's still working the door at your place, right?"

"He's there."

"I'll have him take your bags up to your condo."

"Thank you so much, Eric." Emily blows him kisses, grabs Sara's hand, and the two jog another couple of blocks down the street to the entrance of the iconic Brooklyn Bridge just as the sky settles into a warm shade of pink.

"This is it," Emily says, eyeing the bridge cables up to the tippy top.

Sara's wide eyes tell Emily she's mesmerized. "Come on!" Sara yells, hurrying up ahead. Emily trails close behind as the two dodge dozens of tourists and selfie sticks and cyclists and eventually squeeze in between two couples against the side railing. Their arms are pressed against each other as they watch the sky unravel into shades of peach and red and eventually a dark lavender.

"This is one of the oldest suspension bridges in the United States. Completed in 1883," Emily says.

Sara doesn't take her eyes off the Manhattan skyline, but Emily can see a sweet smile form in her peripheral vision. "Tell me more."

"This is silly, but my mum tells me I was named after her grandmother. My dad, however, used to tell me that I was named after Emily Roebling, the first woman to walk across this bridge."

Sara finally turns her head to face Emily. "No way."

"It was designed originally by John Augustus. When he died, his son Washington took over. But he, too, fell ill, and his wife, Emily Roebling, took over the operation. Saw it to its completion and was the very first to walk over it."

"So which parent is telling the truth?"

Emily shrugs her shoulder. "Not sure."

"Amazing." Sara's eyes are beaming with wonder and magic and joy. Emily knows the look, as she has it too. She gets it every time she comes here.

"Your dad was from here?" Sara asks.

"Born and raised. Did an internship at Oxford in England. That's where he and Mum met. That's where me and James were born. Spent a few early years in London, but other than that, he spent his whole life here. He loved this city."

Emily stares out into the skyline a moment, remembering the first time her father took her here, to the Brooklyn Bridge. She was young, maybe five. It was just the two of them. A dad and daughter date. They had greasy pizza and ate chocolate soft-serve ice cream in cake cones, and she remembers him lifting her into his strong arms and sitting her atop his shoulders so that she could see what he saw: the Manhattan skyline against a brilliant peach sky.

It looked then like it looks tonight.

Emily inhales deeply before rubbing the moisture from her eyes. "Come on," she says, looping her arm into Sara's. "Let's go grab some dinner."

They walk the stretch of the bridge into Manhattan and grab two slices of large New York pizza. Two dollars each. Sara leaves a ten-dollar bill. Emily tries to pay, but Sara insists. "Oh, come on, you bought the flights here and you're taking me to this fancy event, and the whole private driver thing? I mean, I have tried to keep it cool, Em, but this is all pretty amazing."

"Pizza makes me feel this happy too." Emily nudges her over to a high-top red table with no chairs. The two stand opposite each other and bite into the gooey thin crust pepperoni joy.

"Oh," Sara moans. "This is so good."

Emily looks at her with wide eyes and bursts into laughter. "Orgasmic?"

Sara looks up, her cheeks now flushed red. "I need to get out more, huh?"

On the walk to Emily's apartment in Tribeca, Emily shares all about her childhood in the city. Afternoon walks where her father would show off the various buildings, streets, even entire neighborhoods he had a hand in developing or revitalizing. He was a fan of Latin architecture and would bore James and Emily with the various influences throughout the city. She remembers him pointing out dentils, in particular. She shares this with Sara. "Dentils are these small tooth-like blocks. All evenly spaced. Right there." She points up to the top of a brick building. "That decorative band along the top of the building. Those are dentils."

Sara listens intently to all of it, both their smiles as wide as they were on the Brooklyn Bridge.

CHAPTER TWENTY-FOUR

Sara

"All right, Sar, this is it."

Sara grew up in an upper-middle-class family. Never wanted for a thing, but Emily Brynn's life is much larger than hers. Almost to a degree that's hard to fathom. This especially hits home when they pull open the copper handle and walk into a gleaming marble lobby.

"Hi, Paula!" Emily beams.

"Hi, Emily, how was your trip?"

"It's going well. I'm just in for the weekend. The big fundraiser is tomorrow."

"Ah! You guys are amazing. I know it will be a great success. I heard the one on Washington Heights has a basketball court?"

"Oh yes, that was all James's doing. Paula, meet my friend Sara."

"Hi, Paula."

"Are you going to the gala?" Paula asks.

"Emily is taking me along."

"Oh, so fun! I went three years ago with Emily. The open bar is fun." She winks and laughs at herself. "Have you ever seen what they do?"

"Not yet."

"They built an amazing park in our neighborhood. Gosh…" Paula presses her hand to her heart in a sign of gratitude. "Our baby still loves that monkey bar course."

Emily looks to Sara. "We made it special for her daughter, Carlita. Big fan of the monkey bars."

Sara's heart warms with sight of their clearly beautiful friendship. "I'm really looking forward to learning more about their foundation."

"Well, I won't keep you, ladies. I know you need to rest up for the big day. Mike brought the bags up earlier."

"Thank you, Paula. Great to see you." Emily leans down and kisses Paula's cheek. "Tell Carlita, she owes me a Go Fish rematch."

"She's into chess now!"

"Oh boy. I'll have to freshen up on my skills, then."

"I haven't beaten her yet."

They share a giggle before Emily nods her head at Sara. "This way's the lift."

Sara follows and they ride all the way up to floor twenty-eight. It slides open, revealing just two doors. Emily types in a seven-digit code and shoves open her front door.

"Were you the rider in the Peloton commercial?" Sara is dead serious.

"It was not me." Emily laughs. "But I shit you not, that commercial was shot a few floors down."

Sara is mesmerized and completely unsurprised by the truth in Emily's response. She slips off her shoes and walks directly across the living room toward the fourteen-foot-tall sliding door. She opens it, stepping out onto Emily's private terrace. It's well after ten p.m., but light pollution illuminates the vast Hudson River. A smile unfolds and she lets all the city sounds consume her.

Emily steps onto the balcony and stands beside her. Sara lays her head on Emily's shoulder.

"Thanks for having me, Em."

"I'm happy you're here."

Emily shows Sara the guest room and tells her all about how she had the whole apartment professionally designed in a natural palette with modern touches. Sara loves every detail of the idyllic city vibe, but especially the floor-to-ceiling windows in the guest room she's staying in. Her honeymoon on the Amalfi Coast couldn't top this. Though maybe that had more to do with the company.

"This button here will lower the blinds," Emily says. "But if you don't mind an early wake up, keep 'em open. The sunrise is lovely. Your bag is over there by the closet."

Sara is living amongst royalty. She's sleeping in a Peloton commercial. A private driver hand-delivered her luggage to her glass room that sits twenty-eight stories above the Hudson River. And beyond all the head-spinning wonder, the most beautiful woman in the entire world is leaning against her bedroom doorframe.

She'd like her to crawl into bed beside her, but Emily won't. Sara sees the distance she is keeping. It's likely intentional after their…moment…in Sara's bedroom last weekend. The moment Sara could have let Emily kiss her but did not. Could not. Out of fear.

"See you tomorrow." Emily shuts the door behind her.

At the very first sign of sun, Sara stretches her arms above her head, reassociating herself with the fact that she's in Emily Brynn's multimillion-dollar Manhattan apartment on a Saturday morning. She fluffs her hair a bit, taps the thin skin under her eyes to get the blood moving, and heads out to the kitchen. There's a Keurig on the counter. Just what she was hoping to find.

She brews two cups and quietly taps on Emily's door, opening it just slightly. "Em?" she whispers.

Emily turns her head away from the windows and toward Sara. With a half-grin, she asks, "Is that coffee?"

Sara pushes the door open wider and holds out the two ivory clay mugs.

"You are the best." Emily pulls herself up against the headboard and folds down the covers. "Come, come, sit with me."

Her room is on the corner of the building. Unlike Sara's single glass wall, Emily has two. Two brilliant glass walls. Emily props pillows up against the other side of the headboard and Sara slides in close enough that their legs can touch, but far enough away that she can call it an accident.

"Thanks for the coffee."

"You're welcome. I'm sure I'm not the first woman that's brought you coffee in bed."

Emily squeezes her eyes shut and huffs out a laugh. "It's been a while."

"You haven't given me much about your past. Have you ever been in anything serious?"

"Oh, gosh."

"Spill."

"Parker. She's an artist from Oregon. I was twenty-seven and she was thirty-five when we first met. She was more established. More mature. More worldly. I was taken." A soft smile curls up Emily's face as she seemingly recalls the finer moments of their relationship. "We had a three-year run together. Since her I've dated around a bit, but really nothing substantial."

"What happened with you and Parker?"

"She cheated on me."

"Oh." Sara sips her coffee. "Well, she's missing out on you."

"Yeah?" Emily huffs. "I think she's doing okay. She owns the gallery where we're hosting our fundraiser tonight."

Sara squeezes her eyes and they both laugh. "Well..." Sara sips her coffee again. "She doesn't have you."

Emily leans over, gently nudging Sara's bare arm with her own. "That's sweet."

As the coffee settles in, the sun is now shimmering in golden sparkles along the Hudson. Emily reaches up for a stretch.

Sara would typically enjoy every moment of this quiet gorgeous morning, but she's too busy questioning why she can't just kiss Emily.

I could right now. I could put my coffee down. Grab her face in my hands and kiss her.

The thought sends dangerous impulses directly between her thighs. She's so close to her. She could just make a move. Now. But instead, she sips more coffee, knowing the proximity to a nearly naked Emily is everything she wants but everything she just absolutely cannot have.

She runs through the reasons as she has done a dozen times before.

Her parents will disown her. Her clientele will leave her. Her children will be confused. Maybe even embarrassed. Her friends will claim that her divorce from Steve sent her over the edge. She huffs, forcing out her tortuous desire to have Emily's skin against her own.

"You good?"

Sara must look flushed, but she responds, "Yeah, I just can't believe you left this."

Emily looks around. "It is nice, but not every day is this good."

Is it me, making this morning good? Despite Sara's thoughts sending her on a windy road to *absolutely not*, her body gives in. She slides her leg over, grazing Emily's just slightly. The magnitude of the moment causes her to inhale sharply. She gulps it down, keeping a straight face, but Emily doesn't flinch. She's completely unbothered as if she doesn't even realize that Sara's leg is now against hers.

An anxious bead of sweat bubbles up on the back of Sara's neck.

Maybe she didn't try to kiss me last weekend?

Maybe I'm reading this all wrong?

Emily's alarm rings. It's eight in the morning. "Want to go for a jog?" Emily asks.

Sara nods her head, finding it difficult to speak. She lifts her coffee mug to her lips once more. "Yes," she finally chokes out.

"Great. I've got to swing by the venue, about a mile east."

Sara's thoughts are floating in cyclones between her thighs and her lips and her chest. She hops right up, oddly grateful that Emily has helped end the panic for her.

CHAPTER TWENTY-FIVE

Emily

Outside, the late August weather is cool. Very different from the muggy mornings that still greet them along the Carolina coast. "I think my blood has thinned." Emily chuckles as she wraps herself in her arms.

"I find it refreshing." Sara puffs out her chest dramatically before shaking out her limbs, which makes Emily laugh.

"You ready?" Emily asks.

"Let's do it."

Emily leads the way through a quiet Tribeca neighborhood, up through SoHo, eventually slowing at Parker Anne Art Gallery beside New York University.

"This is it," Emily tells her.

"Is it here every year?"

"We've done it here before, but we like to switch it up. Many of our loyal donors are repeat attendees, so we try to keep it exciting. I love this venue, though. You'll see why. We have access to the whole gallery." Emily pulls on the large glass door. It's unlocked. She steps aside and lets Sara enter first.

"Hello," Em yells from the hollow lobby once the door is resecured.

"Em!" James jogs two by two down the grand staircase and right into her arms.

"I forgot how amazing this place is." His lofty grin matches his boisterous voice. Without a moment's hesitation, he looks to Sara. "Hi, it's Sara, yeah?" He reaches both his arms out and encompasses her single hand with both of his. "I am so happy you could join us."

Emily looks at Sara, her bright eyes wide and cheerful, her golden skin glistening in a thin layer of sweat.

"I'm thankful Em let me tag along," she tells him.

"How was your flight in, ladies?"

"Easy," Emily says.

"Good. Well, come on in here. Maya's just finishing up a few things."

They walk through an oversized arch to a large open gallery with dozens of tables and a podium dressed in florals.

"Hi, Emily!" Maya is wearing white New Balance tennis shoes with green joggers and round red-rimmed glasses. A classic look for her day-of event planning. Much like Sara, she's got a similar light shimmer along her temples, telling Emily that she's been running around since early this morning. Tonight, she'll be in a fitted black suit, modest heels that she can still run around in, and she'll replace her red glasses with contacts. She'll look stunning and all business. Ready to mingle and prepared to do whatever is necessary to ensure the evening goes on without a hitch. Emily's seen her do it many, many times.

"Hi, Maya." It's only been a few weeks, but Emily has missed her and brings her in for a tight hug to show her just that. "All coming together like you imagined?"

"Of course. I absolutely love this venue." She releases Emily and reaches out to Sara. "Sara, it's so, so good to see you again. So happy you could make it." Maya gives her a warm hug before Parker barrels in from a swinging kitchen door.

"The great Parker Anne, everyone!" Maya says, waving her over.

Parker still has a bubbly pep in her step. She's in her midforties now, and the silver streaks that run through her dark bouncy hair give her a dash of sophistication that feels foreign to Emily. She's always been quirky, but it appears she's really embraced it. She's sporting wide-legged jeans, a long whimsical necklace, and bright-green cat-eye-shaped glasses.

"Brynny, how are you?" Parker says casually, as if they see each other often.

Sara peers over at Emily when she hears "Brynny." Emily sees it in her peripheral vision and knows she is wondering why the woman she dated for three years has a nickname for her.

"Parker, you look lovely," Emily says before kissing each of her cheeks.

"As do you. You don't age, do you, woman?"

"Well, Botox helps, yeah?"

All the women laugh. James playfully presses his palms to his ears, which makes them laugh more.

"And who's this lovely lady?" Parker glances at Emily with a look of assumption that she and Sara must be together.

"This is my good friend Sara." Emily perks up, gesturing toward Sara with her hand.

The two shake hands before Parker gets down to business. "We were just trying to figure out where we're going to put the auction items."

The five of them spin around, taking in the layout of the room. "Where'd we have the tables last time?" James asks.

"Not a good spot," Maya says. "Remember, it was too close to the dessert table? Not enough room to walk around over there."

"Yeah, that's right," Emily concurs.

Sara chimes in. "You have the whole space, right?"

"Yes," they all reply.

"Why not spread them out? One in the entry, one by the cocktail bar. One in the dessert area. It'll force people to enjoy the space, the art, mingle around a bit."

Parker instantly chimes in. "I like that!" Of course she does. Emily knows she wants to show off her brilliant gallery and all the wonderful artwork she's curated.

Maya squints inquisitively. "I'm hiring, you know."

Sara chuckles. "I've got a little experience in designing practical rooms."

Emily is beaming with pride, and when she glances over at James she realizes he's taken note of the joy she can't seem to hide. "Em, fancy a brief chat?"

She never notices his thick British accent unless she's been away a while. Hearing it now, it feels like home. She follows James up to the podium. "So, you'll open up tonight," he tells her. "Offer the thank-you. And then I'll close with our accomplishments over the last year and our goals moving forward. Good, yeah?"

"Brilliant."

James leans in and whispers, "You fancy her?"

"I do not." Emily can't stop a smile from creeping along her lips.

"You do, and she fancies you." His eyes are wide and genuine.

Emily shakes her head. "She does not."

James's eyebrows furrow. "Wicked lie."

"She really doesn't. I tried to make a move a few weekends ago and was totally shot down."

Emily recalls the morning, feeling Sara's body so close to hers, and how desperately she wanted to lean over and just kiss her but chickened out when Sara looked away. She wouldn't dare try now. Not ever again.

James cocks his head to the side. His eyebrows furrow. "I don't believe you."

"God's honest." She presses her hand dramatically against her heart.

He giggles at her theatrics. "Didn't you say she's recently separated? Maybe she's just not ready. But I see what's going on between you two." He pulls her into a big bear hug. "In time, little sis."

She pulls away. "Oh, stop it. We're friends."

He doesn't push it any further. "Well, if she doesn't work out, you can always shoot your shot with Parker again. She looks great, yeah?"

"What is your deal with her?"

"What? She's so cool!"

"Mm-hmm." She shoves him as they walk back to the group.

"All right, team." Emily interrupts the trio. "Anything else we need to do here?"

"Nope," Maya says. "Eric will pick you ladies up at a quarter to five."

"Thanks, Maya. This all looks wonderful, per usual." Emily raises her voice to address James and Parker as well. "See you all tonight."

The cool morning air has been replaced with a warm August breeze racing through the buildings.

"We've got to get bagels," Emily insists.

"Yes." Sara nods her head in complete agreement at the abrupt statement. "Pizza last night. Bagels this morning. Should be no issue getting into my dress this evening."

"Great," Emily says, ignoring the sarcasm.

Emily urges Sara to get the everything bagel with cream cheese, lox, capers, and a tomato. Sara doesn't fight it. They grab their foil-wrapped breakfasts and sit on a metal bench under a single London plane tree.

"Why are New York bagels so famous?" Sara says, examining the glob of cream cheese sandwiched between the warm halves.

Emily tells her that they're often boiled before baked and carefully hand-rolled and formed. And they're extra dense and doughy. "And it's nostalgic, in a way," she says. "Eastern European Jews brought over their recipes when they immigrated to the States back in the late nineteenth and early twentieth centuries." She holds up her bagel. "There's more history than calories in these bagels, Sar."

"Makes me feel better about eating it. I'm basically inhaling knowledge."

"Precisely," Emily confirms.

"Can I ask you something?"

"Of course."

"What did you like about Parker?"

Emily chuckles. "What do you mean?"

"I guess I'm just curious about your type. She's beautiful and accomplished. It's not hard to see why you'd like someone like her, just wondering, really."

"Well…I dunno. Looking back now, it seems there wasn't much to us, really. She's beautiful, obviously. We ran in similar circles, similar acquaintances. She was fun, and talented, and taught me about food, and art, and finer things. It was all new and intriguing to me at the time. But we were always missing the big things."

"Like what?"

"Family, for one. She didn't crave stability like I did. Didn't care for kids. I thought we'd find our way together, build a little life together, and I'd be happy because I'd have her. And she would be enough. But she didn't want that." Emily turns to Sara as she continues, "You know, I always knew that too. I look back sort of…disappointed with myself. I knew what I wanted, and I knew who she was, and I didn't listen to what was really in my heart."

Sara looks away, her cheeks flushed. She takes a small bite into her bagel and so Emily readjusts herself and does the same.

When she finally swallows, she changes the subject. "Let's get going. I've scheduled us for hair and makeup at two o'clock. It's my treat."

Sara doesn't reply right away. First the strange questions about Parker, now a tentative response to free makeup and hair.

"I left that out. Are you okay with it? We don't have to do it. Well, actually, I do. Look at me." Emily flicks her ponytail to the side.

It causes Sara to break her stern look with a chuckle. "Oh, stop it. You're beautiful."

Emily holds her gaze, knowing that Sara feels this too. The something wonderful pulsing between them.

"You are too," Emily responds in a near whisper.

A breath.

Another breath.

Emily pats Sara's thigh, recalling her awkward attempt at a kiss and not daring to fall into another similar situation. "Now let's go spoil ourselves."

CHAPTER TWENTY-SIX

Sara

Hair and makeup arrive early. They drink champagne out of crystal flutes. Emily is friends with these artists. Sara can tell by the way they laugh about old memories and share about their families. The three of them welcome her into their conversations as they carefully touch up her brows and pat her cheeks with blush. They ask about her daughters, and they talk about marriage and divorce and all the stickiness that comes with it.

By 4:00 p.m., the condo is empty again. Sara admires herself in the full-length mirror as she shimmies up her dress. Her long blond hair cascades over her shoulders in loose curls. A dash of an earthy gold eye shadow accentuates her blue eyes. In this moment, she feels so whole, so alive, so put together in way that has eluded her for too long.

Emily shouts from the other room, "Sar, should we do a reveal like they do in the weddings?"

"Why don't you do a grand reveal? I need your help zipping me up." Sara pushes open her door and steps into the hallway, holding her dress securely against her breasts so that it doesn't fall. "I'm ready for you."

Not a moment later, Emily walks out from her bedroom with her hand against her emerald silk dress. Sara remembers that Emily has spent at least one night on a red carpet with a celebrity, and it's obvious. The single-shoulder, sleeveless sparkling bodice is connected by a pleated waist. Her lips are a bold red and her dark hair is pulled into a low ponytail, the curls hanging loosely over her right shoulder. She spins in all her confidence and sexiness.

"My goodness, Emily, you are stunning." Sara hasn't moved. Hasn't even blinked. She knows she's staring but can't stop herself.

Emily curtsies, thanking her with a bit of sarcasm for the compliment. She walks behind Sara.

"You look lovely as well, Sara Dylan," she tells her softly as she zips up the same dress she zipped up nearly a month ago.

Sara feels Emily's fingers against her spine. She recalls the same moment nearly a month ago and wonders: If Emily tried again, would she kiss her back this time?

Yes. Yes. She would.

Emily doesn't attempt. Instead, she grabs Sara's hand and spins her around, stepping back to take in her completed outfit.

"Gorgeous," Emily says, her tone matter-of-fact. "You ready?"

"I am ready."

When they arrive to the gala, Maya is sprinting from the back room with a vase of florals.

"Last touch, ladies."

Emily and Sara watch her place it carefully on the table. Peonies, calla lilies, and an array of vibrant greens fill the vase. "It looks really beautiful, Maya." Emily leans in and kisses her cheek. "Thank you for all you do."

"For you, I'd do anything." She winks. "The fam's all here. Head on in. I'll see you ladies soon."

Emily and Sara walk side by side through the floral arch and into the main room where her family awaits.

"Woowee!" James yells obnoxiously. "You ladies are looking good!" His wife, Lilly, and their mother, Charlotte, start clapping as if Sara and Emily just won the Academy Award for best entrance.

"You people are ridiculous," Emily says. Sara watches Emily reach for her mother first and hold her tightly for a long moment.

"And I assume you are Roger?" Emily looks at the man that has accompanied her mother.

"That's me," he says in a nasal tone. He holds out his hand and Emily shakes it. "It's nice to finally meet you."

"Family, this is my friend Sara." They all bring her in for big hugs except Roger, who offers a handshake. It's not long before they are bombarded with elaborate gowns and bow ties.

"This is your night," Sara whispers to Emily. "I don't want you worrying about me. Go shake hands with all your guests."

Sara frequents women's networking events and small business owner meetups. She's never been shy in these types of situations and made it clear to Emily earlier that she doesn't need babysitting.

When Emily is off, Sara grabs a cocktail and makes small talk with a cardiologist from Long Island. He's going on about how politics has infiltrated medicine. She hears him, but she's distracted, enthralled with Emily's every move. There's a magnetic vibrancy that Emily radiates, and it's not just Sara drawn to it. Sara notices that there's not a moment Emily is left alone for breathing. People are lined up to hug her and kiss her and shake her hand.

This doesn't surprise Sara. How could they not be enamored with her?

Eventually, a handsome young man with a youthful glow asks the attendees to be seated and introduces the former VP of Acquisition and majority stockholder of The Brynn Company Foundation, Emily Brynn.

Emily takes the stage, not an eye wandering from her exquisite poise and commanding attention. She talks briefly about her father, her grandfather, and their mission with The Brynn Company Foundation.

"I remember when my brother had kids," she says. "There was a newfound joy in his life. He wasn't unhappy before them. In fact, he was doing quite well given he had somehow managed to convince my beautiful sister-in-law, Lilly, to marry him." The crowd chuckles. Emily lets the crowd simmer down before she continues.

"But the birth of his children added a layer of joy he hadn't known was even possible. Yet, there he was, feeling it. And I remember my mum telling him that happiness, all of a sudden, becomes so simple when you have children. Take them to a park. Hand them a ball. Let them splash around in a sprinkler or a drinking fountain. Push them on the swings. Watch their faces light up, listen to their laughter. That is happiness. And that is precisely why we do this. We are creating simple, beautiful places for children to be happy and for their parents to experience that same simple happiness alongside them."

Emily's speech makes Sara think of her own girls. She remembers how they would race to the swings, joy in their eyes, and she'd push them, and push them, and push them, while they giggled and shouted about who was going higher. She remembers the first time Sophie jumped off the swing and landed on her feet. The first time Joanna made it all the way across the monkey bars.

Emily closes her brief speech. "Thank you all for coming, from the bottom of my heart. We appreciate you. Each of you."

The crowd roars in applause, and Sara looks around in disbelief that she knows this brilliant, thoughtful, beautiful woman. She watches Emily's every step from the stage to their table, and when she finally sits down beside her, Sara leans in and whispers, "You are amazing, Em."

Emily reaches under the table and squeezes Sara's hand in response. The gesture moves mountains in Sara.

Emily doesn't take a single bite of dinner. She and her brother only stick around long enough to say hello before they begin their rounds to thank each table. Sara spends the dinner with Charlotte, Roger, and Lilly.

They ask about Sara's business, and she tells them all about the origin. Lilly asks if she can get Sara's design input on their sunroom when she visits for brunch tomorrow morning. "Of course," Sara tells her. And they spend most of the remaining dinner talking about their children, a topic Sara and Lilly find great commonalities in.

After dinner, Sara excuses herself to tour the gallery. She makes her way up the grand staircase and works through landscape paintings, sculptures, and textile arts, eventually finding herself in a chamber of portraits. Emily Dickinson, Indira Ghandi, Eleanor Roosevelt and her speculative lover, Lorena Hickok. Unlike much of the other artwork, these are all painted by Parker Anne. They're all women. Famous women.

Except one.

Sara stops in front of a portrait titled *Wonder*. It bears a striking resemblance to Emily. Velvet skin. Midnight hair. Autumn eyes. Lashes that extend gracefully.

"It's her...if you weren't sure."

Sara spins around. It's Parker. "I painted it four years ago. When they last held their gala here."

"You're talented."

"Thank you. I painted it from memory." Parker steps forward to stand beside Sara.

"How?"

"I looked at her when she was on the podium. Just like tonight. I took a photograph in my mind." A smile curls up her cheek, visibly proud of herself. "I sectioned her face off in six parts."

Parker points. "Her forehead." She moves her finger as if it's a brush, tracing it along each feature as she names them. "Each eye, her nose, here, where her jawline meets her ear, and then her chin."

"Impressive."

"She's a masterpiece."

"She is," Sara says in a near whisper.

The two stand together in a comfortable silence, retracing every single detail of the flawless painting. It's impeccably recalled, even down to the single dark freckle under Emily's right eye and the crow's feet that fray out from beside it.

Parker had managed to paint her grace. Her power. Her striking beauty that only a woman could possess. This isn't just art, it's a work of love. Passion.

"I saw the way she was looking at you during the cocktail hour." Parker doesn't part from the painting as she speaks. "She always had a knack for pulling in just about anyone she desired, but I don't remember her ever looking at anyone the way she looked at you."

"Not even you?"

Parker takes a short breath, spins on her heel, and heads out of the room. "Good luck to you two."

Sara doesn't reply; there is no need for a response. Parker's sentiments are painted concretely on the canvas before her.

When Sara hears the young man's eager voice return to the microphone, she makes her way back down the stairs for what she assumes will be the start of the silent auction, but before she can reenter the main room, Emily swoops up from behind her and links her arm into Sara's. "Follow me," she whispers.

Through a back door they jog, and just outside an emergency exit with no alarm, Eric is awaiting them. Sara chuckles when they settle in the car. "You had me thinking we were in some museum heist."

"That would have been more fun, yeah?"

Sara smiles at her own hands folded together in her lap. Without looking up, she tells Emily, "You were wonderful tonight. It was a real honor to see you in your element. To meet your family. To be a part of this whole thing."

Emily tilts her head, perhaps taken aback by the wholesome comment. "Thank you. I was happy to have you with me."

A few blocks of neon lights pass by before Eric lets them off in front of Emily's building. She praises him for the getaway before leading Sara into the front door. Sara can nearly hear her heart beating as she steps into the elevator behind Emily. She wants to kiss her. She's going to. Tonight. She wants to unzip her emerald evening gown. Lie bare with her. Kiss the freckle beneath her eye, her jaw, her red lips, her neck. Sara's body is so anxious it's not possible to resist any longer.

Emily leans against the back of the elevator. Sara steps beside her. A rush of heat pours down her spine.

The elevator beeps up one floor, up two, up three.

Sara looks down at Emily's hanging hand, her thin fingers, her plum-painted nails. She reaches over, just slightly touching the back of her hand to Emily's. Her touch sends a jolt through her. Emily feels it too, as Sara sees her shift her gaze downward, hears her breath grow heavy. Sara moves her hand so that her palm and fingertips are against Emily's. They raise their gazes from their hands to their eyes just as the elevator door opens.

They are motionless. Lost in a nervous ache for each other.

When the elevator door starts to close, Emily reacts quickly, releasing her hand from Sara's and grabbing the door to open it back up. Emily shakily types in her front door code. Sara stands just behind her, attempting to steady her breathing.

She's crossed the line.

Emily pushes open her front door and heads directly over to the wine cooler under the kitchen island. "You, uh, you want a glass of wine?"

Sara doesn't respond. She's still standing at the front door.

Emily kneels, examining her collection. "I've got a bottle of syrah? A malbec? You know, I have this dessert wine too. I've had it forever."

Sara continues her silence, causing Emily to eventually stand and face her, letting the wine fridge swing shut.

Sara's heart is beating faster than she can ever remember it beating. It's hard to hear her thoughts, but she doesn't want to hear them anymore. She doesn't want to think anymore. She just wants to be. Here. Now. With Emily.

She starts walking toward her. They don't break eye contact.

Sara places her hand against Emily's bare shoulder and slides it gently down her arm, feeling every inch of her smooth skin, until she reaches her hand. Sara looks down, her fingers tangled in Emily's. Her whole body is on fire with desire and tension, but her nerves are preventing her from lifting her gaze again.

Emily must sense Sara's apprehension. She slowly reaches her free hand up to Sara's face, runs her thumb along her bottom lip, and brushes a curl behind her ear before softly placing her hand against her cheek. She wraps her fingers around the back of her neck, lifting Sara's gaze just slightly.

Emily steps forward cautiously, their stares unwavering. Sara has every opportunity to say no, but she won't. Not tonight. She leans in to meet Emily.

Their lips touch softly.

Sara's body ignites. She can't ever, ever, in her entire life, remember this kind of yearning and bliss all in the same moment. Emily pulls back just slightly, leaving the next move to Sara. Sara doesn't hesitate. She lifts both her hands to Emily's face and brings her back in for another kiss. Harder this time, and with certainty. With every single ounce of her being.

Emily reciprocates, pressing her tongue into Sara's warm mouth. A shiver runs through her and she thrusts herself into Emily. Emily grabs her hips and presses her against the kitchen island. Their lips are unbroken, Sara's nerves dissipating. Their intensity grows, their gowns in the way of every holy thing that has ever existed.

Emily moves from her lips to Sara's cheek, to her ear, down her neck, her collarbone.

"I want you," Sara whispers in Emily's ear.

Emily looks up, grabbing Sara's eyes. Sara's imagined this moment. Kissing Emily. Undressing her. But it's hard to grasp that it's happening.

"I've wanted you since the night I met you. I'm sorry for taking so long to admit it to myself."

Emily smiles softly and wraps her arms around Sara, nuzzling her face into her neck. Sara can tell in the way she holds her tightly that she didn't mind the wait. Sara shifts her body just slightly and lifts Emily's chin upward.

"Unzip me," Sara whispers in a sultry tone, her lips just slightly turned up.

"I'd love to." Emily grins and turns Sara around. She unzips her slowly, tracing her index finger down her spine. Emily uses both her hands to lower the straps from Sara's shoulders down past her elbows, until the dress falls to the floor. She spins Sara back around. Sara is now standing in a strapless bra and lacy blush underwear, and the eager look in Emily's stare insinuates that she can hardly wait to undress what's left of her clothing. Emily leans in for a kiss and tells her, "Let's go to my room."

Sara clumsily follows her through the hallway in kisses and in laughter.

When they enter the room, it's as if they've been naked together a million other times. There is not an ounce of fear or hesitation left in either of them.

Emily presses a button on the wall that turns on a dim yellow light from behind her bed before laying Sara down. Sara props herself up against her elbows and watches as Emily steps out of her dress and then removes her bra and then her underwear. She hopes her heart does not literally hop from her chest. Emily stands completely bare, letting Sara take her in before crawling on top of her.

Emily kisses her lips, then her neck, which causes Sara to inhale deeply. Her whole body is on fire. Hungry for Emily to do what she pleases. She reaches under Sara and unlatches her bra. She's well practiced. Sara can feel her confidence, and she likes it. A woman in control.

Emily grabs Sara's full breast and puts her mouth around her nipple, bracing herself with one hand and sliding her other down between her legs. Softly rubbing her fingers up the insides of Sara's thighs and over her soaking underwear. She moves her mouth to the other nipple. More touch, more taste. Sara wants all of it. Her nipples are hard. She's soaked with desire. She's trying to minimize her moaning, but she wants to shout in joy.

She cannot believe she has been missing out on this woman for her entire life.

Emily slides her mouth down Sara's toned belly. When she gets to her underwear line, she uses both hands to shimmy the lace down over her thighs, past her knees, and off to the floor. Emily spreads Sara's legs, but before she can taste her, Sara brings Emily back up to her lips and kisses her passionately before rolling over and on top of her.

Despite months of feeling so unsure, she's never been surer about how and where to touch Emily. How and where she wants

Emily to touch her. She pulls Emily up into a seated position and crawls onto her lap, wrapping her legs around Emily's torso and pulling herself in close.

Sara whispers in Emily's ear as she runs her fingers through her hair, "I want all of you." They sit like this, naked and vulnerable, and willing, and hungry, minute after minute, exploring each other firmly with their hands, their lips not daring to miss a single inch of skin.

"I want you inside of me," Sara says, her back heating up.

Emily, still seated, slides her hand from Sara's breast down between her legs and slowly moves a single finger inside her. She's warm, dripping with desire. Emily adds a second finger moving in and out, her thumb now circling where Sara craves it most. Their mouths are rich with tongue and Sara's moans become more strained. She's close, so close.

"Not yet," Emily whispers. "I want to taste you."

Emily pulls her fingers out of Sara and puts them in her own mouth. Sara watches, thinking about how she's never been naked with someone she has wanted so desperately. It's both sad and thrilling, like being trapped under a tidal wave and finally coming up for air. This. This is life. This is what it feels like to be alive.

She's finally alive.

Emily lays Sara down and crawls out from under her, steadying herself on top. She makes her way down between her legs again. Sara spreads them wider as Emily opens her and firmly presses her tongue inside. Emily's tongue moves slowly upward and starts to circle. Sara tries to hold off, sinking into the warmth of Emily against her, but in what feels like seconds, she arches her back in a moan and yanks Emily upward, holding her tightly around her sweaty body in pure bliss.

"My God." Sara allows herself a few deep breaths, before announcing, "I don't want to stop." She smiles slightly. "I've waited forty-two years for you, Emily Brynn."

CHAPTER TWENTY-SEVEN

Emily

Emily's arms explode with goosebumps. "I'm all yours."

Sara rolls them over. On top and in control. She kisses Emily softly, lifting after each kiss, allowing Emily to take in Sara's round, wanting eyes, her smooth skin, her perfect breasts.

Sara lifts herself off, rolls Emily onto her side, and crawls behind her, pushing herself up against her.

She sits up on one elbow and brushes Emily's hair to the side, gently kissing her neck, her shoulders, her spine. Emily's played out this whole moment alone in her bed at night—the moment she could take Sara in her arms and touch her wherever she desired. But she couldn't have predicted the desire she'd feel from Sara taking the lead.

"I can't believe how much time I've wasted not kissing you," Sara says as she wraps her arm around Emily and grabs one breast, then both of them. Emily can't resist a smile. As she feels Sara's hand push lower and lower between her thighs, she wants her hands everywhere, each sensitive space of skin from ear to toe.

Sara presses herself more tightly to the back of Emily as her fingers make their way inside of her. Emily gasps and Sara presses harder, moving her body in a steady rhythm against her. They move together. The two of them as one.

Emily's moaning gets louder and more desperate, begging Sara not to stop. Sara turns her over, crawls on top of her. "I want to see your face," Sara whispers.

Her fingers are still gliding around Emily. Emily's back bridges upward. Sara doesn't stop, not until Emily grabs Sara's wrist firmly and pulls her on top of her, collapsing together into the bed.

Sara pulls Emily's arm out and lays her head on it, curling up beside her.

"How do you feel?" Emily asks after many moments of silence.

"Alive. For the first time. Maybe ever."

Emily looks over at Sara. She's sleeping soundly. The Sunday sun through the glass walls has colored her bare arm in glitter and gold.

She hops in the shower, replaying every moment of the night with a grin she can't wipe off her face. She dresses in a baggy T-shirt and underwear, brews two cups of coffee, and crawls back into bed, kissing Sara's nose once, then twice before she finally opens her eyes.

"Good morning," Sara says, a soft smile curling up her cheek.

"I have fuel." Sara pulls the white sheet up over her bare chest as Emily hands one of the coffees to her.

The two are having Sunday brunch with Emily's family before they head to the airport. Emily can't wait. She's missed her family's weekly get-together and is eager to spend the morning with her niece and nephews. FaceTime is no replacement for big hugs and kisses.

"Did you sleep okay?" Emily asks. She wants to cut to the chase and ask if she's waking up full of regret but doesn't want Sara to feel uncomfortable.

"Yeah, I slept great."

"Good. You, uh…you feeling okay about what happened between us?"

"Are we an us?" Sara's eyebrows raise.

"No, no." Emily tries to gulp down a grin. "I'm not insinuating we are anything. I'm just making sure you feel okay about what happened between us."

Sara looks down at her coffee. "I feel great."

Emily leans over and nudges her. "Good."

"Can we take the subway today? I've never been on one."

Emily looks over, completely unprepared for this request but ready to fulfill it.

"A weekend of firsts for you, yeah?"

They both chuckle.

Emily looks over at Sara, wanting desperately for this to be her every morning. Coffee beside a naked Sara Dylan. Sunshine.

Sara returns the gaze and leans in, letting the sheet fall from her chest to her lap. Emily meets her and they kiss softly, holding steady for a long moment before Sara backs off. She puts her coffee down on the pinewood end table and crawls on top of Emily. She takes Emily's mug from her hands and places it down as well. Emily wraps her now free hands around Sara's waist.

Sara kisses her forehead. Her rosy cheek with the single freckle, her rounded nose, her full lips. Her lips again, and again. When she slides in her tongue, Emily's body ignites.

"Do we have time?" Sara whispers.

Emily takes in Sara's sea-blue eyes, thinking the word *time* sounds so limited with a woman like Sara Dylan. They could have tomorrow. They could have next Sunday. Forever. But she knows Sara well enough to know that the Sara this morning exists in a city where no one knows her.

She knows their time is now and maybe there won't be any more of it later.

"Yes," Emily tells her, pulling Sara's hips into her.

CHAPTER TWENTY-EIGHT

Sara

Sara's phone pings in her pocket. It's Rebecca. She swipes it open, wondering what her tennis teammate wants on a Sunday morning.

I'm with Ang. We're filling in at a doubles tournament today at Valley, but I was telling her about this new cocktail bar in Southport. She told me you are helping to design it and you're with the owner now in New York!

Sara feels her face heat up. She must have read the same article Carrie Mae read, which means they both now know Emily is a lesbian.

I'll let her know she's already got fans. Good luck to you and Ang today!

Almost instantly another text comes through.

I read that Emily has made her rounds with hot women, watch yourself Sara! (Laughing face emoji?) Ang was shocked to find out she was a lesbian. Too hot. She said you've been into Thursdays with her. How fun that you've become such good friends! We can't wait for the new spot to open!

The lump in Sara's throat drops to the pit of her stomach. She isn't sure if her face is ghost white, but the tension in her entire being makes her feel as if it is. She rereads the message as she follows Emily on the walk from the metro station to James and Lilly's home.

"You doing okay?" Emily asks. "Need to make a call?"

"No, no." Sara could tell Emily about the message and she would likely have some sage advice, but instead, like she's done for months now, she slides her phone and secrets into her pocket. "I uh, it's…uh." She coughs before continuing, "It's probably best to keep whatever we are between us, right?"

The comment takes Emily back, visibly. She stutters for a moment before continuing to walk. "Did you think I was going to tell my mum we slept naked together?"

Sara exhales, finding it difficult to laugh at Emily's joke due to the tension eroding her rationality.

"I figured it was a matter of time before you started questioning things. Don't worry though, Sara. Secret's safe." Emily doesn't laugh or mince her words. She sort of seems… hurt.

"No, I don't…You know I don't mean it like that."

"Well, you can tell me how you meant it later. This is it." Emily waves her up the concrete stairs.

Sara pauses for a moment to admire the grand brownstone. The closest she's ever been to one is a *Sex and the City* episode but here she is, about to share a meal in one beside the billionaire woman she's just undressed. "He lives here. In this one?"

"Yep." Emily tugs open the door and before they're fully inside, the children rush to her. She bends down to hold them all in her arms at once, kissing their heads and laughing with them.

Sara smiles at the wholesome, endearing interaction, allowing herself to further banish Rebecca's text messages from her thoughts.

James, Lilly, and Charlotte greet the ladies with big hugs and a kiss on each cheek. Charlotte urges them all to sit for a hearty brunch, which is already prepared and sizzling warm.

Around the wooden table, Sara listens to them chatter on in their thick English accents while dipping her sourdough bread in a small bowl of beans and sipping green tea from fine china adorned in yellow lemons. She went to London shortly after college and remembers this familiar feast.

James interrupts the banter with a demand for attention. "Can we talk about Parker's painting?"

"She's always been so generous," Emily replies. "Was not expecting three paintings. One has always been more than enough."

"No, no, love," Charlotte says. "Not the donated paintings. James is talking about the portrait of you."

"You didn't see it?" Sara asks.

Emily shakes her head. "I've no idea what you all are talking about."

"Yes, the portrait," James reiterates, his eyes wide.

"Look." Lilly pulls out her phone and scrolls through her pictures from the evening, settling on the one of the portrait. She hands it to Emily.

A wide grin takes over her face. "Wow, I look good." They all chuckle.

"You do," Lilly agrees.

Lilly takes her phone back. "I talked to Parker about it. She said she's had it up for a couple of years now. Not selling it, though. She said there were a few paintings that she's done in her life that bring her joy, this is one of them."

"Woowee!" James shouts. "She's definitely still got the hots for ya, Em. Bummer she left ya for that ol' bloke."

Charlotte grabs her floral napkin from the table and smacks her son's arm with it. "It is amazing, James, the company you are running with the ignorance you spew."

They all laugh. Sara, too, but less for his comment, or the smack, and more for his vernacular. She can't get over how much thicker his accent is than Emily's.

"You saw it too?" Emily turns to Sara.

Sara nods. "It's really beautiful." The two share a sweet smile. "She painted it by memory," Sara says, looking up to address the rest of the table.

"Not a chance," James responds.

Sara nods again. "She did. She said the last time you had the gala there, four years ago, she took a mental picture of Emily while she was up on stage."

"A mental picture?" Lilly repeats.

Sara looks at Emily as she recalls her conversation with Parker. "Your forehead, your eyes, your nose." As Sara talks, her Southern drawl slows, taking in each area of Emily's face as she names it. The masterpiece it is. "Where your ear meets your jawline. And your chin." She stares at Emily a moment, thinking how she'd like to kiss her before remembering she's surrounded by Emily's family and hastily looking away.

A long, inquiring pause is followed by a simultaneous, "Wow."

CHAPTER TWENTY-NINE

Sara

"This was the best weekend I've had in a long time," Emily shares as they settle into their airline seats.

"Thanks for letting me tag along." Sara's been a bit on edge since the message from Rebecca came through.

"It was so good to be with my family. I missed the kids so much."

"They're big fans of you. Did you end up winning that game of chess?"

"No, Blake got me. She's much better than I remember."

As they exit the jetway and step into the terminal back in Wilmington, Sara reaches to grab her purse from Emily, and at the touch of their hands, Sara smiles.

"Sara Dylan!"

Sara yanks her arm back to her side, removing the smile from her face. "Oh, hi, Mary. How are you?"

Mary Lewellen, head of the tennis program and the Valley Club. Nosy and nitpicky and gossipy and really good at her job.

"Who's this?"

"Yeah, yep," Sara awkwardly replies, her face flushed. "This is my friend Emily. We were just returning from a fundraiser in New York."

"Wonderful." Mary looks from Emily to Sara and back to Emily. "Why aren't you playing tennis with us, Emily? You look like an athlete."

"Oh…" Emily sort of hesitates, seeming to find it odd that they're in the middle of a busy airport gate starting a conversation about tennis. "Been busy, but maybe I'll tag along next week."

Mary huffs. "Well, I took the girls to see a Broadway show." No one had asked her, but obviously she felt inclined to share. "*Wicked.*"

Sara can't think straight, so much so that she hadn't even noticed Mary's daughters standing next to her. She doesn't care about the Broadway show. Mary was on the flight, and all Sara can think about is if she saw Emily's hand on her leg. Did she see them at LaGuardia giggling together, standing too close together? How could she have missed her? How could she have not heard Mary Lewellen's squeaky voice shrilling through LaGuardia?

Sara manages to regroup enough to ask, "Did you enjoy it, girls?"

"Yes," they reply in unison.

"Well, it was great meeting you, Emily. I hope you'll join Sara on Tuesday at tennis."

Sara doesn't speak while they wait for their bags. Emily must sense the anxiety because she doesn't ask any questions. Every bone in her body is aching in fear. She doesn't want to be the divorced woman that is now with a woman. What will her friends think? She does not want a single person to think that she and Emily could possibly be together as more than friends.

When they get in Emily's car, Sara relaxes into her seat, huffing out what she recognizes as a lifetime of stress.

"You okay?" Emily finally asks, avoiding eye contact.

"Not really. Did you see them at LaGuardia? Mary and the kids?"

"I didn't."

"Did you know they were on our plane?"

"No."

Sara huffs out another deep, loud breath.

"I didn't see them either. You sure you didn't see them?"

"Sara, stop."

They drive the twenty minutes back to Wrightsville Beach in silence. Despite the two of them talking about staying together, when they turn on their street, Sara says, "I think I'll just go home tonight. You know, I want to unpack, get ready for the week."

Emily doesn't put up a fight. "I understand." She pulls past her house and up to Sara's condo complex. "Can I help you take your bags in?"

"No, I got it." Sara hurriedly jumps out of the car and grabs her bag from the trunk, so distraught over seeing Mary that it's as if she's forgotten about their weekend. Forgotten about the sunset on the Brooklyn Bridge. Their ten-dollar dinner date. The love they shared under the glow of the city lights.

Timeless, yet fleeting.

"Bye, Sara."

Emily's sweet voice causes Sara to slow her pace, her emotions. She turns around and peers in the front window, catching Emily's gaze. She stays there, perfectly still, for a long moment, hands full of her bags. Neither of them even blink.

"I'll see you soon, okay?" Sara says.

She lugs her bag up the stairs, undresses, and steps into a warm shower. She wants nothing more than to rewind this weekend, take back every kiss, her gown, the feel of Emily's skin against hers. Tears pour from her eyes and salt fills her mouth.

She hardly recognizes this version of herself. The woman she knows she is now. The woman that loves Emily Brynn.

CHAPTER THIRTY

Emily

According to Sara, Mary Lewellen insisted, through a handful of text messages, that Emily join her to their Tuesday evening tennis league. That's why, Emily assumes, Mary is still in her job. It's unlikely that her bullish personality is drawing women to join the club, but she does a hell of a job bullying the ladies into recruiting for her.

And it's clear why so many stay. The facility sits amongst a dozen or so large oak trees. The courts are well kept, and after a sweaty couple of hours the women are showered in lemon cocktails and champagne.

Emily questioned tagging along. Sara didn't seem too enthused. They didn't speak on Sunday night at all. It was late Monday when Sara finally reached out via text. *Mary Lewellen is driving me insane. Please join me for tennis tomorrow.*

Emily had responded, eager to see her again: *I'd love to.*

When Emily asked if she wanted to ride over together, Sara had told her that she had some errands to run after work and would meet her there at five.

Emily spent all evening and most of today thinking endlessly about the strange tension bubbling between them since the Mary incident at the airport. She has told herself repeatedly that Sara's instinctual desire for distance is all normal. It's probably a lot for Sara, coming to terms with herself. Her sexuality, her life as something different than she's always pictured it.

Despite the rationalization, Emily decides to do her best to pull Sara back in.

She wears her white tennis skirt and white sleeveless shirt that she bought just over a year ago while attending Wimbledon for a customer appreciation event. Her skin is well-tanned from hours of work at The Pirate's Hideaway. She knows she looks as good as she's ever looked in the perfectly fitted outfit. But that isn't all. She showed up early to the courts. It's been a while since Emily volleyed let alone played a tennis match, but her years of childhood lessons prove worthwhile.

"I'm stealing you from Sara next week," Ang states as she pours four flutes of champagne. One for Emily, one for Sara, one for Rebecca, and one for herself.

Sara looks at Emily for what feels like the first time all night and offers her a relaxed smile. "I suppose I could share the good fortune."

"Ladies!" Mary Lewellen interrupts in her high-pitched squeal. "I know many of you already got to meet our new star, but, Emily, I was hoping you could formally introduce yourself. Tell us a few things about yourself."

Emily, fortunately, isn't shy in a large group. In fact, she thrives when put on the spot. "Thank you, Mary. I understand you peer-pressured Sara to bring me in tonight."

The ladies chuckle.

"I, uh, I'm thirty-seven. New here. Living just over the bridge on Wrightsville Beach. I like to build things. Learn new things. And I'm happy to be here with all of you tonight. Hopefully I can join again next week."

The ladies shout "Welcome" in unison.

"So, no partner?" Rebecca asks.

Sara's eyes jolt to Emily. Emily briefly acknowledges her before letting out a chuckle. "No partner."

"Well, I for one am thrilled you are not interested in men. I'm sure Sara is too. Right, Sar?"

Sara so obviously forces a strained smile, but Rebecca doesn't seem to notice, as she carries on. "It's already hard enough out there finding good men in your forties."

Emily can't look at Sara again. The awkwardness is eating her alive. Instead, she embraces the conversation.

"Imagine trying to find a woman!"

Rebecca and Angie laugh hysterically. When they finally simmer down, Emily can't help herself from asking, "How did you know I was interested in women? Am I that obvious?"

"No!" Angie shouts. "Quite the contrary, and I know how shallow that sounds so ignore I ever said it, but Sara here didn't even tell us. We read about it in the newspaper. Celebrity lesbian buys up real estate…it was something like that, right?"

Rebecca hasn't stopped laughing.

"Ah, yes. The infamous article. This really is a small town."

"Ladies, I'm going to head out." Sara stands from her barstool abruptly and slides it back in. "Got to get the girls. See y'all next week." She smiles her sweet smile, glancing briefly at Emily but careful not to offer any additional attention.

"Bye, Sar," Emily says as Sara walks away.

"She seemed a little off tonight, right?" Angie leans in toward Emily, clearly hoping to get the scoop.

Emily just shrugs her shoulders. "I didn't notice."

Emily is nearly asleep when her phone buzzes.

I didn't want to worry you before the big gala, but Carrie Mae called it quits on us. Just received the signed contract from our new amazing firm. Right on track with deadline.

Not the message Emily hoped to see from Sara, but she responds: *What did her in?*

Not really sure.

It was the newspaper article, wasn't it?

Small dots appear, and then disappear, and then appear and disappear again.

Emily, impatient, probes further: *Is she against the lesbians or does she think I'm going to be involved in some financial scandal involving the city?*

More than ten minutes pass before Sara responds, and it's a total change of subject.

Did you find the conversation tonight regarding your sexuality intrusive?

No, Emily responds instantly, trying to indicate she's been staring at her phone.

Again, small dots appear, and then disappear.

Emily texts again: *People are inherently curious. I don't find it offensive. It's nice to talk so openly about it. Who I love does not embarrass me.*

CHAPTER THIRTY-ONE

Sara

"How was the fundraiser?" Steve is attempting small talk. Sara is uninterested.

It's been nine days since she returned from New York. Seven days since she last saw Emily. There's no makeup cure for this kind of exhaustion. She's buried herself in work, declined one invitation to have dinner with Emily, and now here she is trying to wrap up a few odds and ends at the Food Hall, and both Steve and Margie are in the building. Of course they are.

"It was great. Thanks for asking."

"Emily said the same. She said they raised the most money to date."

Sara shoots up in attention. "When did you talk to Emily?"

"I uh…She helped me out with a business predicament this past Friday. I thought she may have mentioned it to you?"

"She didn't mention it."

Not that she's had the opportunity. It's not like Sara has given her an ounce of attention since she whispered in her ear if there was enough time to have sex before breakfast.

"I've been busy." Sara looks back down at her pad of paper. "Why'd you come today, Steve?"

Steve widens his glare, taken aback by Sara's strange response to the mention of Emily and her even more ridiculous question. "Well, I own the building, Sara. I come often to see the progress. I had no idea you'd be here today."

Sara looks up and nods. She knows this but wants him to leave her alone and hopes he'll take the hint. But he doesn't. He's clearly determined to break through to the woman he once spent his every day with and likely wondering how long she could carry on like this—stubborn and cold in his presence.

"I saw Mary Lewellen at Sophie's soccer practice last night. She said she ran into you and Emily at the airport and then you brought her to tennis."

Sara replaces her annoyance with anxiety, wondering why on earth she brought this on herself. If she only could have restrained from Emily. "Yeah." She doesn't look up from her task, but she can feel her face burn. "We saw her."

"Yeah…okay. Well, I'm glad you had a good time in New York."

Sara looks up at Steve, her eyebrows furrowed, her cheeks feeling a touch redder than normal. "Did Mary say something about me and Emily?"

Steve looks confused by the question, or maybe just the haste in how she asked it. "No. No, I just, you know…I'm trying to have a conversation with you, Sara. We're raising daughters together. Remember?"

Sara's shoulders droop. She exhales loudly, a common trend these last few days. "Sorry." She really is sorry. It's not his fault she can't get her emotions together. "I've got a lot going on right now, Steve. Let's chat later, okay?"

Steve holds her gaze for a moment. "Okay, Sara. I'll see you this weekend. Tell the girls I love them." He heads to the back of the building where Margie is diligently making notes.

Sara speeds through her task list before either of them can make their way back over. She shouts goodbye from the front door and hurries off to her Jeep before she sees another person that might mention Emily or New York or Mary Lewellen.

She's greeted by two messages. Emily's name sends a rush of uncontrollable butterflies through her. It's painful how much she misses her. There hasn't been an hour stretch that Emily's hands against her skin hasn't crossed her mind, but she's in no state to see her.

I can't come to tennis tonight. I've got a plumbing issue at The Hideaway. Yoga Saturday?

Sara presses her palms to her tired eyes, rubbing the ache from them before breathing out deeply.

I'll be there.

She didn't go last Saturday. She blamed it on the girls, but it had nothing to do with them and everything to do with facing Emily. She woke up that morning, looked in the mirror, called herself a coward, and crawled back into bed to sleep the day away.

Sara slides open the next message, from Angie. *Come over this Saturday. Remember that friend I told you about? His name is Brandon and I want to introduce the two of you.*

Without a second thought, Sara responds: *I'll be there.*

Back at the office, Jared is clicking away. He's recently set up a third large monitor to improve his workflow, so he's buried behind a wall of screens when Sara enters his office.

"What'd Margie have to say today?" he asks.

"Steve was there."

"Oh." Jared releases his hand from his mouse and slides his chair to the side to give her the attention he knows she needs. "And?"

"Steve's trying to be friendly. I just feel...I dunno. Overwhelmed. It's hard for me to think about being his friend. He was talking about my New York trip and some lady from tennis that he ran into at Sophie's soccer practice. Some meeting he had with Emily."

Jared nods. "Can I ask about New York?"

She looks at him. They are both, without a doubt, recalling the conversation at Shark Tooth Tavern.

Sara's whole body slouches. She's exhausted with her double life. With her emotions. "I can't be with her, Jare."

"Did something happen between you two?" Jared's tone is calm, his face nonjudgmental, unsurprised.

"No." Sara's eyes dart around the room, pathetically paranoid that someone may overhear them while knowing there is no one else in the office. In her office. That she owns. "Yes."

She drops her head into her hands as her eyes fill with tears. She wants to tell him everything. Get it off her chest.

"You don't have to be alone," he says. "This doesn't have to be some big scandalous secret." Jared sits up straighter. His tone is deeper, more direct. "In fact, I'm a little hurt that you think it is. You have feelings for a woman. Why is this something you are ashamed of?"

"I'm not ashamed. I'm…I'm confused."

"Sara, I know you, and I've been incredibly patient with you about this topic, but you sat down in my office today because this is eating you alive. If you can't talk to me, let's find someone you feel comfortable talking to."

Jared isn't mentioning it, but she knows he sees the heavy bags under her eyes. He knows the stress she's feeling.

"You haven't said more than a sentence at a time since coming back from New York. I know that you're holding on to this secret alone. You haven't told anyone, have you?"

She shakes her head.

"Why? Because you're embarrassed? You're scared? You're worried? These are incredibly valid feelings, but you are forty-two years old. You are in the prime of your career, Sara. You are a badass professional and mother and woman. Why on God's green earth are you keeping yourself from happiness?"

"My parents. What will they say?"

"They may need time, but they love you."

"My friends? My children? Steve?"

Jared exhales, like he's reminding himself to be gentle with her.

"They may also need time, but they all love you, Sara."

There are tears streaming down her face now. She's not sure how there are even tears left to cry. She's had a constant headache from tears. She's depleted from the tears.

"Sara. Hun." She looks up at him, sure that her eyes are bloody red. "You need to get to a point that you love yourself more than you love other people's opinions of you."

She doesn't respond. She doesn't know what to say. Is he right? Does she not love herself enough to be happy?

"You are one of the greatest humans I have ever met. I love you. I also think you are harboring some deeply poisonous ideas about what makes a good life. You deserve a great life. Let yourself have that." He sits up from his seat, walks to her, and pulls her up out of her chair for a hug. They stand in embrace for a long moment.

"I love you," she tells him.

"I don't want to harp on therapy again, but will you please explore it?"

"Okay."

CHAPTER THIRTY-TWO

Sara

Sara takes great care in placing her mat just slightly ahead of Emily's, a poor attempt at limiting her peripheral vision because all class long she finds herself drawn to Emily's strong form and graceful movements. The body she had the privilege of touching almost every part of.

As the two are rolling up their mats at the end of class, Emily asks, "You want to come have a coffee at my place?"

Sara hesitates a moment. She's thought hour after hour about her conversation with Jared and hasn't come to a place where she feels comfortable approaching Emily. Approaching herself. She's a ping-pong ball, bouncing between desire and aversion. Fear and courage. Happiness and responsibility. Freedom and expectation.

"Sure, that sounds nice."

The two walk silently in step to Emily's.

"Are you hungry?" Emily asks as Sara takes a seat at the counter. "I can put on some eggs."

"No," Sara replies. "Just a coffee, please."

Emily starts the pot and leans against the butcher block opposite Sara.

"Have you been doing all right?"

"Yeah." Sara nods her head and offers a tender smile. "I'm doing okay."

"You've been texting me so often, I thought we should just talk in person." Emily smiles at her and spins around for the coffee. Sara chuckles. Her wittiness is unavoidably funny. Emily is clearly pleased. "I was hoping that comment would break the awkwardness."

They look at each other.

"You're the same Sara I undressed two weeks ago."

Sara closes her eyes, huffing out a chuckle. The comment swirls desire within her.

"I'm sorry." Sara is struggling to look Emily in the eye.

"No need to apologize." Emily slides a full steaming cup along the counter.

"Steve said you two met up."

"We did."

Sara takes a sip. She isn't quite ready for this conversation. Despite how simple Jared made this whole thing seem, Sara hasn't been able to gather rational thoughts since the moment they landed back in Wilmington. Since the moment Mary Lewellen and her pompous posture shoved Sara right back into the square house on the cookie-cutter road that she's spent her whole life on.

"We don't need small talk, Sara. I mean, I've seen you naked. I think we're past that." Emily's tone has changed. It's not as light and airy as it was a moment ago. "I'm not asking you to come out to your friends, or your family. I'm not asking you to be my girlfriend. I want nothing from you that you don't want to give. I haven't said a word about us, not that I have anyone to tell, but I like you. I like hanging out with you and I think you feel the same. I don't want to be some burden you're lugging around. I was your friend before we were…whatever we are now. And we just shared this incredible weekend together and it feels as if saying hello has become an impossible task for you. What on earth is going on?"

Sara grabs Emily's eyes, noticing her confidence, her sophistication, her certainty. Sara envies all of it. Her heart beats heavily against her chest. She feels physically ill, nauseous. "I, uh…I'm not going to be with a woman, Emily. I can't be with you."

"What?" Emily shakes her head, letting out a sarcastic chuckle. "It is not the nineties, Sara. Majority of the country does not care in the slightest if two women end up together. Why are you even saying this? I didn't ask you to commit to me."

The two stare at each other. Sara steels her face to stone-cold indifference.

"Tell me. Please!" Emily begs.

"Because I have a business. And two kids. And parents that won't ever understand. And I can't risk this all for some…feeling I have about a woman from New York that's on some wild hiatus from her billions of dollars."

Emily looks like she's been physically struck, and for a moment Sara can't believe her own harshness, her audacity.

"A wild hiatus? Do not use my desire to live a life that is more meaningful as your reasoning to walk away from us."

"We aren't an *us*, Emily. I'm nothing like you. You are proud of your sexuality. You've dated celebrities, for God's sake. You're living in some fairy tale, buying up properties, and starting all these new endeavors. For how long? Until you get bored? Until you go back to New York and pick up where you left off?" Sara doesn't let Emily respond. She's convinced herself of these lies enough times that they are flowing from her lips. "I am someone here. I was someone here before you came."

Emily's eyes raise. Sara sees her gulp down a heavy lump of sadness. She wipes the tears that have trickled down her cheek with the back of her hand. She clearly wants to talk. She probably wants to say a million things. She finally asks, "What can I possibly say to a woman that is too scared to love herself?"

A stagnant silence weighs down the room.

Sara steps up from her chair but is stopped by Emily's low voice. It's nearly a whisper. "You are angry with yourself, Sara. You are angry that you are different now than you once were, and I understand you need time to process this, but it doesn't require you to project your fears onto me. I am very proud of the person that I am and the person I'm becoming. I work hard for it. And despite what you've said today, I like you. I'm not scared to say that. But you've got a lot of soul-searching to do. You don't have to worry about me showing up to tennis or yoga. I need you to leave now."

Sara says nothing, because her heart breaking is clouding all thoughts. She pushes her stool under the counter and doesn't even look back at Emily as she steps out of the kitchen, down the hall, and out the front door.

CHAPTER THIRTY-THREE

Sara

"That's him." Ang nods in Brandon's direction through the group of people gathered in her home. Sara takes note of his stats. Just under six feet. Clean cut. Similar to Steve in build and style.

"He's handsome," Sara tells her, flatly.

Angie nudges her. "You doing okay?"

"Oh, yes." Sara paints on a grin. "Busy week with work and the girls. You know. The normal."

"All right. You should have brought Emily tonight. When is she coming back to tennis?"

Sara shrugs her shoulders. "I'm not sure."

"I friended her on socials. She's like…a low-key celebrity. Did you know she dated Michael Perry's daughter?"

Sara's eyes crinkle. "I've heard."

"I'm a terrible human, but I had no idea there were so many hot lesbians."

The comment bothers Sara in a way it shouldn't. The shallowness of it. The idea of what beautiful is. The idea of what a woman should be. She knows Angie didn't mean it in a hurtful way, though. She loves all people. She just also loves a gossipy comment every now and then.

"Yeah, I imagine there are plenty of beautiful women who like women out there." Sara knows, because in the comfort of her bed one evening she did a Google search for lesbians and a long list came up: Portia de Rossi, Sarah Paulson, Cara Delevingne, Michelle Rodriguez, Ali Krieger. Then she deleted her search history.

"What's gotten into you?"

Sara bites her lip, realizing how defensive she sounds. "Nothing." She forces a witty smile. "I'm gonna go talk to Brandon."

Angie tilts her head in what appears to be confusion before cheering her on. "Go ahead, girl."

Sara walks over. There are no nerves. She spent the afternoon crying herself into a sort of zombie-like state. She curled her hair and hid all her feelings behind a coat of powder and blush. She hasn't really thought about it much before, but she knows now that this is something she's been doing her whole life. Hiding herself behind blush and a smile.

Brandon greets her joyfully. Angie must have told him about her, as it seems like he was expecting her company. They talk through the night about her girls, about his son. His work as a financial advisor. Her work as a designer.

She doesn't feel a spark. She doesn't feel much of anything at all.

"What's your favorite job you've worked on recently?" he asks her.

"Hmm..." Thoughts of Emily's lips against her collarbone swirl around her head. "The Pirate's Hideaway. It's different from most of the work I do. It's a new bar in Southport. But also kid-friendly. Interesting combination, I know, but so many cool touches. It's been a fun one."

"Can't wait to check it out."

He means it, she can tell by his perky grin. It's genuine.

"Yeah, me too," Sara says. She doesn't really know if her response is genuine. She sort of just wants to curl up in a ball and disappear for a while. She knows as this thought hits how unhealthy it is. She commits to finding a therapist in the morning.

Angie yells from the kitchen, "Question time!"

It's her infamous game. Pull a card, read a question, and either choose to answer or take a shot of liquor. In their twenties it was shots for everyone, but they hit age thirty, the shots became far less popular. And now that Sara is forty-two, a shot sounds like a dose of ibuprofen.

Angie kicks it off.

"Favorite sex position?" Angie screeches. "Why do I always pull this one?" She squeals in hilarity. "Y'all already know the answer!"

The cards pull and the questions flow.

"Celebrity crush?"

"If you had to marry an ex, who and why?"

"Favorite vacation?"

The room is full of laughter. Even Sara finds herself chuckling along. It's her turn now. She pulls a card and reads, "What is the best date you have ever been on?"

Brooklyn Bridge, peach sky, pizza, Emily.

Sara looks up and scales the room. She's known most of the people here for over twenty years. Most are married. Some dating. Some in love. Some sticking it out for the kids. Then her. In love with a woman that she doesn't know how to love. Standing in a room of people that don't know this about her.

She smiles softly, picks up the shot of whiskey, and shoots it. The room roars in laughter.

"Come on!" a man yells. Another woman jokingly boos her.

Angie scoots down the kitchen island and nudges her. "Love you," she whispers, and Sara is thankful her friend knows that questions about love and dating and marriage might be triggering given her recent divorce.

The room is clearing out. It's getting late. Brandon asks, "Any interest in grabbing a coffee tomorrow, Sara?"

She looks at him for a moment. He's been kind. He's handsome. He's a man. Why not?

"Sure." Sara nods kindly.

He doesn't hug her, which she appreciates. He just smiles warmly and leaves. "I'll call you in the morning."

Angie walks in and offers another nudge. "It's weird getting back out there, huh?"

Sara huffs out a chuckle. "You have no idea."

"You sure you're doing okay?"

"I am."

Angie furrows her brows.

"I am! I promise," Sara says with conviction this time.

Sara hugs her. "I'm gonna head out, too."

"All right, babe. Let me know how it goes with Brandon tomorrow." Angie winks.

CHAPTER THIRTY-FOUR

Emily

November

Emily ties up her sneakers, pulls on a tightly fitted lightweight sweater, and heads down her front steps into a chilly November morning.

It's nothing like a New York November. She's not teeth-chattering cold where the ends of her fingers stiffen up and it's hard to make a fist. It's in the low fifties here. No snow. Seagulls still chirping away, the smell of salt amongst the browning blades of zoysia grass.

Emily starts her run.

At the end of mile one, she lifts off her sweater and ties it around her waist.

At the end of mile two she's tracking a 7:53 pace.

At the end of mile three, she sees Sara. She knows it's her before she can even make out the shape of her eyes, the roundness in her cheeks. The way she stands, her height. It's her. She's next to a dark-haired man.

Without changing her pace, Emily searches quickly for the first possible side road off the bridge she is running. She desperately wants an out from the woman she hasn't spoken to in two months.

There's nowhere to go. Sara Dylan and the brown-haired man are walking over the bridge and Emily is running toward them. Sara will notice her soon.

Emily has thought about running into Sara. It was only a matter of time, after all. They're both runners. They live only a few doors from each other, but what Emily didn't expect is that she would run into Sara with a man.

She runs through the possibilities of who it could be. A cousin, maybe. A friend, a client, a new coworker. A love interest.

Emily continues. She can now make out Sara's creamy V-neck knit sweater with big brown buttons down the front. Her dark wide-legged jeans. The man wraps his arm around her shoulder.

They're dating?

At his touch, Sara looks up. She sees Emily instantly. Her eyes widen. Neither of them turns away. Neither blinks. Their gaze is magnetic. Emily's pace stays steady. Her breathing grows heavier and heavier as she gets closer and closer. Sara's lips part as if she is about to say something. Emily passes. And continues. Faster, lost in the conversation they just shared with their eyes.

Hi.

I miss you.

How have you been?

CHAPTER THIRTY-FIVE

Sara

"I saw Emily, Rupa."

Sara has been doing online therapy for ten weeks now with a woman named Rupa from Charlotte. She went through two others before finding her. First there was Lauri from the Outer Banks, but she reminded Sara of her middle school principal. Obligated to smile, but clearly overwhelmed and far too formal. Then there was Bonnie from Hampstead, the neighboring city. Too close in proximity for Sara to feel comfortable getting personal.

Rupa is perfect. Warm. Firm. And three-and-a-half long hours away from Wilmington.

During session one, Sara shared her hopeless dating attempt with Brandon. She expressed how he wanted more, and how she sort of did too, but there was no desire to fuel it. At least not yet.

In session four, she carried on more about Brandon until Rupa blurted out, "Is there maybe someone else?" Which led Sara to finally divulge about Emily. Before she spit it out, she wiggled in her seat, letting a rush of heat circle her chest and work its way up her neck and her ears. When she finally said, "Her name is Emily," she found herself laughing with eyes full of moisture. "I haven't told anyone except for Jared. And now I can't imagine having to tell anyone else. I'm...I'm flustered."

Rupa offered her a reassuring grin and told her, "Sometimes angst and relief are tough to differentiate. I'm glad you felt comfortable enough to share. Now we can decide which one it is that you're actually feeling."

"When did you see her?" Rupa asks.

"Yesterday." Sara is slouched in her seat.

"How did it make you feel to see her?"

"I, uh." Sara presses her fingertips to her temples before running them through her golden hair. "I felt everything."

Rupa stares at her a moment, letting Sara simmer in the distress.

"You live by the water, right?"

"Yes."

"I want you to start thinking of yourself like the sea. The sea is still the sea when it is calm, when it is wild, when it is ripping itself sideways. You are you in all your ways. In your strength, and in your weakness. In your joy and your sorrow. In your bliss and your grievances. It is all you. Even if one of those emotions is dominating in a particular moment, you are never just that one thing. You are all the things. Always."

Sara nods along.

"So go ahead and straighten yourself back up. We'll get through this." Rupa smiles gently.

Sara sits up straight. "Can't imagine my mother's disappointment if she'd seen me sitting like that."

Rupa nods. "That's a good segue. We've talked a good bit about your more traditional Southern upbringing. A lot of beauty. A lot of expectations. And a bit of judgment."

Sara nods in agreement. Prior to therapy, she'd never put much thought into her past, but they've been dissecting it week after week. It's been an almost religious awakening hearing Rupa describe her childhood in all its joy and stickiness. Her life back then is so clearly intertwined with who she is today.

"What you're feeling right now, about Brandon, about seeing Emily, it might be fueled by what you're juggling, or rather, what you're trying to hold on to."

"I don't understand."

"Is it time to call it quits with Brandon? Correct me if I'm wrong, but it appears that you're holding on to him because he checks the boxes. But we're moving away from that version of you, Sara. The new Sara does not need to check the boxes that please her parents or her clients or anyone but herself."

Sara inhales, knowing every bit of what Rupa is telling her is the absolute truth.

"All right, so task for the week…I know in your evening journaling, you write about the things that you want for your daughters. I want you to include yourself in that too. I want you to start thinking like you have a big life left to live. More living. More growing. More learning left to do. Because all of these things are true. You are not just a mother. You are a human. You are a woman. You are an incredible designer, you are an entrepreneur. You are the whole damn sea, Sara. Can you do that for me this week?"

Sara chuckles. "I will do that, Rupa."

She flips through the journal she's been keeping at the direction of Rupa. She finds the evening routine enjoyable, resolving after each long day. She flips back a few weeks, scanning her entries.

Sophie and Jo,

If you're feeling fragile, pull out the Christmas ornaments and toss them in the street. I did this once in college. It felt freeing.

Don't ever coat your words with lip gloss. Don't hide your emotions with blush.

You are brave and you are beautiful and you are perfectly designed.

When you stand along the shore, watching the waves wobble in and crash before you. When you stand amongst the redwoods, or alone in your room long after nightfall, know that you belong. You are needed. And you are deserving of all the good things. All of it.

At the top of the page next to Sophie and Jo, Sara writes her name. At the bottom, she writes: *You are the whole damn sea. The calm and the hurricane. All of it. All the time.*

CHAPTER THIRTY-SIX

Emily

"Wow, wow, wow, Ms. Emily," Jared cries out as he walks through the nearly completed Pirate's Hideaway. "This is absolutely incredible."

Emily pops out from the bathroom by the bar. She's dressed in overalls and boots, a brown tool belt around her waist. She's working alongside Carlos, a contractor recommended by Jared and Sara. They're wrapping up the floor tile that was changed, and then changed again, until Emily was certain it was the perfect fit. It's one of the final steps before their grand opening in December.

"And you look incredible too. Overalls and manicure. You do it all, Emily Brynn." Jared winks.

Emily looks down at her outfit and pats away the dirt from her pants. They both chuckle. Jared offers a side hug before addressing her coworker. "Carlos, how are you, buddy?"

Jared's been here biweekly to monitor progress. Hanging bamboo blinds, delivering doorknob samples and tiles, and various fabrics for the custom barstools.

"Emily, is your next venture a contracting business?" Jared asks.

Emily hasn't missed a day on the job. Everything from pulling weeds, to hanging pendant lighting, to today's tiling.

"I'm gonna hire her," Carlos chimes in.

They all chuckle.

She walks up to the main bar area as she unhooks her tool belt. Jared follows. Excitement is steaming from her. She's just a few short weeks from her grand opening.

"You're happy, aren't you?" Jared looks at her.

"I am." She nods.

"Good. Can you sneak away to join me for lunch?"

"Sure."

They ask Carlos if he wants to join, but he shares that he's got to head out early today, so he wants to knock out a few more things.

"He's probably happy I'm out of his hair. Teaching me is slowing him down," Emily says as they close the front door.

Jared and Emily walk a few blocks toward the waterfront and pop in a small café with a large outdoor pergola. It's high fifties today. Gorgeous for an outdoor meal of soup and salad under a heat lamp.

As they sit, Jared begins to tell her that he and his husband are headed to the Cotswolds in the countryside of England for their tenth wedding anniversary. "I got us a room in Stow-on-the-Wold."

"I know it well. Went on holiday there many times."

Jared beams with joy, perhaps assuming she'll be able to save him from hours on Google. "Tell me everything," he says.

"The Queens Head Inn is one of my favorite pubs." She offers a few suggestions for afternoon tea, a walking trail in Lower Slaughter, which is another village just down the way, and she makes him promise to find the hidden pub in the basement of the oldest Inn in England.

He obsessively writes it all down in the note section of his phone.

When she's exhausted her advice, he chimes in abruptly. "So, I won't be here next week." It's clear based on the urgency in his voice that he's been wanting to get this off his chest. "Sara is planning to swing by to ensure the delivery of the outdoor furniture is fulfilled properly. Are you okay with that?"

Jared and Emily haven't spoken of Sara. Jared seamlessly took over the account after Emily and Sara's chat a couple of months back. Emily didn't ask questions. What was the point? Jared is equally capable, charming, and professional. Ultimately, she hired Sara Dylan Design to help bring alive her visions and they've far surpassed her expectations.

Emily holds eye contact. Jared doesn't blink, though the inflamed veins along his temples tell her he's itching to get through this conversation. She wonders what he knows. He knows something happened because he's here in her place. But does he know that Sara was the one who held her hand in the elevator? Does he know that they slept together? Does he know that she told her being with her made her feel alive?

"How is she?" Emily asks.

"She's okay."

"Is she seeing anyone?"

"I don't believe so, anymore." Jared is matter-of-fact in his response.

Emily looks down. "I saw her recently walking with a man."

Jared stares for a moment before responding. "I believe she's just ended it with him. It wasn't anything serious."

He reaches over and cuffs Emily's hand with his.

"Between the two of us, Sara is harboring a lifetime of expectations. Harmful ones, even, that she's cradled at the demise of her own happiness. I find it hard to comprehend myself and I've spent entirely too much time thinking about it. She's getting there, though. Taking steps to feel more comfortable in her own skin."

Emily nods, unsure of what those steps entail.

"I don't know if this helps or hurts, but I know Sara and I know she was happy when you were around."

"What's unfortunate is that I was happy being around her." Emily forces a laugh, a defense mechanism to prevent herself from releasing a waterfall of tears.

"You'll be all right?" he asks.

"It's perhaps pathetic to say, but I'm looking forward to seeing her."

He huffs out a giggle before hugging her tightly. "She's a good one. But a pain in the ass, huh?"

CHAPTER THIRTY-SEVEN

Sara

"I've got to make a quick pit stop, ladies."

"Why?" Sophie whines as Sara pulls into a parking spot in front of the grocery store.

Sara isn't fine, but what she's discovered through therapy is that she hasn't been for many years. She's grown to be very effective at harnessing the joy of her daughters and the passion of her work and using these two bright spots to mask the rest of her being.

She is a good mother and a successful businesswoman, and it would have been enough had she not met Emily.

But things are different now.

At night, when she's alone, when it's only her and she doesn't have to put on a mask for the public, she loses herself in memories of Emily. Her lips against her lips. Her lips against her neck. The two of them laughing on the subway. The way her hand felt in Emily's. Too often, she's fallen asleep with tears running down her cheeks and the promise that tomorrow will be the day that she tells Emily, that she tells everyone.

But each day she wakes with enough strength to keep it bottled up inside.

"I've got to get flowers for Ms. Emily. I've got a site visit tomorrow. Her new bar is about to open."

"I miss her!" Joanna shouts.

Sara smiles at her in the rearview before unbuckling her seat belt.

"I do too," Sophie says. "Since you started hanging out with Mr. Brandon, we never see her."

"Mr. Brandon? We've only hung out a handful of times."

"So what? The timing aligns, Mama." Sara grins at the sass Sophie displays. Reminds her of herself.

"Well, I told Mr. Brandon that I've got a busy rest of the year with you girls, and he said he'd be busy too, so you don't have to worry about him taking our time up anymore, all right?"

When Sara told Rupa about calling it off with Brandon, she said that she felt a massive relief not having to put on a silly front anymore.

"It's sad I'm still doing this, isn't it?" she had told her.

"No," Rupa had replied. "It's exciting you're finally figuring it all out."

As they walk across the street into the store, Joanna says, "I want my own flowers, Mama."

Sara kisses the top of her head. "You'll have them. You too, Soph."

Sophie goes for a three-pack of sunflowers. Joanna chooses a small bundle of purple tulips.

Sara can't decide.

She customized one gift for Emily months earlier with the intention of giving it to her before opening day. So much has happened between then and now. There were weeks when she wasn't sure she'd have the courage to face her again, but she does now. She must, now. And she can't wait to see her sweet face again.

She spoke to Rupa about it.

"There can't be expectations," Rupa told her. "From what you've told me about her, she's very sure of who she is, so there may be an element of lost trust due to you needing a bit more time to figure things out. But, I'd guess she's rational, so she'll come around. No expectations, though. This journey is not about you and Emily. It's about you, Sara. You getting ahold of your happiness, your wants, and your needs. And if one day that includes Emily, then great."

Sara is consciously preventing her excitement from boiling over by repeating Rupa's advice on expectation. How could she possibly have expectations after the way she treated the woman that welcomed her into her home, her friendships, her family, her bed, and her heart?

She can't think too much about it now, though. Her reason for seeing Emily is business, first and foremost. With that in mind, it shouldn't be so hard to pick out flowers.

"Mom," Sophie tells her. "Just pick something."

Sara looks at her girls. "I want it to be special."

Joanna grins widely. "Can you invite Ms. Emily over soon?"

Sara offers a side smile. "She's been busy, but maybe soon. Which flowers do you girls think she'd like?"

"Get her the best ones!" Joanna shouts.

"Well, which ones are those?"

Sophie scans the selection. "Those." She points confidently to a large bouquet, a kaleidoscope of color: golden sunflowers, lavender, orange roses. Lush greenery of fern and eucalyptus. A dash of purple irises for contrast. It's the perfect mix.

"It looks like Emily, huh?" Sara says.

"It does," Joanna chimes in, excitedly.

"It does," Sophie agrees.

Sara picks out a glass vase to compliment it. She ties a thick string of burlap from behind the floral counter around the top of the vase and steps back to admire.

"It's perfect."

Sara shuffles through her clothes. She's thinking too deeply about what to wear for her site visit to The Pirate's Hideaway. To see Emily.

Jeans. No, a dress. No, jeans. Definitely jeans. A fitted top and a wool peacoat. Pointy flats.

She dresses herself in late fall attire, looks in the mirror, and approves. Even smiles. She pulls her hair into a ponytail. More casual now, but still professional. Professional is important. Business only today.

It's hard to not let her jaw drop when she pulls up. She's relied on Jared for updates, but seeing The Pirate's Hideaway in person has Sara feeling giddy. She had originally expressed concerns about Emily's aggressive timeline. Emily had been so adamant about a December opening, but sure enough, almost nine months after purchasing the land, The Pirate's Hideaway will be open for business.

The rounded wooden door is already propped open. Inside, there are three bartenders mixing cocktails. Training, Sara assumes.

She introduces herself and asks, "Is Emily here?"

"She's out back," one of the men, with a perfectly trimmed beard, tells her.

Sara stands for a moment, spinning slowly around the space, admiring how her designs have come to life. The pirate map on the aged wooden floor is her favorite, but every single detail feels thoughtful. Intentional. It is, by far, her favorite job. After she's scouted every nook and crevice, she walks out the back door to find Emily in loose black jeans, high-top Chuck Taylors, a blue jean jacket, and a beanie. A stark difference from the Emily in the emerald-green dress, yet no less stunning.

"Hi, Sara." Emily greets her without standing from her bench seat, like it's easier to keep her distance than decide whether a hug or a handshake is appropriate.

"Hi," Sara says with a shy smile. "Can I sit with you?"

"Please."

Sara sits on the opposite end of the table. "Patio looks great. Are you happy with all the furniture?"

"Very happy with it."

"Can't believe how incredible this place looks."

"You shouldn't be too surprised. You designed it."

Sara huffs out a chuckle. "It doesn't ever get less exciting seeing the 2D renderings come to life."

Emily nods at her. Reserved. Protected.

"I got you this." Sara hands over the flowers and the gift. "A little gift before the big opening."

"Thank you, Sar. These are beautiful."

The pit of Sara's belly flutters at the sound of her name from Emily's lips. "The girls helped me pick them out."

"Yeah?" Emily looks up, connecting with Sara. "How are they?"

"Good." Sara nods.

"Good." Emily stares for a second, then two, then three, before setting the flowers on the far end of the table, allowing her space to address her gift. It's wrapped with care, the brown-paper lines precisely trimmed, the burlap string tied in a neat bow.

As she begins to open it, Sara talks. "I had an artist in town create it."

The artist, Brooke Bowen, has become a friend of Sara's. She's commissioned him for numerous projects she's worked on. His intricate line work is immaculate. She knew she wanted the best for Emily, so she got it.

Emily pulls the picture from the paper while Sara continues talking. "That frame is carved from the wood on the property. I picked it up back in April, before you cleaned things up."

Emily looks up at her. Her face is pale in apparent disbelief at the artwork.

Sara knows what she's thinking. She knows that Emily knows this gift was thought of with love, made with love, wrapped with love. She knows that Emily knows that this isn't just a business exchange. This is something more.

Emily looks back down at the pencil and watercolor picture. It features the silhouette of a little girl with dark brown hair in yellow boots holding the hand of her much taller father, the two of them splashing around in rain puddles. Various shades of blues and pinks color the evening sky around them.

Emily gulps and looks up at her again. "This is the nicest gift I've ever been given. You didn't…" She presses her lips together as she visibly gulps down her emotion. "You didn't have to do this."

"I wanted to."

The two hold eye contact for a long moment.

Eventually Emily diverts her gaze and places the frame atop the brown wrapping paper so the trash doesn't blow away.

"Do you have plans for the holiday?" Sara asks, not wanting their conversation to derail quite yet.

"I'm heading up north. I wasn't planning on leaving until Wednesday, but I just switched my flight to Sunday morning to miss this big hurricane rolling through. Have you been following it?"

"Yeah, it's looking like a Cat 1 for now. If it changes, I'll take the girls up to my parents in Durham. We've got Thanksgiving with them, too, though, so I'm prayin' we don't get caught up there for the whole week."

Emily smiles, looking down at her fidgeting hands.

"How's the tree house coming? All wrapped up?"

"Yeah." Emily waves off the question. "But, hey, I've got one last project for you. I don't need it done by opening day. Maybe January or February timeframe. There's no rush, really, but come on back, let me show you."

They walk along the back of the property to a small metal building. The outside is nearly covered in bamboo, blending it into the lush garden.

"Can you help design this space for storage?"

It's a tight squeeze. Disorganized. It looks like Emily threw a bunch of needed items in here without much thought during the rush of construction.

"I want a commercial-grade fridge in here," Emily tells her. "We're going to serve premade charcuterie boards from Pine Market down on Pike Street."

Sara's eyes widen. "Love that. I can definitely help." She steps forward, diligently eyeing the space from top to bottom. "We'll frame in a fridge here. Floor-to-ceiling shelving here. Let's put a small chest freezer in. It'll fit here." She points. "They're inexpensive, don't take much room, and if we're running electricity, then it'll be worth having. On this side, we'll do open shelves for additional liquor, paper products, whatever kind of storage you need. Hooks here next to the door for cleaning products."

Sara is like a computer, scanning the space and spitting out a detailed understanding of what's needed and useful. Emily looks impressed but she bites her lips, and Sara wonders what she's trying to stop herself from saying.

"Wonderful. Let's move forward."

Sara turns to face Emily. There's not much space between them. She hides her awkwardness by grabbing the strap of her tote as she speaks. "Jared said Carlos has been great for you. He can handle the buildout on a space of this size." She says it confidently, not offering an alternative option, which Emily looks completely fine with. "I'll get the specs drawn up over the holiday and chat with him about it."

"Thank you," Emily says as she steps out of the storage shed. Sara follows.

"I saw that the crew inside seems to have everything stocked and ready for next week. The bookshelves look great too. That was Jared's work, wasn't it?"

Emily smiles. "It was."

The bookshelves are loaded with local pirate novels, ghost stories, gorgeous novelties like ships in bottles, and wooden carvings of yellow-booted fishmen with pipes hanging from their mouths. It's all for sale. Jared displayed everything so that the eye is unavoidably drawn to it. A masterful skill.

"He's the best. That's why we make a good team. I design, he decorates."

Sara is following Emily toward the back exit.

"You two have been exceptional. Thank you."

They're now standing by the tall privacy fence door. Lingering. Sara senses both of them can feel it: the need to leave, the want to stay.

"Here, almost forgot." Sara reaches in her bag and hands Emily a binder of warranty requirements and maintenance guidelines for every single piece of furniture and equipment in The Pirate's Hideaway. "Everything is registered, this is just for your records. Jared will run through a final punch list after

Thanksgiving, but you're just about there, Em. Is there anything else I can help with? Before I get going?"

Emily shakes her head. "We're all set. Are you planning to stop by on opening day?"

Sara has thought a lot about attending opening day but still isn't sure if her appearance would feel more like a distraction than a showing of support. But now that Emily's asked, her mind is spinning. *I should go. I want to go.*

"Do you want me to come?" Sara feels her face heat up, but she stands sturdy and wide-eyed, refusing to look away.

"If you're not busy, sure, it be nice to have you here." Emily looks around. "You've been a part of it all, you know."

"I'll be here."

"Great."

"Okay." Another quiet moment hovers by. "Okay, I'll get going." Sara tries to unlock the gate but struggles with the lever.

"Here, let me help. It's a bit tricky." Sara steps aside and lets Emily unlatch the hook. She can't help herself from taking in Emily's strong arms, her dark hair, her curves. Emily pushes the door open and holds it for Sara.

"Have you been well?" Sara asks, frozen.

"Not bad." Emily hesitates a moment before visibly deflating. Her typically firm demeanor cracks as she chokes out, "What happened with you? With us? You disappear and then you come here with that painting, talking to me like we're old friends, like nothing ever happened between us."

Sara feels all the blood drain from her face. Emily must know she's flustered her because she steps forward but then appears to rethink and steps back, straightening up, protecting her own heart probably.

A lump grows in Sara's throat. "I uh…" She can't talk. She'll cry if she talks. She spits out a feeble, "I'm so sorry, Em."

She steps through the gate, wanting to find the strength to tell her everything. To tell her that she hasn't gone a single hour without thinking of her, that she wants to spend time with her, that she's been seeing a therapist and she's spent the last ten weeks working through forty-two years. And forty-two years can't heal in just ten weeks.

Emily nods her head. "Are you seeing anyone? The man I saw you with?" Immediately after she asks, she presses her hand to her forehead in what appears to be embarrassment. "Don't answer that. It's really none of my business."

"It's okay." Sara is thankful she inquired. It tells her she cares. "I'm not seeing anyone. That man you saw me with was nothing."

Emily doesn't respond. She's apparently probed enough, and Sara can't muster up the strength to come out with her thoughts, so she crumbles. "I'll see you around, Em."

CHAPTER THIRTY-EIGHT

Emily

"Brynny, so lovely of you to grace us with your presence this evening."

Parker hands Emily a short crystal glass with a single round ice cube. "It's Woodford's. Double oaked."

Emily accepts it. It's her third of the evening. She didn't bother to pack her inhibitions in the luggage she carried on her flight up to New York this morning.

She gives Parker a kiss on the cheek. "I understand you are to thank for these tickets?"

Maya had asked Parker to get the tickets for the exclusive Monday evening launch of Bloom Cardaway's new lingerie line. Maya has been eager to network with the Cardaway entourage, and she knew Parker had the in with Bloom's father, the esteemed financier Bharat Cardaway.

Naturally, she got it done. Three tickets. VIP access. Top-shelf cocktails.

Emily was unsure she wanted to join the duo at first, but as soon as she stepped into her high-rise apartment, she could only think of kissing Sara by the wine fridge and thought it would be best to drown herself in strong liquor.

"You're welcome." Parker offers a half-ass curtsy before heading off toward her seat. Emily falls in step. They sit second row, toward the entry of the stage. Their chairs are so close that their upper arms touching is unavoidable.

Bloom Cardaway steps out first, thanking the crowd for their interest in her clothing, or lack thereof. The music starts, the models begin.

"That's Kirena," Parker whispers. "She slept with Carrie Buhler's husband."

"Scandalous." Emily has no idea who Carrie Buhler or her husband are, but she assumes that they are no different from everyone else in this room. Wealthy. Famous. Part of the elite city establishment.

Parker sees the blank stare in Emily's eyes and fills her in. "Buhler is the multimillionaire owner of the steakhouse chain Bullers."

The next model walks, and Parker knows her too.

"This is Bianca. I got high with her last weekend at the opening of Sharise's new gallery out in Queens."

"Sharise?"

"You know her. It's Sharise."

Emily shrugs her shoulders, another elite she does not know. But she asks Parker, "Did you and Bianca hook up?"

"God, no. She's nineteen."

"Age has never stopped you."

"It's not her age I'm concerned with, Brynny. It's mine. I'm not the woman I once was." She nudges Emily playfully.

Not a single part of Emily is curious as to how Parker knows nearly every model. She's always been this person, interwoven in these elite political and pop culture bubbles. She's the ideal top-shelf New Yorker. Unabashed, beautiful, gifted, and loaded with dollar signs.

Parker slyly points off to the other side of the stage. "Didn't you and Amelia have a moment together?"

Emily finishes off her whiskey. "A moment?" She rolls her eyes.

Parker chuckles. "I'll grab you another drink."

Emily is four whiskeys in when the show comes to a close. The floor opens for drinks and mingling. She hasn't seen Maya all night. Predictable. Maya came with an agenda, and she's busy completing it. Emily also came with an agenda.

Parker.

The room starts to close in a bit as Emily pulls her fifth whiskey to her lips.

"Here," Parker says, trading her a water for her whiskey. "We're switching. You're not in your twenties anymore."

Emily doesn't complain, and she chugs the water back with zero class. "I need to see this painting."

"What painting?" Parker says, sitting on the stool beside her.

"The painting of me at your gallery."

Parker chuckles. "Did your lady tell you about it?"

"My lady?"

"Sara, your date to the gala? Isn't she your lady?"

"We're not together."

"Hmm." Parker glares over to Emily, seemingly trying to read her blank stare. She sips back the rest of Emily's fifth whiskey and places it gently on the counter. "Okay, let's go see it."

Emily says nothing as she pulls her phone from her clutch and texts Maya. *Leaving. Love you. Talk soon.* She shoves it back in her purse, pushes her barstool in, and heads for the exit, knowing Parker will follow.

Outside, gusts of heavy wind toss her hair clumsily. Parker links her arm in Emily's. "It's cold," she tells her, but Emily knows it's also to help keep her balanced. The whiskeys did her in, though she feels herself sobering with each frigid step.

They walk the half mile to the gallery, and after a moment's digging, Parker yanks out a key from her purse and unlocks the large glass door.

Just inside, she flips on a series of lights, locks the door behind her, and slips off her heels. Emily does the same, her toes in need of a fire to thaw them out. Parker waves her up the stairs. Emily follows closely, taking in all its architectural glory until they reach the room full of portraits.

"You didn't actually paint this on memory, did you?" Emily absentmindedly brushes her fingertips along her own cheek, half expecting the woman in the painting to mimic her.

"I did."

"You never lacked in talent."

"I hope in more areas than just painting."

Emily allows a smile to unfold on her face, and in her peripheral vision, she sees Parker mimic it.

"Questionable."

"Oh, come on. I had some shortcomings, sure, but I made up for it in other ways," Parker says.

A breath passes before Emily turns from the painting. "Old news." She leans in, pressing her drunken lips against Parker's. Despite eight years between this kiss and their last, they fall right back into an easy rhythm. Parker tastes the same. Same cold, thin lips. Same cold hands against the back of her neck.

Parker pulls away from her lips. She kisses her cheek and takes her earlobe into her mouth before whispering, "I'd make love to you here, Brynny, but I'm forty-five now and I like to drink tea after I orgasm. Come home with me?"

Emily backs up a step. "I'd like tea first, actually."

CHAPTER THIRTY-NINE

Sara

A blaring ringing startles Emily awake. She's in Parker's California King bed, naked, olive-green sheets wrapped around her. Parker's gone, fumbling around in the kitchen, from the sounds of it. Her gas fireplace is roaring in the bedroom. It smells like cinnamon.

Emily coughs up her exhaustion, her hangover. She slides her finger across her phone, mustering up every bit of energy to answer. "Jared, how are you?"

"I'm so sorry to bother you, Em. I know you're visiting family in New York this week, but this storm is gearing up to cause a little more chaos than originally expected." There's hurry in his voice. "I don't want you to worry about a thing. Me and Sara are heading over to The Pirate's Hideaway to ensure everything is good to go before we head out of town. I just wanted to check that the lockbox is still around back and the code is the same?"

"Yes. It's there. I did push all the tables and chairs against the back of the building. Is that not enough?"

"It's gearing up to be a Category 2 now, maybe even Cat 3. We've got Carlos coming to assist. We don't have time to board up all the windows, but we're going to address the two windows by the bar to at least protect most of the valuables. We'll tie down the rocking chairs and toss the umbrellas inside the building. Make sure everything is up off the ground in case there's any flooding."

"Oh, gosh. I'm so, so sorry, Jared. I'm embarrassed. I should have planned better. I hate that this is on you. I'll send a payment, of course."

"Emily, you do not need to worry about a thing. We want to do this for you. Enjoy your family. Happy Thanksgiving."

"You are amazing. Happy Thanksgiving."

Emily drops the phone on the bed when the call ends, pressing her palms to her forehead and massaging the pounding away.

"Everything okay?" Parker barges back in with two teacups.

Emily pushes herself up to lean against the headboard. "Not exactly. There's a hurricane coming in. I took basic precautions at The Pirate's Hideaway, but it's apparently gearing up to be much worse than initially expected."

"What needs to be done?"

"Boarding up windows. Tying things down. It's probably best left in their hands. I don't know the first thing about hurricane prep."

"Who's they?"

"Jared, Sara, and Carlos."

"Sara's pulling through for you, huh?" Parker hands Emily her tea.

Emily looks at her in contempt, making it clear she doesn't want to discuss Sara with her.

"Okay, killer. We don't have to talk about your scorned lover."

Emily ignores her, pulling up her phone to check the weather.

"Shit. Category 3. That's not good, is it?"

Parker reaches over and pulls the phone from her hand. "They've got it handled."

Emily nods. "I suppose you're right." She picks up her tea.

"Any interest in joining me this evening to Queens to check out a new exhibit?"

"No."

Parker chuckles. "So, you've made me wait eight years and I only get a single night?"

Emily closes her eyes. "I'm sure you'll find another to go with."

"Still not over it, huh?"

"I had a ring for you, you know."

"I know."

Emily looks over, her gaze locked on Parker. "You knew?"

"Not until after you left for good. Maya told me. My memory is a little hazy, but it was something along the lines of, 'She bought you a ring, you fucking dimwit.'"

Maya never shared that with Emily, but she can't help herself from grinning. "She's a good friend."

Parker nods and sips her tea. "Well, if you change your mind tonight, let me know. I'd love to have you as my date."

Emily gazes at her again, holding her eyes a moment before standing to get dressed.

CHAPTER FORTY

Emily

"Nice of you to show."

Parker walks up beside Emily as Group One is boarding. A classic Parker move. To be on time. Barely.

"Wouldn't miss it."

On Tuesday morning after Emily left Parker's home, Parker texted once an hour with the same message.

Join me tonight.

Join me tonight.

Join me tonight.

Until Emily finally responded, *Fine.* Regret boiled over immediately after she hit send on the message, knowing Parker was on the receiving end wearing a haughty smirk of victory.

That evening they drank espresso martinis, and when other attendees bombarded the distinctly talented art connoisseur Parker Anne, she introduced Emily as her date.

"This is my lovely date, Emily."

Emily had to resist rolling her eyes at first, but after the fourth introduction it began to feel strangely nice hearing the accomplished woman so proud to show her off. They went back to Parker's townhome. They undressed each other. They had sex. Parker made them chamomile tea. They gossiped about her family and their old acquaintances until very early in the morning.

On Wednesday they met up for a late afternoon coffee. Emily's eyes were heavy with exhaustion. Too many months away from the city had her feeling like a stranger to the late-night shmoozing.

She didn't miss it.

"Can I visit you?" Parker had asked.

"What are you talking about?"

"Did I stutter?"

"No. But what are we doing here, Parker?"

"I guess I'd like more time to find out."

"Parker, we had our time." Emily had sipped her coffee, struggling to take her seriously.

"I'll remind you that I'm not the one who made the first move the other night. Why not give us a little time to see if we can make this work again? I like us together."

Emily had peered up, holding her gaze, recalling how effortlessly convincing Parker had been so many years ago. How her striking green eyes filled her with a life of promise. How those same eyes had deceived her.

Maybe she's different now, she'd thought.

Maybe she's not.

"I'm not in a place to commit to anything, Parker. Not now."

"I'm not asking for any commitment."

Emily had huffed out a laugh. "That would be right up your alley, yeah?"

Parker had reached across the round café table and lifted Emily's chin with her soft cold hand, forcing her to make eye contact. "This dimwit would like an opportunity to prove herself to you, Brynny."

A half-smile curled up Emily's face. Parker always had a way with words. "Fine."

On Thursday, while Emily was enjoying an early Thanksgiving dinner with her family, she'd texted Parker that she had switched her flight to head back to North Carolina on Friday. The news circulating about the Carolina coast damage had Emily eager to get back to The Pirate's Hideaway.

Parker had responded: *What time are you leaving?*

Early. 6.

The return text arrived in a moment: *Booked. See you tomorrow, Brynny.*

Emily had chuckled in flattery, knowing Parker was one hundred percent serious. When Parker set her mind to something, or someone, she got it.

CHAPTER FORTY-ONE

Sara

"Mom, you really have to start calling," Sara says, whining.

"I know, I know, I'm sorry for just popping in. I wanted to check the damage from the storm for myself."

"I told you the condo was fine."

Though Linda was expected to pop in once a month, they had literally just celebrated an early Thanksgiving together two days earlier, on Wednesday. They had to do it a day early because in a late arrangement, Steve convinced Sara to let him take the girls on Thanksgiving Day to his parents' home in Virginia.

"The trip in was a little iffy," Linda shares. "Tons of branches and power lines down. I saw the Flamingo Café lost its flamingo."

Sara doesn't respond. She knows exactly how the roads are, as she drove them back yesterday. She resettles herself into the couch, wrapping a warm knit blanket around her tightly.

"Get dressed, sweetie. Let's go have lunch."

"I really am not up for it today, Mom."

Her mother looks her up and down. "Well, this makes it easy. That's why I really came here. What's wrong with you?"

"I'm exhausted. I miss the girls. I really just wanna to sit on the couch today."

It's a chilly Friday, a bit cloudy out. It really does make sense to bundle up under a load of blankets and flip through a magazine, watch a little television.

"Hmm." Her mom takes off her jacket and hangs it on the coat rack. "I'll sit with you, then." She heads into the kitchen, noticing that coffee isn't made and putting a pot on herself. This surprises Sara. Linda's role of caretaker ended years ago. But here she is, recognizing she's needed again.

From the warmth of her couch, Sara watches her mother spray and wipe down the counters. She moves on to the dishes in the sink and dries them all before the coffee's made. When the machine beeps, Sara's mother grabs two mugs, pours coffee into both, and adds a dash of mint mocha creamer.

She hands Sara a mug. "Lots of calories in that creamer."

"It's the holidays. Calories don't count."

"That's true. Let me tell you about Suzanne, you know, from my book club? Her pumpkin cream pie is outta this world. Wow, delicious."

Sara chuckles as her mother goes on and on about the rich, milky taste and how it paired so well with her decaf coffee blend. She pauses briefly, oblivious to the fact that Sara has yet to speak a word, before switching topics. "Are you going to tell me what's going on now?"

Sara looks at her mother. She's been crying on and off since she saw Emily last week. Mostly on, today. Her eyes are puffy and red. It's a blessing the kids are with Steve because functioning, even in the most basic manner, has exasperated every ounce of her existence.

"Honey." Her mother reaches over and grabs her daughter's hand. The touch causes a rush of moisture to flood Sara's eyes. "Sara, honey, what on earth is going on with you?"

"I love a woman," Sara replies, the words spilling from her lips with the ease of asking for a glass of milk, devoid of any contemplation.

Completely unexpected.

Her secret is out now.

Linda doesn't budge. Her hand stays wrapped around Sara's. But for the first time that Sara can remember, she is completely, dreadfully silent.

"I haven't told anyone other than my therapist. And now you." Water is drooling from Sara's eyes. Here she is outing herself at forty-two years old and still feeling obligated to say that she hasn't told anyone because she doesn't want her mother to think that she's been prancing around with rainbow flags trying to embarrass herself and her family.

"Honey, I...I don't think you like women. You're just grieving the loss of your husband."

"No, Mom. Steve's not dead. I'm not grieving our divorce."

"Of course you are, sweetie." Her mother pulls her hand back and repositions herself properly on the couch.

"No, Mom, I'm grieving my life." Sara is so weary from the thoughts hammering away at her body. "I am grieving me." Her voice is quiet but absolutely sure. "The me I have been hiding for forty-two years. I am so tired of hiding, Mom. I don't want to be this person anymore. A woman that hides who she is."

Linda, to Sara's surprise, leans in and hugs her. Holds her. Eventually, she leans back to wipe away the moisture that has now built up from her own eyes.

"You haven't told Steve? The girls?"

"No."

"I...I know you seem upset, Sara, but what about your clients? Have you thought about them? How they'll react? Your company?"

Sara looks at her mother, fire igniting her eyes. Through gritted teeth, she tells her, "Mom, I have thought about everyone except for me for my whole fucking life."

"Sara! There is no need for cursing." Sara's mother stands from the couch, stomps toward the door in a fury, then stops, turns around, and walks back toward the couch. "Honey, you are going through a lot right now. You don't have to make any decisions today."

Sara doesn't reply. She has very little energy beyond what it's taking to just breathe. She's thought a lot about telling her mom. How this moment would play out, how her mother would react, how it would make Sara feel. It's as horrible as she imagined it would be.

Linda exhales frantically before taking a seat in the chair across from Sara. No amount of Botox can hide a seventy-year-old woman's age when she's in distress.

"Is there a…specific woman?" Sara can see on her face that it was painful for her to ask this. To say the word *woman*. It's a disgrace to her. An embarrassment.

Sara answers matter-of-factly. "Yes." Another flow of tears rushes from her face. She can't control it, feeling as if this entire discussion with her mother is for nothing. It's too late for her and Emily, anyhow. How on earth could Emily ever trust her again?

Sara's mother watches her sob. Her heart aches for her daughter, which Sara knows from the way she presses both her hands to her heart. "Did something happen with you two?"

"I don't really wanna talk about it, Mom."

"Okay." Linda relaxes her shoulders, likely relieved she didn't have to stomach further discomfort.

The two sit in silence for many minutes. Her mother's legs are crossed, her back is straight. Her hands are placed neatly atop her knee, as if she's staged for a childhood ballet recital photograph. Biting her tongue from spewing homophobic worry, and fear, and maybe even hate.

The same homophobic worry, and fear, and maybe even hate that Sara knows she is harboring as well.

Linda, after nearly ten minutes of dreadful silence, finally stands. "You know my friend Margaret?" She doesn't allow Sara time to answer. "Her son is gay. He's married now. She loves him and his partner very much."

The two make eye contact. Sara looks up at the woman that raised her. For a moment, she's a child again and Linda is twisting Sara's blond hair into foam curlers. She is telling her to marry a rich man. Begging her to sit straight, to stop slouching, no cursing. Fix her attitude, iron her shirt. Linda is tucking her into a pale pink comforter, telling her she loves her more than all the specks of sand on all the beaches in the whole wide world.

Sara smiles softly at her.

Linda's comment sounded like a mother that is trying her best to digest the fact that her adult daughter is on a different path than the one she imagined so long ago. She is just a human, after all. Humans need time to process things that are different from what they know.

"I don't know what your father is going to say," Linda says as she leans down to give Sara a kiss on the forehead. "He's an old grump these days anyway, hun. I love you."

Linda rises and walks to the door. "You said you're in therapy?"

"I am."

"Hmm."

Sara knows what she's thinking. Therapy is for weak women who cannot juggle their emotions, and the laundry, and their full-time job, and also putting a hot meal on the table. Therapy is for the woman whose husband cheats on her.

"Okay, Sara. I'll see you soon."

CHAPTER FORTY-TWO

Emily

Emily presses her hands to her eyes, rubbing them fiercely, praying what she's seeing isn't true.

Parker steps up beside her. Emily is glad she doesn't attempt to touch her in comfort. This isn't the kind of pain that can be healed with any words or any touch.

"We were set to open in two weeks." Emily knows the distress is seeping pathetically from her quiet voice.

Parker stays silent.

Emily lifts a single book from the floor, its pages glued together, its ends curled up from bathing in a pool of unwelcome flood waters. In the bathroom, she avoids a pile of glass from the small broken window. Splotches of mud are caked into the tile. Out in the garden, she finds a key culprit. A loblolly pine at the edge of the property has split into pieces. It looks as if the hurricane had hands that shook its core and tossed its branches like baseballs across the property.

The shed is crushed. A massive branch, at least a foot thick, is lying down in the center of it. The short-term rental tree house has at least one broken window. The roof is missing half its shingles.

Emily chuckles in defeat. "Guess this is my sign that it's time to head back to New York."

"Oh, come on," Parker says. "God was just having a little fun with you."

Emily screams in frustration, picking up a branch and tossing it into the fence.

"Well, the fence is one of the few things still standing, so let's avoid changing that."

"Stop it, Parker. This was all a damn waste." Emily is filled to the brim with frustration and Parker's humor isn't what she needs right now. Her dad, her move, her company, Sara, the hurricane. She feels everything that made up the last year of her life boiling up inside of her.

"You stop it." Parker stomps up in front of her. "The year after your father died, you led your department to a ten percent increase in sales. You were on two magazine covers, and you just held what I'd guess was the largest Brynn Company Foundation fundraiser to date. So what? A few trees decided to challenge your little business venture? Get over it! Build it again. Make it better."

Emily stares for a moment. "How did you know about the increase in sales? And the magazine covers?"

"I keep my eye on you, Brynny." Parker twirls herself back around. "That shed was hideous, by the way. You should be thanking God for laying that branch there."

"The shed was literally the only thing I picked out and purchased for the property without discussing with Jared and Sara."

"Well, you made a terrible choice."

Emily stares at Parker, her body decompressing as the truth in Parker's words sinks in. "You have changed."

"Life will do that to a person."

"You want to go drink tea?"

"Yes."

Nearly every plank from the dock was wiped away into the sea, but the rest of the rental house is fine. Hurricane shutters and stable stilts kept it from debris and high waters.

"You know if you give up, you and I could give it a real go," Parker says.

"A real go, yeah? Did you have this planned all along? You and me rekindling over Thanksgiving?"

"Once I knew you were coming solo, I figured I'd shoot my shot."

Emily raises her eyebrows, wanting the whole story. "Humor me."

"You know when you left me eight years ago—"

"You mean when you left me no choice but to leave you because you cheated?"

"When I made a mistake eight years ago that you have yet to forgive me for, I always thought that maybe we'd find a way to reconnect. Four, five, six years passed by, and you were always dating around but it was never anything serious. There was always hope. And it always felt that way until your brother told me that you had moved to North Carolina. Then it felt permanent. You were gone. That was it for you and me and my silly fantasy." Parker sips her tea, evidently swallowing her pride. "Not gonna lie, kinda crushed me to see you show up with a woman to the fundraiser. You moved to North Carolina. Found yourself a beautiful Southern belle. But then to see you last week. To hear you say that you and Sara weren't a thing. That was it for me." Parker looks up from her tea, a smile stretching across her face. "I knew I was going to get you naked again, Brynny."

Emily tosses a pillow across the couch, hitting Parker's feet. "You can't take anything serious, can you?"

Parker puts down her tea and crawls on top of a sitting Emily. She kisses her softly. Slowly. Emily lets her. It's nice to feel wanted. Cared for. Appreciated.

"I can *seriously* think of nothing I'd rather do than undress you."

CHAPTER FORTY-THREE

Sara

"Do you have plans to tell anyone else?" Rupa asks.

"A plan?" Sara chuckles halfheartedly. "I need to tell Jared, but between him and my Mom, it feels like enough."

"Why is that enough for you?"

"I don't have the energy to out myself to the world until I have the courage to tell Emily what I'm thinking. I dunno how to even approach it, though. She's probably devastated by the damage to her new business. The last thing she needs is for me to crawl back into her life after how terrible I've been."

"It's not your job to manage her feelings. Only your own."

"I know, I know. I just don't want to overload her."

"I understand. How are you feeling about the public component? Being seen together? Going out to run an errand? Grab coffee? Have you put much thought into it?"

"I don't know for certain, but I've been really, really sad for the last few months. I think I'm ready to try to not be so sad, and that's gonna require me to not be so worried about what everyone else is thinking."

Rupa shakes her head, a reserved grin on her face. "Good."

At the close of her virtual session with Rupa, she powers down her computer and heads right over to Jared's office.

"Jare?" Sara steps in slowly. "I wanna share something with you."

"Ooh!" Jared slides out from behind his wall of screens. "Spill."

"It's nothing too exciting." Her eyes begin to swell with nervous tears. "I like Emily, Jare." She huffs, irritated by the persistent weight of her emotions. "Damn it." She presses her palms to her eyes. "I've done nothing but cry the last few months. I'm so annoyed with myself."

Jared gently reveals a restrained smile. "Sounds like it's been an eventful weekend."

"A whole lifetime unraveled."

Sara tells him all about spilling her woman crush to her mother, how she needs to share her feelings with Emily, how she's watching a lifetime of secrets burst at the seams.

"You've come a long way, Sara Dylan. Tell me what my sweet Linda said."

"She's gonna need some time."

He walks around Sara's desk and wraps his comforting arms around her. "Most parents do. I'm proud of you."

"Proud? Ugh," she says, her arms tightly around him. "I'm embarrassed. The things I've said, how I've acted toward Emily. Toward you."

"Listen, Sar, we're all just trying to do the best we can. Give yourself a little grace." He steps back, returning to the chair. "Have you thought about your next move with Emily?"

"Well, I stopped by The Pirate's Hideaway yesterday. It's an absolute mess, Jare."

His face drops. "Noooo."

"It's bad. I assume she's seen it. I saw her car in her driveway this morning. She's probably devastated. Definitely not the right time to try to win back her heart with everything she's dealing with."

"Feel her out. You'll know the right time."

Sara nods her head in agreement.

"Therapy seems to be helping."

"It is."

"How do you feel? Discovering the Sara you are now?"

"Oh, I dunno. Conflicted. A little sad. Free. I hadn't realized how…poisonous some of my harbored thoughts have been. It's enlightening. Overdue."

"All normal."

"Do you think I'm crazy if I swing on by her place now?"

He whips his hand in grand theater. "Love is always crazy, my dear."

CHAPTER FORTY-FOUR

Sara

Sara has Christmas music playing softly as she drives toward Wrightsville Beach. There's a chance Emily is in Southport, but she'll check her home first. The sun is out. This kind of weather is why she loves living in North Carolina. Every home is dressed in colorful wreaths made of buoys. Every palm tree is swathed in multicolored lights, and there's an inflated Santa on a surfboard as she crosses the bridge onto the island.

Emily, I love you.

No. No.

Emily, I'm sorry. I'm so, so sorry for being too scared and embarrassed to tell you how I feel.

Ugh. No.

Emily, I'm an idiot.

Goodness.

Sara turns the music up louder, drowning out her pretend confessions. She parks when she sees Emily's car is still in the driveway. She inhales deeply and heads up the stairs.

Emily opens the door instantly. "Hi." She looks as if she's preparing to leave. Going somewhere casual, based on her joggers and hoodie.

"Hi, may I come in?"

"Uh…" Emily pauses and looks over her shoulder. "Sure, sure."

The hesitation in Emily's response has Sara reluctantly following her inside. On the living room end table, Sara notices that Emily has propped up the painting she gave her. Emily must see her staring and comments, "It looks good there, yeah?"

Sara nods, a soft smile forming across her lips. "It really does."

"So, what's going on?"

"You've seen the damage, I assume?"

"I have."

"Have you thought about what you plan to do?"

"I'm going to push back the opening date a couple of months," she answers straightforwardly.

"Is there anything I can do to help?"

Emily's eyes are shifty, hurried. She's making it blatantly clear in her cold demeanor that she does not want Sara here.

"Not at the moment."

"Okay, I'll head out. I just…I saw your car out front and wanted to, uh…" Sara reaches into her leather satchel and pulls out the matchbox with the letter in it from The Pirate's Hideaway. "I wasn't sure how bad the flooding would be from the hurricane. I didn't want you to lose it."

She hands it over, their fingers brushing each other's. Emily stares at her for a long moment, releasing the stern look in her eyes. "Thanks, Sar. That was really thoughtful."

Sara reaches out, softly wrapping her hand around Emily's forearm.

"Hey." Sara is nearly whispering. "I want to help you. Jared does, the girls do. We all do." She lets go of Emily's arm, returning her hand timidly to her side. "I'm here for you. I just need you to know that."

Emily holds her gaze. "Okay."

"Ready, Brynny?" Parker steps from Emily's bedroom.

Sara's eyes widen. "I'm so sorry. I didn't know…" Her vision shifts between Emily and Parker. It makes sense now why Emily looked so on edge. Her ex-girlfriend has been camping out in her bedroom during the entire conversation.

"I'm ready," Emily tells her before redirecting her attention to Sara. "I've got to take Parker to the airport. We'll catch up later."

The way she says *later* does not warrant a follow-up. They'll catch up. Maybe. At some point. But maybe they won't.

"Yes, of course." Sara nods at Parker, hardly able to make eye contact. "Safe travels, Parker."

Sara hurries out the door, flustered. A million questions run through her head, the most prominent being: why on earth is Parker Anne in Emily Brynn's home?

CHAPTER FORTY-FIVE

Emily

"Brynny." Parker grabs Emily's right hand and kisses the top of it. "You are still a terrible driver."

Emily smirks.

"You like her. What happened with you two?"

"What makes you say that?"

"Because I stood in your bedroom door and saw the way you looked at her."

Emily huffs. "The way I looked at her?"

"A way that you've never looked at me."

A twinge of sadness sails right through Emily, but there is no need to argue with Parker. They both know it's true.

"It doesn't matter," Emily says. "She doesn't like women. She made it clear."

Emily pulls up to the curb of the airport. They both hop out. She grabs Parker's bag from the back seat, hands it over, and watches Parker sling it over her shoulder with the kind of grace only an artist could have.

"She likes you. It's clear." Parker tells her this with a straight face, without a hint of jealousy. As if this is absolute fact, and now that Parker knows this is fact, she knows that the idea of her being with Emily is done.

"Why do you say that?"

"I saw the way she looked at you, Brynny." Parker leans in and kisses Emily's cheek. "If it doesn't work out, you know where to find me."

Emily stands at the trunk of her car as Parker walks through the sliding airport doors.

"Bye," she says to no one.

CHAPTER FORTY-SIX

Emily

December

"What did you get your niece and nephews for Christmas?"
"Entirely too much," Emily shares.
Sara chuckles.
This is the fifth Saturday in a row that Sara has shown up to help bring The Pirate's Hideaway back to life. On the first Saturday, she showed up with rakes and big black trash bags.
"What are you doing here?" Emily had asked her.
"I told you I wanted to help and I haven't heard from you, so I thought I'd just show up."
"I hired landscapers. The yard cleanup is done."
"Okay." Sara looked at the unpredictably expensive rakes. "That will save me seventy-three dollars. What else can I do?"
In a moment of contemplation, Emily had entertained the idea of putting on a hard exterior. Sending her home. Refusing to open the door to the woman who made her feel so profoundly confused.

But she'd decided against it.

Sara looked so ridiculously adorable in her boots with her rakes and her garbage bags that Emily couldn't resist smiling at her. "The shed is being removed today. I could use some help relocating anything that's salvageable."

They had worked all day without much discussion and absolutely zero talk of Parker. In the evening, Emily thanked her and asked if she could help her pick out a shed. On Sunday they did just that.

"This shed is much better, Em," Sara told her. "That last one didn't fit the aesthetic."

"It was the one thing I picked out."

"I know."

The following weekend, Sara showed up again at eight a.m. sharp. They designed the interior of the shed. Hung shelves and hooks and shimmied in the new refrigerator.

During week three, they grouted one of the bathrooms that required new tiles.

Step by step over the last five weeks since Thanksgiving, they've brought life back into Emily's new bar.

"Did you and the girls spend Christmas with your parents?" Emily asks.

"No. We had a quiet Christmas this year. Just the three of us."

"Really?"

"My parents and I are going through a little something."

"Oh." Emily stops working to turn toward Sara. She was hardly thinking as she was talking, just rambling on as they have been doing week after week. "I'm sorry to hear. Anything you want to talk about?"

"It's a story."

"I've got time."

Sara stops what she's doing. She makes eye contact with Emily, straightens up her posture, and takes one deep breath in.

"I told my mom that I have feelings for you."

Emily's heart comes to a standstill. She's frozen. "You what?" Emily nearly whispers.

"Emily!" Carlos's voice rings through the small bar, interrupting their conversation. "Come up here, por favor!"

Emily holds a single finger up. "Hold on. I'll be right back."

The ten minutes away removes the rosiness that rushed to Emily's cheeks after hearing Sara's declaration. "The tree house is complete," Emily shares. "Carlos did amazing. Just need a final inspection from the city."

"Great," Sara replies.

"Want to grab lunch?"

They haven't grabbed lunch, or dinner, or even a coffee over the last five weeks. It's been all small talk and business. Easing back into a fractured friendship. This is progress. This is a door.

"Yes," Sara says decisively. "I've got a cyclone of emotions spinning around my head right now, but yes. I do."

This makes Emily laugh, which makes Sara smile.

Both pull on their jackets and knit hats. It's cold for the eastern shore of North Carolina—forty-two degrees. A bit overcast. Avoiding the hefty wind along the waterfront, they head downtown, and Emily leads them into a casual restaurant with large windows and black-and-white checkerboard floor tile.

"Get the burger."

Sara obliges. They order burgers on lettuce wraps with a side of carrots and hummus.

"What do you think about the décor here?"

Sara looks around. "I find it nauseating."

"I knew you would. But I also knew you'd like the burger."

"I do."

"How'd your mum take it?"

"She's still coming to terms with it." Sara is fidgeting, tapping her toe against the tile. "I thought it might be all right at first, but it seems the more she thinks about it, the more it agitates her."

Emily nods her head and asks, "How are you?"

"Good. Therapy helps. Before Thanksgiving, you asked what happened between us and I couldn't tell you because I didn't really know." Sara's eyes water up, but her voice remains steady.

"It's the God's honest truth. But I've been working through some things that I've been holding on to for a whole lotta years. Meeting you, Em, changed me in a way I can't unknow. I told my mom because I was bursting at the seams. I still have a long way to go, but I'm feeling more like myself than I ever have."

Emily reaches across the table. She's forcing herself to take deep, full breaths. Forcing herself to resist grabbing Sara up out of her chair and into her arms. Her heart's been through enough for now. Best to stay calm.

"That must have been difficult for you. Thanks for telling me."

The two women take a long route back to The Pirate's Hideaway, enjoying the brisk, salty December air. As they pack up for the day, Sara asks, "Do you have plans tonight?"

"I do, actually. My employees are taking me on a cocktail tour of Wilmington." Her staff of six, all of them far more adept to work in the hospitality industry than she, had told her that she needed to be familiar with their neighboring competition. They were right, of course, so she agreed to treat them to a night on the town with the promise they'd show her the very best spots.

A look of brief disappointment on Sara's face is quickly erased by a smile. One that's probably forced. "That's awesome. I'm sure you'll enjoy the team bonding."

CHAPTER FORTY-SEVEN

Emily

January

"I just want to point out that your love life hasn't been this exciting since that time in college when you slept with that NFL player's girlfriend."

"Maya, please."

"He was on the Jets, right?"

"Maya."

"A rekindling of Parker…Gotta be honest, that was weird. And now the woman that said she couldn't love a woman has outed herself to her mother and expressed her love to you, it's a sitcom!"

"Ugh, I don't know what to do about Sara."

"What do you mean? I saw it when I visited. I saw it at the gala. Everyone saw it. You deserve her. She deserves you. Now, I wouldn't go out and buy a ring. We know how that goes for you."

"Really?"

Maya chuckles. "Sorry. Take it slow. She's not done adjusting. Meet her where she is. And if she blows it this time, Em, then you tried and you move on, but my guess is she won't."

"I suppose I wanted to hear it from you to ensure my sanity was still in check."

"There's a billion-dollar business in New York with your last name on it and you left it to build a bar in a small beach town, so your sanity is questionable, but your judgment of Sara? Nailed it."

"Mm-hmm." A slight pound in Emily's forehead reminds her of the drinks she indulged in last night. Four bars. Five cocktails. And Uber rides home for everyone. She steps out onto the front porch as she listens to Maya carry on about a drunk uncle at a quinceañera she worked. Instead of being greeted with a hopeful gush of frosty air, she's met with a nearly sixty-degree morning. She sits on her top step as a mob of seagulls caw their way by her.

"All right, Em, I've gotta run. Ben is yelling at me for something. I said I'd let him stay up for New Year's if he cleaned his room, so I'm guessing he's wondering where things go because why on earth would he know where his own toys go? He never puts them away."

"Oh, the joys." Emily chuckles.

"Are you going to text Sara and see if she's got plans for the evening?"

"I want to." A single raindrop falls into Emily's palm. Then another.

"Is there a reason you wouldn't?"

"Nerves?"

"You're Emily Fucking Brynn. Where the hell is that confidence you had when you closed that billion-dollar deal in Brooklyn last year that no one said you were going to close?"

"Very different scenario."

"Oh, hush. I'm hanging up now. Go call her immediately. Happy New Year, Em."

Emily sits with the phone in her lap a moment. *Why the hell not?* She hops up from the steps, hurries back inside to slip on her yellow rain boots, then heads down the street to Sara's.

Sophie answers her knock. "Emily!" She leans in for a side hug before yelling, "Mom! Emily is here!"

Sara walks from her bedroom, wearing half a smile. Everyone is still in their pajamas. "What are you doing here, Em?"

"I came to see if you guys wanted to walk on the beach."

"It's raining, isn't it?"

"Yes, it is raining."

"Can we, Mom?" Joanna begs with her best puppy dog eyes.

"All right, let's go."

On the beach, both girls slip off their shoes and socks, burying their bare feet into the cold sand before running off toward the water. Emily and Sara fall in step behind them.

"You're a nice surprise this morning." Sara nudges Em. She hasn't wiped the smile from her lips since she saw Emily standing at her front door. A soft rain is drizzling, leaving tiny craters in the sand before them.

"Well, I know you outed yourself to your mum, but I was up all night wondering if it's still true."

"If what's still true?"

"Do you still have feelings for me?"

Sara giggles. "You're gonna make me admit it?"

"Yes." Emily nods.

"I like you, Em. A lot."

A wave of warmth starts in Emily's toes and reaches the top of her head. "That's so sweet, Sar." Emily nudges her and sprints off in front to catch up with the girls, leaving Sara in a fit of laughter.

Not even fifteen minutes into their soggy walk, Joanna gets caught up in a wave while digging for shark teeth and emerges completely drenched by the sea. Emily tosses the shivering girl over her shoulder and the four of them trudge back inside where they settle into an afternoon of board games.

Around four o'clock, Steve arrives to grab the girls. After Joanna pleads, he joins them for their final round of Telestrations. His lack of artistic ability has the whole group in hysterics. As the girls pack, Steve asks all about the rebuild of The Pirate's Hideaway.

"Wow, that was a heck of a turnaround. Sara was telling me the damage was pretty intense."

"The team has been impressive." Emily hasn't taken much time to digest how far they've come, from repairing broken windows and missing shingles to installing a whole new shed. Her and Carlos's team have worked tirelessly to get the bar up and running. "Should be another seven to ten days for permitting. We're planning for a February first opening. My birthday."

"Ooh!" Steve's genuine excitement is apparent in the way his dark eyes illuminate with enthusiasm. "That's a perfect way to celebrate. I look forward to being there."

The girls make their way back into the living room as Steve hops up from his seat. "All right, ladies, what can I grab?" Joanna hands him everything except her stuffed penguin.

Sophie rolls her eyes. "That's lazy, Joey."

Sara kisses them both. "Happy New Years, ladies. Have fun with Dad."

When they leave, Sara stands against the door for a long moment as she always does. She'd shared with Emily ages ago that she says a silent prayer in her head for their safety and takes a moment to grieve the fact that she must share time with them, reminding herself, as always, that this isn't easy on Steve either.

"Em," Sara finally says when she emerges from her silence. "Will you come with me to a New Year's party tonight?"

Emily's eyes widen. "I didn't know you had plans tonight." She peers down, a bit flustered. Of course she has plans—she's Sara Dylan. Born and raised here. She was probably invited to a dozen New Year's parties. "You go, have fun. I don't need to tag along."

"No." Sara walks over toward Emily. "I would bail, but Angie is on the board of the women's networking committee and that's who is hosting it, so I feel obligated. Come with me, please. There's not a person I'd like to bring in this new year with other than you."

Emily holds her gaze. She's serious. Sara wants Emily to join her at a public party. She wants them to go together.

"Okay, I'll go."

"Perfect, it's at 1452, the event space downtown. I know you probably have a dozen cocktail dresses lying around, but if you want to look through what I have, you're welcome to it."

"I'm sure I have something. Can never be too prepared," Emily says with a flip of her hair. "I'll see you soon, Sar."

CHAPTER FORTY-EIGHT

Sara

Sara's phone pings. She ties her hair up into a towel, preventing it from dripping all over the hardwoods. It's from her mom.

Sara, I know this is overdue, but I don't want to go into this new year without telling you. I love who you are. The girls you are raising. The business you've created. And because of these things, I know I will enjoy the company of the person you choose to love. I got a therapist. I think it's helping. Happy New Year, sweetheart.

Sara squeezes her eyes shut, pressing her phone to her chest. It's almost humorous that her mother is seeing a therapist, something she downplayed indirectly for as long as Sara could remember. And yet, it is the sweetest act of commitment and love she could offer Sara. Her message was crafted with intention, and Sara knows this. Sara knows she is trying.

She texts her back. *This means a lot, Mom. Happy New Year. Give Dad a kiss from me.*

First, Emily shows up unexpectantly at her front door, then she receives this message from her mom. It's almost too good to be true. Sara puts her phone down, feeling a buoyant energy rise within her. This isn't the end of her mother's journey to acceptance, but it sure feels like the beginning, and if her mother can embrace this new perspective, this level of respectful understanding, then so will others.

Sara blow-drys her hair, curls it carefully, paints her lips in red. She slides on a golden sequined skirt and an off-white sleeveless knit turtleneck. Classy fabrics with a fun twist. Empowering.

She pulls on a peacoat and walks the two blocks to Emily's.

"Now how in the heck did you just have this lying around?" Sara inquires as her eyes unconsciously move from Emily's spiraled dark hair to her hips. Emily curtsies for her in jest. She's wearing an emerald sequined fringe dress that she knows fits her in all the best places. It's screaming roaring twenties, but with a contemporary, sexier twist.

"You look gorgeous, Sara." Emily leans in and kisses her cheek, but before she can pull away, Sara catches her eyes.

"I missed you."

"I missed you too," Emily says, grabbing her hand and spinning her around. "Our Uber should be pulling up now."

Sara wants desperately to kiss her again, but it appears Emily is going to test her patience this time around.

In the Uber, Sara tries to provide as much insight as she can on the crowd she expects to see tonight.

"Jared and Matthew will be there. Ang and her husband will be there too. The women's network coordinated this whole thing. They do it every year. You know how these things are, a little forced business chatter, a little fun."

Sara takes a deep breath before they step through the propped-open glass doors. She notices the easiness in Emily. The confidence she carries herself with. The beauty she resonates.

Sara quickly squeezes Emily's hand, telling her she's absolutely sure that she wants her here. Emily flashes her a sweet smile.

Upon entering, two nicely dressed men, likely the unfortunate husbands of women in attendance, take their coats.

"I'll grab us a round," Emily says.

"Jared and Matthew are in that corner. I'll wait for you there."

Ivy and café lighting is looped around the ceiling rafters, up and down the columns, and along the brick walls. It's charming. Sara wonders if Emily thinks the same. She's probably spent dozens of New Years in lavish New York City venue spaces.

"I didn't know you were bringing Emily." Jared greets her with a kiss of the cheek.

"Me either." Sara talks calmly, forcing her rapidly beating heart to slow.

His eyebrows perk up.

"It's a story," she says.

He waves over a server with a platter of champagne flutes. Jared grabs two, handing one to Matthew.

"You look stunning." He clinks his glass to hers.

"As do the two of you."

Both men would feature well on *GQ*. Chiseled jawlines, precisely tailored navy suits, cute matching bow ties—one blue, one red with blue crabs. Jared has described his style as coastal chic, and it would be tough to argue that in his current attire.

"This is where the celebrities hang, huh?" Angie butts into the circle. Emily is right behind her, two drinks in hand, one for Sara. "You all look gorgeous," Angie tells them as they exchange hugs and kisses.

"Now, Em," Ang continues. "I'm just gonna pull this Band-Aid off and ask what the fans have been wondering. What celebrity are you dating now that has kept you from coming to tennis?"

"Celebrity?" Emily chuckles. Her bright white teeth accentuate her red lips.

"Oh, girl, I stalked you on social media and you've had flings with scores of hot women, some of them very famous." Angie talks with her finger, pointing to further emphasize her findings.

Matthew spins around swiftly and leaves the circle, clearly unable to stomach the looming awkwardness. Jared seems to hardly notice his absence, too enthralled with what's going to happen next.

Sara sees that Emily bites the inside of her lip to keep herself from laughing at Angie's abruptness. "I'm laying low these days." She winks.

"Ooh la la. A woman who keeps her cards close to her chest."

Angie lifts her flute to Emily for a cheers while Sara throws back her champagne in a single gulp.

"Ang, she's with me."

Angie chuckles and dismisses Sara's remark as fitting comedy with a flick of her hand until she notices the wide-eyed stares glued on Jared and Emily.

"Wait, what am I missing?"

Sara just nods, unable to speak.

"I suppose the secret is out," Emily says, leaning in to kiss Sara's rosy cheek. "I'm with her."

"What?" Angie squeals. The whole group swivels their heads around the room, expecting it to be at an absolute standstill from the shrill exclamation, but it seems Angie's outburst went unnoticed.

"I'm so sorry." She uses both hands to visually push down her own volume. "I'm sorry that was loud and obnoxious." In a normal volume—and octave—she continues, "I need clarification. So, you, Emily, and you, Sara, are together?" She nods her head. "Dating?"

Sara still can't speak, but she nods, her lips clenched in a reserved smile.

Angie presses her hands to her heart. "Awww." She pulls Emily and Sara in for a very awkward, very tight hug. Champagne splashes, no one is comfortable, but this is what love feels like sometimes.

When Angie finally releases the two of them, she leans back in to hug Sara individually and whispers, "So happy for you. She's perfect." Angie winks, spins on her heel, and heads off to another conversation as if Sara didn't just use every ounce of her being to reveal her deepest secret. It's as if she has just told her that she's lost an earring. No big deal at all.

Jared and Emily look intently at Sara, watching the tension in her face melt away. "You know I've been working myself up all evening to tell Angie, and I'm wondering if maybe no one really cares anymore."

"Most won't," Jared replies with a shrug of his shoulders. "Where's Matthew?" Without awaiting a response, he scurries off to find his husband.

Emily steps in closer to Sara, talking low enough for just the two of them to hear. "That was sweet what you said to Angie, but please know that there's no pressure to share about us unless you're ready."

"Are we an us?"

"Well." Emily smirks, her drink against her lips. "I was thinking I'd like us to be."

Sara grabs her free hand and kisses her palm. "We're an us, then. And thank you for saying that, because despite my heart beating outta my chest, I like showing you off."

Pop music propels them through the night. The evening has been far more enjoyable than Sara could have imagined. She knows it's because of Emily. Anywhere is more enjoyable with her.

Sara takes a seat at a high-top table to rest her feet while Emily heads off to the bathroom. Angie dashes up beside her, clearly wanting a moment alone to chat.

"Why didn't you say something?"

"I wasn't ready."

"I understand, but I'm sorry if I ever led you to think you couldn't share something so exciting and important with me."

Angie should have been the first person Sara chose to tell. She owns a coffee shop. Her employees look a lot like her customers. Some clean-shaven and buttoned-up. Some blue-haired and some tattooed. She serves lawyers and art education majors the same whole milk cappuccinos. She serves tech gurus and carpenters and snowbirds from New England the same mild house blend. This kind of day-to-day diversity inevitably does something good for the soul. Not that Angie ever needed some grand awakening—she's always been a good person. There's a reason she and Sara have made it so many years as friends. She's one of the kindest, funniest, most outspoken women Sara knows.

"No. It was all me. Me and my insecurities. Worrying too much about everyone else's opinion instead of trusting my own."

"Have you told the girls? Or Steve?"

"I plan to tell Steve soon. I'll share with the girls in time."

"You're happy."

"I am."

"I can tell."

"One-minute countdown!" the DJ shouts.

"Where's Emily?" Angie asks.

"Off to the loo, as she calls it." Sara can't imagine ever getting used to some of the words Emily says.

Angie chuckles. "I'm gonna go find my husband."

The large timer on the wall ticks to forty seconds.

Maybe it's best she's late.

Thirty-five seconds.

Then I wouldn't have to think about if we should kiss or not.

Thirty seconds.

Oh gosh, what will people say?

Twenty-five seconds. Sara stands from her chair, too anxious to sit.

Who cares what people think? Come on, Em. Where are you?

Twenty seconds.

There you are. Gosh, you are beautiful.

Sara's racing, worried heart slows instantly as she watches Emily hurry across the wooden floor.

"Ten! Nine! Eight!"

The room is full of roar and yet it is only the two of them. Sara standing beside the high-top table. Emily walking toward her with a sweet smile stretched along her gorgeous face.

"Seven! Six! Five!"

A promise shines from Emily's golden eyes. She wasn't ever going to miss this. There was never a reason for Sara to worry.

"Four! Three! Two!"

Emily grabs Sara's face and whispers, "One" into her mouth before pressing her warm lips firmly against Sara's.

"Happy New Year!" Emily shouts in jubilation as she spins Sara around, laughter engulfing them.

And Sara thinks of nothing except for how absolutely perfect this moment is.

CHAPTER FORTY-NINE

Sara

"Hey, Steve, you got a minute?"

"Sure, of course."

The girls hurry out of her office to the coffee nook, where they keep a pile of toys and books and puzzles under the storage bench.

Steve takes a seat in one of the chairs that she typically reserves for her visiting customers. "Gosh, these are so much nicer than the ones I have in my office."

"Of course they are." She chuckles. She's a bit flustered, but she's trying not to show it. "Emily's opening is tomorrow."

"Yeah, I'm excited. The girls are super pumped too. I'm sure they've been hounding you about it as well."

"Oh yes." She chuckles. "That's, uh…that's what I wanted to talk to you about. Emily."

Steve cocks his eyebrow up.

"Emily and I have been…" Sara tries to employ Rupa's advice. Be assertive. Be precise. Be clear. Leave no room for misinterpretation. She inhales deeply. "Steve, I like Emily. As more than a friend."

A timid smile curls up over his face. "I kinda heard."

"Heard?"

"It's not that big of a city, Sara. People talk." His gaze doesn't stray from her eyes. There's hurt…maybe frustration too. Hard to tell. "I wish you would have told me sooner. Gotta be honest, I was thrown off at first. Denied it, even. Really made me look silly. But hey…I, uh…I understand this probably has been challenging for you, but I do want you to remember that we're raising our daughters together. I don't want to be completely blindsided by things."

All fair points. She hears him. He's right. Sara wants to ask, *Who knows? Who said what? How did he respond when they asked?* But none of it matters. "I'm sorry that I've made you feel uncomfortable, but I wasn't ready and I'm telling you now. I'm not asking you to understand or for your acceptance. I'm telling you because it's important."

His face is flushed. "I know it's important. And you have my support and my acceptance, because support does matter. And we don't have to turn our relationship into some business transaction. We are raising kids together, Sara. I want us to be on the same page."

Sara slouches in her seat. Despite his frustration, she's relieved. She huffs out the tension in her shoulders, amazed out how silly she was to think she didn't need his support.

"I think very highly of Emily. I'm happy for you two. I can see why you like her, and I know why she likes you."

Despite his buttoned-up success, Steve's a product of western Virginia sweet potato farmers. Hippies. He's never said an ill word about anyone except commercial poultry farmers.

He is a good man, at his core. She sees that now. Remembers it, now.

"Thanks, Steve. Thank you, really."

Steve walks around her desk and wraps his arms around her. It's the first time they have touched each other since he walked out of the house so many months ago. He's warm, and safe. Just as Sara remembers him in their fondest days.

"Have you told the girls?" he asks as he makes his way back to his seat.

"Not yet."

"Let me know when you do. I can be there, if you want. How about your parents?"

"They know."

His eyes widen, clearly surprised she's already shared with them. "Oh, boy. How'd they take it?"

She doesn't feel like expanding on the multitude of daily draining texts prior to New Year's Eve.

Are you sure?

We still love you.

This is probably just a phase, honey.

I'm worried for your business.

I'm worried for the girls. Do you think they will be teased?

We'd like to meet Emily.

Are you going to start dressing differently?

We support you, but are you absolutely sure?

We love you no matter what, sweetie.

"They are coming around, but they're gonna need some time."

Steve nods. "How long have you known?"

"With Emily, since the day I met her."

He asks again. "But, before Emily. When did you know?"

She knows what he's wondering. Did she know the day they met that she liked women? Did she know the day they were married? Did she know and try to love him anyway?

"I don't know." She shrugs her shoulders. It's an honest answer, one she hasn't quite been able to work through in therapy. "What I do know is that I'm thankful to have met you, Steve. Thankful for our two beautiful girls, for my business, for your business. We've been blessed. We did all of that together."

Steve's closed lips curl up into a grin. "Me too."

"So, I'm gonna throw more on you. I've got a little secret about Em's big day tomorrow and I need your help. You up for it?"

"Spill."

CHAPTER FIFTY

Sara

February

"Happy birthday." Sara barges in and kissed Emily's nose before placing a steaming cup of coffee on the end table.

Emily stretches her toned arms above her head and Sara can't help herself from running her hand up it as she leans down to kiss her. She doesn't dare get back into bed. It would be too easy to fall into Emily's intoxicating kiss, her hips, her hands. Replay what they did to each other last night.

There's too much to do.

"I've got to run into the office."

"Don't leave," Emily begs, lifting the coffee to her lips.

"If I didn't have to submit a contract before heading over to your grand opening, I'd be crawling back in."

Sara has to look away as she tells the lie. She's not going to the office. She's going to pick up table rentals and call the limo with the fifteen-minute late arrival time of Emily's mother, brother, sister-in-law, niece, two nephews, and her friends Maya, Ben, and Donovan.

Emily has no idea, and Sara's gritted teeth are on the verge of giving the surprise away. She leans in hastily and kisses her forehead. "I'll see you at The Pirate's Hideaway at noon."

The plan is for Emily to meet her at noon so that she can assist with any last-minute items before the mayor of Southport shows at 1:45 for a 2:00 ribbon-cutting ceremony, but Sara plans to derail the calm before the ribbon-cutting with some additional helping hands—all of her family and her very best friend.

The idea had been simmering since New Year's Day, when they took a walk to Shark Tooth Tavern for Bloody Marys because they deemed it was the only suitable remedy they could fathom coming off New Year's Eve.

"Why wouldn't you want them there?" Sara had asked Emily.

"It's not that I don't want my mum and brother here, it's that they've already arranged travel down here once and then, of all things, a hurricane hit."

"That's not your fault."

"Feels a little karma-esque, no?"

"No!"

"Regardless, this time around the grand opening is on a Tuesday. The kids would have to miss school. My brother would have to miss work. I'm not telling them to come. It's silly. They're going to come in March, when they can enjoy a weekend here."

"It's not silly. You've worked hard for this."

"Okay," she had said. "You're right. It's not silly, but it is an inconvenience that they don't need."

Sara disagreed. Perhaps she was biased, but Emily and all her doings, whatever they may be, couldn't possibly be seen as an inconvenience, especially to the people that loved her most.

So, she meddled.

Behind Emily's back she coordinated plans with Maya to have Emily's family show up at 11:30 on February first. Opening day of The Pirate's Hideaway, and more importantly, Emily's birthday.

When Sara gets into her car, she goes right to work. First, she calls Steve, who had kept the girls home from school for the big celebration.

"Balloons are ready for pickup."

"Jo has forgotten how to put on her shoes, it seems, but whenever she figures it out we'll be leaving."

"Put me on speaker."

"On."

"Joey, I need you, and Daddy, and Sophie to be big helpers today. You've got to pick up Emily's birthday balloons and cake! Remember, you picked out that pink cake for her?"

"Yes! Cake. Cake. Cake. I want cake!"

"Well, that worked out," Steve says. "Shoes are on. We'll see you there at ten thirty."

Sara hangs up with a boastful grin, satisfied with her efforts in corralling her six-year-old over the phone. Her relationship with Steve deepened instantly after spilling about Emily. "You're carrying one less secret," Rupa had told her. And Emily found that it was easier to walk with less to carry.

She texts Maya next: *There will be a limo out front when you land. It's about a 40-minute ride to Southport from the Wilmington airport. Let me know if there are any hiccups, otherwise I'll see you when you arrive.*

Sara pulls up to The Pirate's Hideaway at 9:45. Jared is already there with table linens and charcuterie platters. Over the next forty-five minutes, Jared directs Sara where to put the almonds, the salami, the green grapes, the pomegranate. He had purchased mini pirate ships of varying sizes to place around the tables, and instead of standard glass platters or risers, he purchased old navy-blue novels and stacked them at various heights, using wooden cutting boards atop them to complete a genuine work of art.

Jared and Sara step back to admire their work.

"This should be on the cover of *Food & Wine* magazine," Sara says. Despite knowing Jared since they were young adults in college, his artistic mind never ceases to amaze her.

"I know."

Steve honks as he parks. The girls are sporadic with joy. Replacing school with cake on a Tuesday is as good as a trip down to Disney World. Emily's heart is beaming as they help her tie up pods of mylar ballon bouquets before heading into the beer garden to play.

"Hey, Sara," Jared yells from the parking lot. Sara looks up, baffled by the sight of her mother and father stepping from the car. Her heart picks up pace.

How on earth did they know?

She hasn't seen either of them in over two months. She approaches them, her heart racing in a mix of confusion and excitement and worry. Excitement to hug her mom, to see her dad's sweet face. Confusion about how they knew to come here today. Worry about how awkward this may be.

"Hi, Mom," Sara says, leaning in for a hug. "I'm, uh…I'm surprised to see you guys here."

"We're here to celebrate Emily's opening with you and Jared." Her mother's voice is unfaltering, as if they have been carrying on over the past two months without incident.

Sara leans in to hug her father. He hasn't said a word. She's certain he won't. But he's here, stoic and poker-faced. That's good enough for her.

"How'd you find out about this?"

"Jared called us. He said it was important to you, so we wanted to show up."

"Mom, I—"

"Sara, honey, if it's okay with you, let's skip any important discussions today. We know this is Emily's big day. We're not here to disrupt anything. Your father and I just want to sit back and enjoy in the celebrations."

Sara looks at her mother, dumbfounded for a moment. Part of her can't believe how rational she sounds. Part of her is unsurprised. This is the woman, after all, that sang her to sleep every night as a child. That braided her hair through high school, that brought her warm home-cooked meals in college.

"Okay," Sara says. She glances up at her father. His face has relaxed a bit. He smiles gently at her.

Within a few minutes, the limo shows. Emily's family hops from the car at the urgency of Jared, whose sole job is to provide ample notice of Emily's arrival. According to him, she is "Ten minutes out, folks! Let's move!"

Introductions are extremely brief. Sara yells for Joanna and Sophie to join them by the tables, and everyone stands at attention as Emily's Mercedes SUV clunks onto the gravel parking lot.

CHAPTER FIFTY-ONE

Emily

Emily steps out onto the front porch to await Sara, who'd texted her to let her know she was on her way over with coffees. It's just after seven. The sun is slow to wake the frosty overcast sky, but when Sara comes into sight, she lights up the whole street. Her hair is pulled back into a smart ponytail. A brown peacoat. Bright blue pointed flats.

Emily feels a rush of joy flutter through her as she thinks about the mastermind behind her birthday surprise yesterday.

She'd pulled up to The Pirate's Hideaway to those she loves most shouting, "Surprise!" The moment had literally frozen her in the driver's seat of her car. Sara hurried over to open the door for her. When she stepped out, her eyes overflowed with the happiest tears and Sara pulled her in for a tight hug. "Happy Birthday."

Emily meets Sara at the base of her steep front steps.

"Hi." Emily kisses her cheek and leads them into the warm home.

"Are the kids still asleep?" Sara asks.

Everyone stayed at a bed and breakfast nearby except her niece and nephews, who insisted on crashing in the triple bunk bed in Emily's spare room.

"I imagine they will be for a while. We were up until nearly one in the morning playing Telestrations."

Sara chuckles, tossing the Port City newspaper on the island countertop. "Check this out."

"Is it any better than the first?"

"Better, yes."

On the front page, in bold:

Books, Booze and Pirate Ships
Wealthy investor opens pub the whole family can enjoy

"Wealthy investor?" Emily looks at Sara and rolls her eyes. "I knew he wouldn't be able to help himself." The squeamish journalist that showed up to the ribbon-cutting ceremony had already done his due diligence on Emily Brynn. He was so caught up in her family history that she'd had to redirect him multiple times during their discussion.

"Are you writing a biography?" she had asked him.

"No, ma'am."

"Then why don't you inquire about Southport's newest pub? It is the reason we are all here today, correct?"

Sara walks behind Emily, who is sitting on a barstool at her kitchen island. She massages her shoulders. "Good investigative journalism, if you ask me."

"Rubbish! One more of these articles will put me out of business."

"Oh, there's nothing to worry about. If they actually take a few moments to read the article, they'll see I designed it and they'll ease up on ya."

Emily's eyebrows raise as she cocks her head around to catch a glimpse of this foreign dose of cockiness from Sara. Sara winks at her with a chuckle.

Emily stretches up from her seat and Sara leans down to meet her for a kiss. "Thank you for everything yesterday," Emily says. She turns back toward the counter, eyeing the paper once more. "I've had some really great birthdays, but none as special as yesterday."

"I'm happy it all worked out. You see the picture?" Sara says, pointing to it.

In it, Sara and Emily are front and center, holding their hands high up toward the sky in celebration. Everyone else is crowded around them. Joanna has a piece of cheese in her hand. Everyone is grinning, and some appear to be laughing.

"Your parents were so sweet. I look forward to talking with them more when it's not so chaotic."

"Look how happy they are in this picture." Both of Sara's parents are seemingly elated.

"I see. Your mom gave me a hug before she left last night."

"Are you serious?" Sara's eyes widen, clearly in shock. Emily nods her head. "Wow. They showed up. That was a big step. I'm happy they were there."

"Me too, Sar."

Sara removes her hands from Emily's shoulders, but not before kissing her cheek from behind. "I've got to run, but I found a house in Southport that I'm planning to check out tomorrow morning. Would you want to join me?"

"Would it look good pink?"

Sara smiles sheepishly. "It would. With a white picket fence and a front porch swing."

"I'd love to join you."

Emily stands, following Sara to the front door and grabbing her hand then spinning her around to face her. She uses both her hands to grasp Sara's face and kisses her passionately. Not in a way that's asking for more in this moment, but in a way that tells her she needs her. She wants her. She loves her.

Despite the intention, a familiar shiver runs up Emily's arm.

"I love you, too."

Bella Books, Inc.

Happy Endings Live Here

P.O. Box 10543
Tallahassee, FL 32302
Phone: (800) 729-4992
www.BellaBooks.com

More Titles from Bella Books

Mabel and Everything After – Hannah Safren
978-1-64247-390-2 I 274 pgs I paperback: $17.95 I eBook: $9.99
A law student and a wannabe brewery owner find that the path to a
fairy tale happily-ever-after is often the long and scenic route.

Integrity – E. J. Noyes
978-1-64247-465-7 I 28 pgs I paperback: $19.95 I eBook: $9.99
It was supposed to be an ordinary workday...

The Order – TJ O'Shea
978-1-64247-378-0 I 396 pgs I paperback: $19.95 I eBook: $9.99
For two women the battle between new love and old loyalty may prove
more dangerous than the war they're trying to survive.

Under the Stars with You – Jaime Clevenger
978-1-64247-439-8 I 302 pgs I paperback: $19.95 I eBook: $9.99
Sometimes believing in love is the first step. And sometimes it's all
about trusting the stars.

The Missing Piece – Kat Jackson
978-1-64247-445-9 I 250 pgs I paperback: $18.95 I eBook: $9.99
Renee's world collides with possibility and the past, setting off a tidal
wave of changes she could have never predicted.

An Acquired Taste – Cheri Ritz
978-1-64247-462-6 I 206 pgs I paperback: $17.95 I eBook: $9.99
Can Elle and Ashley stand the heat in the *Celebrity Cook Off* kitchen?

Printed in the USA
CPSIA information can be obtained
at www.ICGtesting.com
JSHW080028060624
64403JS00001B/1